Randomness

Written by

Austyeno Babyeno

DEVCOM

All rights reserved.
Randomness of the Universe
© Austyeno Babyeno

ISBN 978-0-9935237-7-9

First published in May 2023

No part of this publication may be reproduced, stored in a retrieval system, or transmitted, in any form or by any means without the prior written permission of the publisher, nor be otherwise circulated in any form of binding or cover other than that in which it is published and without a similar condition being imposed on the subsequent purchaser.

British Library Cataloguing in Publication Data:
A record for this book is available from the British Library.

Copyediting by Suzie Mason
Proofreading by Rita Okeke

Cover designed by Suzie Mason

Published by
Devcom Media, Jersey, CI, United Kingdom

I appreciate the efforts of all those who contributed to the development and completion of this novel. I also appreciate all the kind people that support me, and I give God the glory for making the book see the light of the day.

Dedicated to Belushi, the muse.

Chapter One

It was a cool evening in early-October 1984 in Beijing. Pockets of dead leaves were heaping up under the trees as the autumn weather still hovered across the city. Though the foliage season was not favourable to the florals, it was a blossoming time for the hotels. Most of them were fully booked as the holidaymakers sought to take advantage of the last mild weather before freezing chills blew in from the Gobi Desert.

That evening, it had passed rush hour and the sun was dreamily glowing in the horizon. The public transport that was often jam-packed was now less crowded without the Chinese labour force aboard, most of who had already reached their homes after a hard day's grind. The diurnal residents gradually prepared for their rest time as daylight faded away to herald nightfall. Despite the day passing, the city was still busy welcoming foreign visitors that were arriving in their numbers.

A grey minivan was driving through the city towards Hebei district, carrying a passenger from Nanyuan Airport. The van navigated through Tianjin to Xifang Tian Tang, slowing down for the speed bumps along the street as it drove past the hotels that spread on the thoroughfare like sands on a beach. It eventually pulled to a stop outside Xtopher Hotel, a three-star bed-and-breakfast lodging particularly sought after by English-speaking tourists. Xiamen Christopher got out and went to open the back door; he let down a ramp for the passenger to wheel himself out. After the passenger had alighted, Xiamen returned the ramp and closed the door. He took out a

Delsey wheeled suitcase from the back seat and gestured to the passenger.

'Come with me Monsieur Gilbert, I will escort you to reception and assist you with your bag.' Xiamen walked ahead, rolling the suitcase behind him as Monsieur Gilbert followed. The automatic doors of the hotel slid open as they went over the ramped entrance. They entered the alcove into the lobby where a middle-aged female receptionist was busy attending to guests. When the receptionist had finished with the person she was serving, Xiamen and Monsieur Gilbert approached her desk.

Xiamen greeted the receptionist warmly and stood to one side so she could attend to the guest. After Monsieur Gilbert was checked in and had collected the key to his room, Xiamen led him up the corridor to the lift. A few minutes later, Xiamen came back to the reception lobby and made a hand gesture to the receptionist that he'd be back. He hurried back to his van and drove off.

Xiamen was born in Beijing by Violet and Silver Christopher, a British couple who doubled as the proprietors and managers of Xtopher Hotel. The couple initially taught English language at the University of Westminster before they'd left as expatriates to teach contemporary English at Peking University. After completing their contracts term, they obtained a proprietary certificate for private school ownership and set up an English language tutorial centre with boarding facility. However, the new venture grew with less than one per cent per year and couldn't go beyond breakeven in the first three years. Due to the economic doldrums, they change the business line and reconstructed the school building into an overnight boarding-house with breakfast. Fortunately, the bed-and-breakfast turned out profitable so they acquired a bigger premises and expanded the business.

Xiamen's parents also had a daughter Marlene, who they had three years before Xiamen on their third year of settlement in Beijing. Regrettably, Marlene was frequently sick due to a congenital anaemia and didn't make it to her ninth birthday. That cruel twist of fate made Xiamen an only child.

After completing his middle school, Xiamen left home to study at a university in Hong Kong, where he obtained a bachelor's and a master's degrees. Upon acquiring the necessary qualifications, Xiamen moved to Shanghai and worked as an associate instructor at a college, but he was unable to find his niche in the academic world. After failing to get the hang of the job, he'd quit and returned to Beijing to join his parent's hospitality business.

Now aged twenty-seven, Xiamen enjoyed a full-time job as an all-round guest's chauffeur. He mostly spent his days driving the hotel's minivan and tour coach. He spoke the local language and English fluently; his bi-lingual fluency made him well-suited for the job of a tour guide.

Barely thirty minutes after Xiamen had dropped off Monsieur Gilbert, an airport taxi pulled up outside the hotel and parked in the same spot. The driver got out of the car and swiftly went to open the boot. A tall, young woman with long dark hair got out and stepped onto the pavement, holding a backpack and shoulder bag in her hands. The driver took out a dog-patterned suitcase and passed it to her; she collected it and thanked him. The driver went back into his car and drove off.

The woman extended the handle of her suitcase and made her way into the hotel. Wheeling the suitcase along, she repeatedly stifled yawns as she struggled to keep herself steady. Her carry-on bags felt like they had suddenly become heavier. She was knackered, hungry and badly in need of a bath after travelling since the previous night. She was only too glad to finally be at her resting destination.

The travelling woman had snapped up a last-minute flight deal on cheaptickets.com at a bargain price, but the prolonged transit time at Dubai airport hadn't been any fun. The 7-hour interval had given her plenty of time to reflect on her recent failed relationship. Her ex had cheated on her with another girl and then ghosted her. She hoped the trip would set her heart free and reset her mind to move on. Nonetheless, she still harboured an ill-feeling in the pit of her stomach for his callousness.

'Come on now doggy bag, we're almost there.' Clara muttered as she rolled her bag over the ramped entrance of the hotel and went through the automatic doors as they slid open for her. She went past the alcove and walked into the reception lobby, immediately heaving a sigh when she saw the waiting queue. She joined the line in the sixth position. Feeling exhausted, she considered taking a seat in the lounge to wait her turn but quickly reconsidered it; more guests might arrive and join the line and wouldn't hesitate to give her the eye when she cut in front of them. Her legs buckled under her weight; they couldn't put up with standing a minute longer. Hanging her backpack on the extended handle of her suitcase, she secured her place in the line with it and went to settle in the closest available lounge chair.

From her chair, Clara looked at the line and noted that four people were now standing before her bag. The reception lady was serving another guest; a rather dapperly dressed man who was wearing a fedora hat and a button-down paisley shirt with suspenders clipped on the waist band of his baggy gabardines. From the chatter going on between them, Clara made out that the guest sounded Australian whilst the receptionist spoke in the Queen's English. The receptionist was certainly cheerful and talking too much. Clara thought the receptionist didn't seem to care about the patience of the waiting queuers. She started to feel exasperated and internally pleaded that the receptionist worked a bit faster. In frustration, she leaned back and nestled herself into her chair.

A short while later, the receptionist had finished serving the queue and two further guests before she noticed Clara's unattended bag. She looked around for its owner and saw the dark-haired lady sleeping in one of the lounge chairs.

'Excuse me!' the receptionist called out to the sleeping woman. 'Hey there!' She tried again severally, frowning as the sleeper remained unresponsive to her wake-up calls. The receptionist left her desk and went over to her.

'Hello!' The receptionist tapped her on the shoulder.

Clara started up jumping to her feet. 'What... er, is it my turn already?'

'Of course dear, I have been trying to wake you. Come with me. Let's get you checked in.'

'Gosh, so sorry. I'm exhausted from travelling all day.' She grabbed her belongings and approached the desk.

'May I see your booking receipt please?' asked the reception woman, now sitting behind her desk.

Clara fished out a printout from her handbag. 'There.' She passed it over.

'Can I have your passport as well please?'

'Sure.' Clara took out her international passport and gave it to her.

The receptionist skimmed over the printout and then looked at the passport. 'Welcome to Xtopher Hotel, Clara Jerkins. We are glad to have you as our guest here.'

'Thank you.'

'How was your journey?'

'It was long but well worth it.'

'Have you travelled from England?'

'Yes.'

'' It's always a pleasure to have a guest from home stay with us. I'm from Walthamstow in East London. What about you?'

'East Anglia.'

'Oh really? I was at the Anglia Ruskin University in Cambridge for a programme years ago! Is this your first time in Beijing?'

'Yes! It's my first time in Asia too.'

'Are you here on a business trip or leisure?'

'Hmm, it's a last-minute holiday.'

'I see you've booked for ten nights with us. Do you have any sight-seeing planned?'

'I don't yet, I will make some plans now I'm here. Do you recommend anywhere?'

'Oh yes! I recommend the Great Wall of China. It's among the top seven wonders of the world, definitely a must-see! People come from all over to Beijing just to see the sites. Our hotel organises coach tours to two amazing Great Wall sites in Beijing. The round trip includes visits to other interesting places in the city. If you are interested, there is a flyer in your room with all the details about our scheduled excursion trips.'

'That's good to know… I'll have a look later,' Clara offered a complaisant smile.

The reception woman smiled back. She wrote Clara's details in the booking register. 'I have room number 19 for you. Here is your passport and the key to the room. it's at the bottom of the corridor, just before the stairs. Our complimentary buffet breakfast is available in the restaurant from eight o'clock to ten. The restaurant is open for lunch and dinner. Drinks and snacks will also be available until 10 PM. Do you have any specific requirements, or any other questions you'd like to ask?'

'Do you offer room service?'

'We don't.'

'Is there a bathtub in my room?'

'The one I gave you doesn't have one. But I can check if I can switch you if there's one available. Would you like me to do that?'

'Yes please if possible. I love a tub to douse myself in and unwind.'

'Give me a moment.' She looked through the register. 'So, there's a vacant room with a bathtub on the third floor if you don't mind being that far up?'

'That's great. I'll have it.'

'No problem, let me have that key back and I'll sort it out for you.'

Clara returned the key. The receptionist revised the information she had entered in the booking register and gave her another key.

'Your new room number is 35. You can use the lift or stairs, they are opposite each other at the bottom of the corridor.'

'Alright, thanks a lot!'

'You are welcome dear. Do have a good rest.'

'Sure, thank you,' Clara replied, taking the key. She said good night and walked up the corridor.

A short time later, Xiamen arrived in the van outside the hotel. This time he'd carried a Canadian family of four from PEK international airport. 'We're here,' he said to them as he pulled the vehicle to a stop. 'That's the entrance to the hotel. If you go through the doors and walk in, the reception desk will be to your right.'

'Thank you,' the male parent said to Xiamen. He opened the door on his side and alighted.

Xiamen got out and walked round to open the trunk. The father followed and helped to retrieve the baggage whilst the rest of the family got out; they all helped themselves to their own bags and made their way into the hotel. Xiamen closed the boot and passenger doors of the minivan, got back in and drove it round the back to park for the night.

One of the boys let out an exaggerated yawn. 'I'm so tired Mom. I just want to rest now.'

'Don't we all Jake? We're at the hotel now, be patient,' his mother said to him.

'I've been carrying my backpack all day. I need a break.'

'It's your own fault, you didn't have to pack the bag up like a stuffed animal,' his brother teased.

'I wasn't talking to you Blake. Mind your business.'

'Then quit whining in my ear reach if you don't want my feedback.'

'Don't you know when to keep your beak shut, parrot?'

'Who is a parrot?'

'You.'

'You're the one that's a—'

'Knock it off both of you I've had enough of you two in my ear all day!' their mother cut in.

The father momentarily stopped walking with a raised hand to halt the others. He gave the lads a cross look. 'None of that squawking here.

We are about to go into a hotel, so behave like civilised people now. Clear?'

Blake and Jake both apologised. The man continued to lead the family through the alcove and into the reception lobby to the front desk. No one was being attended to so they promptly assembled before the receptionist.

A short while later, Xiamen strolled into the hotel lobby and waited by the desk for the family to be checked in. When they were gone, he leaned on the counter and greeted the receptionist.

'Hi Ma.'

'How're you doing Xiamen?'

'All good, Ma. I've just finished my last shuttle for the day. I'll be heading up now.'

'Okay, that's good. I am rounding off in a minute and will be right after you.'

'Where's the night staff? Isn't Beibei here?'

'Of course, she is already here. She is just helping an elderly guest take her second suitcase up.'

'That's good. Is Dad back from Shanghai yet?'

'No. He says he will be coming back tomorrow.'

'How come?'

'He called earlier to say that there has been a—'

'Good evening Xansheng Xiamen!'

Xiamen turned to face a smiling Chinese girl walking towards them from the corridor. he grinned at her. 'Ah! Good evening Beibei! How're you?'

'I fine, xiansheng Xiamen, thank you.' Beibei turned to Violet. 'Nushi, I take over from you now?'

'Of course dear.' Violet moved away for Beibei to take her place behind the desk. She turned back to Xiamen. 'I'll head up with you then, okay Xiamen?'

'Sure Ma. Ready when you are.'

'Let's go then. Good night Beibei.' Violet bade her.

'Goodnight Nushi,' Beibei said as she took her position behind the desk.

Xiamen and Beibei said good night to each other too, then he and his mother strolled down the corridor and into the lift. Xiamen fumbled in his pocket for his key card but his mother beat him to it. She inserted hers into the slot and pressed the button. The lift ascended past the two floors of the building before it stopped and opened its doors directly into the lounge of their penthouse suite. They stepped out.

'What were you saying was Dad's reason for not making it back today?'

'He called to say it wasn't possible to seal off the purchase deal today but he will be doing so tomorrow. He should be getting here later in the day.'

'That's great. We'll be getting the ultra-modern coach soon then. That'd be so good.'

'Of course, I'm sure you can't wait to start driving it.'

'You bet,' Xiamen said with a grin.

'Well I'm going to sort myself out and get to bed. There is some food in the warmer for you if you'd like to eat. I suppose you'll be having supper, won't you?'

'Yeah, thanks Ma.'

'Remember to switch off the light in the kitchen after.'

'I will… no worries.'

'Goodnight then.'

'Night-night Ma.'

Violet left for her bedroom and Xiamen made his way into the kitchenette. He took a casserole pot from the hob, retrieved chopsticks from a drawer and started helping himself to the noodles without bothering to sit down. Once he'd finished the food, he cleaned up the dish. He swiftly grabbed his father's Ciu Ciu libation wine from the cupboard and poured himself a shot using his father's favourite cup. Downing the drink in a single gulp, he rinsed the glass and wiped it dry with a paper towel. After returning the bottle and glass to where he had found them, he opened the fridge and took out a bottled water. Moving out of the kitchen, he headed for his bedroom drinking the water. He hadn't remembered to switch off the light!

The following morning, Clara Jerkins stirred in her bed from a restful sleep. Her eyes fluttered open and widened in surprise as they glimpsed at the unfamiliar surroundings. Recollecting where she was, she shut her eyes as a sudden gasp of breath threw her mouth into a loud yawn. She simultaneously stretched and spread her hands like a rood-tree. After arriving the previous night, she had satiated her hunger with some short bread and juice before taking a quick shower and crashing out. Now feeling more awake, she opened her eyes and trailed them around the room.

The room was a standard double with a bed large enough to sleep two adults and a baby comfortably. There were two bedside tables flanking the bed; the inner one stood by the wall with a bed lamp on top it, whilst the outer one carried the intercom telephone and bridged the bed to an upholstered chair. Next to the armchair was a small coffee table. A flat screen TV hung on the wall overlooking the bed and a clock radio sat on a draw cabinet positioned below the TV. A mini fridge stood beside the cabinet with a pile of tourist leaflets sitting on top. There was also a reading desk and chair positioned in the corner. Close to the foot of the bed was a mirrored wardrobe that was fixed to the wall which demarcated the ensuite.

Clara tossed the covers aside and got out of bed only in her birthday suit. She shuffled across the tiled floor to the window and drew back the curtains. 'Urgh!' she squealed, turning away from the slap of sudden sunlight. She glanced at the clock radio; her squinting eyes instantly widened. 'Half past one? How did I sleep in for so long? What the F?' She rushed to her open suitcase, fished out the frothy soap from her duty-free shopping and hurried to the bathroom.

After freshening up, Clara stepped out of her room and made for the lift. When the doors opened she found a lone occupant already inside. Their eyes locked briefly. Clara gave him a good cursory glance, taking note of his tall height, black curly hair and handsome face. The stranger was wearing a V-neck sweater, olive chinos and brown loafers. His friendly smile welcomed her in. She joined the lift without a word.

'Ground floor?' the man asked.

'Yes please,' Clara replied, barely moving her teeth.

'I'm going to the ground floor too,' he said as he pressed the button.

Clara said nothing further and fixed her look downwards as the lift descended. When the doors opened, she left the stranger behind and briskly walked ahead towards the reception lobby. Reaching the reception desk, she stopped to talk to Violet.

'Good afternoon.'

'Good afternoon to you too. I hope you're enjoying your stay so far?'

'Yes thank you. The restaurant is open now, right? I missed breakfast.'

'Of course dear, they will be serving lunch until 3PM. In the alcove, turn the corner to your right, and you will be in the passage to the restaurant.'

'Thanks! I'll head there in a minute. May I also just ask you about the excursion you mentioned yesterday?'

'Of course dear. What do you want to know?'

'I gathered there's one tomorrow. I'd like to book the trip if there's any spaces available.'

'Of course dear. I'll do that for you now if you like.'

'Er, actually I'm starved… I will go eat first if that's ok.'

'No problem. I'll be here whenever you're ready.'

As Clara moved away, Xiamen walked up to the desk. He was the stranger in the lift with Clara and had been standing to the side whilst she chatted with his mother. He trailed her with his eyes as she walked off.

'Xiamen?' his mother called him.

'Yes!' he turned and faced her.

'Are you ready to go get your dad from the airport?'

'Sure, right about.'

'Better get going then.'

'Okay, see you later!' Xiamen walked away.

Further down the corridor, the lift doors opened once more and Monsieur Gilbert wheeled himself out. He too stopped before the reception desk. 'Good afternoon Madame Hotelier. I want to ask you about the trip to the Great China Wall tomorrow if I may.'

'Of course Monsieur Gilbert, what would you like to know?'

'I would like you to book me in please.'

'No problem. Give me a minute, I will have it sorted for you. Let me get the booking list to register you.' Violet riffled through some papers on her desk, found the one she wanted and glanced over it. 'I am sorry Monsieur Gilbert... unfortunately, the site they are going tomorrow is not all that accessible to wheelchairs.'

'I do not understand, Madame.'

'I mean that the ground there is not levelled so it won't be particularly good for your wheelchair. There are hills and slopes there that will make mobility difficult. There are stones along the path too. It is even strenuous for the people on foot to walk there.'

'Okay. Is there any Great Wall site accessible to a wheelchair that I can go?'

'The best one I'll recommend is the Great Wall site at Badaling. We already done that route two days ago. Let me check the date for our next scheduled trip there... Oh, the next one will be Tuesday next week. But, Monsieur Gilbert, if you like, I can book a tour bus with another operator that's going to the Badaling Great Wall site tomorrow if you wish to go with them.'

'Yes I would like that thank you.'

'Great. Let me make a call to get the details and I can tell you where to go. Bear with me for a moment.' She reached for the telephone.

'Madame, while you do that, excuse me to go fill up in the restaurant before it shuts. I will come back to you after.'

'Of course. You do that. I will have all the information ready for you when you return.'

'Many thanks Madame. See you later.' He wheeled himself away.

Chapter Two

Early morning of the following day, Xiamen parked the coach at the front of the hotel and waited in his seat for the excursion guests to get on board. Some excursionists from nearby hotels were also there to join the trip so the queue snaked along the path like a long python. The Canadian family were present amongst the group; when they reached the front of the bus, they showed their tickets to Xiamen who took off the stubs and waved them on.

The next passenger stepped up and Xiamen stared into Clara's eyes. She momentarily faltered in her steps and drew in a sharp breath as she recognised him. Offering a small smile, Xiamen took her ticket and observed it, making a mental note of her particulars before taking the stub and waving her on. Xiamen soon finished checking in the thirty-one passengers. After all the passengers had settled in their seats, Xiamen started the engine and began the first leg of the day's travels. He turned on the tannoy system and cleared his throat.

'Morning everyone! My name is Xiamen, your driver and tour guide for this trip. As you already know, this excursion is specifically set to see the Great Wall of China. We'll also be making a few pitstops at designated tourists spots where you can get out and have a look around for a bit. There'll be plenty of opportunities to purchase souvenirs and refreshments as well so I hope you bought enough spending money. A lot of the local cash machine's don't accept foreign cards and the local traders only want the renminbi unfortunately. If you have any questions don't hesitate to ask me.'

Xiamen paused for a moment to wait for any questions. The passengers remained quiet so he continued. 'This trip will last for most of the day, we should be back just after five o'clock this evening. There' will be toilets at each stop point if you need to relieve yourselves. I don't recommend using the toilets around the street markets unless you really have to go. In case of an eventuality, just be prepared to come out smelling like a toilet for the rest of the day. As this is a sight-seeing trip, I'll be talking to you most of the time and telling you about the places we'll be passing. So, if you were planning to sleep through the journey, pardon me but you won't be having any peace and quiet on board.'

A roar of laughter suddenly cut across the bus. Xiamen smiled and continued.

'Thank you, thank you. It's not very often I get a bus full of visitors who laugh at my silly jokes. We're going to get on very well if you keep responding with such good feedback. And you don't have to cheer because you think I'm funny, just do it because you like me to kid myself that I am. Make my day and humour me.'

Another uproar of laughter swept across the bus. Clara was one of the passengers who joined in this time; she thought the driver was a funny one. She recollected seeing him in the lift the previous day as his eyes penetrated her like an X-ray beam. His ogling had made her uncomfortable at the time. She had thought he was a guest staying at the hotel so was taken aback when she stepped on the bus to find him at the wheel. She inwardly appreciated his sense of humour and continued to listen to his gags.

'For those of you who haven't been to Beijing before, let me introduce the city to you. Rest assured, what I'll be telling you in this bus is authentic, because I am a son of the soil... In case you're looking at me now and thinking that's a porky because I don't look an inch Chinese, I was born here by British parents. My name is Chinese too, it means gate of China. And in case you forget it, please dip into the seat pocket in front of yours and take out the gratis jotter and pen I'd kept there for you. You can use that to write down my name. I suggest you write in upper case. It's spelt as, X, I, A, M, E, N and pronounced Xiamen. So, since I'm the gate of China, you can take everything I'll tell you about Beijing to the bank, or the lottery house, in case you're a fan of tombola.'

The coach filled with giggles once more. Some of the passengers wrote down the driver's name. Even Clara did. The corners of her mouth crinkled with a smile as she continued to enjoy the driver's comic rhetorics.

'First of all, Beijing in Chinese literally means northern capital. The city has an ancient historic origin dating back over 5000 years and it's been the imperial capital of China going back centuries, since the Mongols and Japanese invaded and occupied it. Back then it was called other names like Dadu, Ming, Qing, Peiping and Beiping. It was named Beijing in 1403 and no one thought to change it after that. Today, as the political headquarter, Beijing is China's major transport hub and quite easy to travel to from any location within China. There're so many interesting and beautiful places to see and I'll be takin you to some of them today. Some of these places are quite huge, a slow walker could take two whole days to go around fully. But since the focus of this trip is to see the Great Wall, we'll only be stopping briefly at each one. But don't you worry, you can always return to wherever fascinates you on your own later and take as many hours as you like to walk around again.'

Xiamen took a brief pause to sip some water. Some of the coach occupants traded small talk about what he'd said. Xiamen gave them a moment then carried on.

'The most adventurous experience for every visitor here is the freedom to walk on the streets and cross without the worry of rushing traffic. The local residents don't appreciate the luxury of driving around themselves like other places around the world, so fewer cars are on the streets. The city does enjoy a good taxi network but I warn you they aren't cheap. People here mostly like to walk or take the bus or Metro. So feel free to walk in the middle of the street if you like to be adventurous, it's unlikely that you'd be knocked down by a car. But this advice only applies to those who understand what at your own risk means.'

Now, inside the coach was strewn with more giggles as the passengers laughed like the audience in a gag show.

'Y'know this driver is really tickling me... he's so funny,' a woman with an American drawl said to the dapperly dressed man in a fedora sitting beside her.

'Yeah, the chap certainly knows how to entertain I give him that,' he replied.

'I think he's gonna do well in stand-ups,' the woman further added.

'You are damn right!' another passenger from across the aisle chipped in. They turned to look at the woman sitting beside their row. She carried on.

'This driver certainly is a good comedian. I was on this bus on the same tour last time and he was so hilarious.'

'You've already been to see the Great Wall?' the dapper man asked her, looking surprised.

'Yep, but not quite. I wasn't feeling well that day so I didn't really go around much. But this driver really made me laugh despite me not being in a laughing mood. He is a funny man.'

Sitting next to the woman, Clara turned to her. 'So, you've really been on this same tour before, how was it?'

'I didn't get much out of it, but that was just me. It was a lot of fun for the others though.'

'Have you been in Beijing for long?'

'Ten days today. But I will be leaving in two days.'

'Aw, that's a shame.'

'Yep, it's why I'm doing this tour again. I didn't enjoy it the last time because I was sick with a stomach cramp.'

'I arrived yesterday and thought to go on the tour because it was highly recommended by the woman at the reception.'

'Of course, That woman! She will tell every guest to go on the tour of the Great Wall because it's business for them.'

'What do you mean?'

'They own the hotel.'

'They... who?'

'She, her husband, and the funny guy at the wheel.'

'You mean the driver?'

'Yep, he is her son.'

'Oh really?'

'Yep. He and his parents run the hotel.'

Clara gave the woman a pointed look and started to say something but stopped short as the driver's voice cut in.

'In approximately six minutes, we'll be making our first stop at Beihai Park, a very delightful place to visit in Beijing! I wouldn't be exaggerating if I said that the place is heaven on earth. The park has been preserved as a royal garden for many years and visitors have been trooping to see it since 1925. The grounds cover a whopping 171 acres so it's easy to get lost if you wander too far out. The stunning temples and palace halls are simply out of this world. There's also a serene lake which blooms with lotus in the summer and freezes over in winter. The water covers more than half of the total park and is believed to have some blessing powers too! You can dip your feet in if you like but I'd definitely recommend going bare foot. I've heard the lake might curse you if you keep your shoes on. Besides that, I don't want you coming back on the coach with wet shoes, it's only just been cleaned.'

A roar of laughter went off again in the bus. Xiamen thanked the passengers for it. He turned off his microphone and didn't speak until they were near their stop a few minutes later.

'Ahem! So far so good, we're now in the Xicheng District. This, ladies and gentlemen, is the famous Beihai Park! I'll be stopping in a moment to let you out; everyone must vacate the coach please. The stop interval here will be for two hours. That's plenty of time for you to see the grounds, but don't wander too far out as we need to stick to our schedule. Take your tickets with you, it's your pass into the park and the other gated entrances. I'm going to have a little nap while you're out but I'm a light sleeper, you won't find me slumbering away when you return. Make the most of the sightseeing. See you later.'

The passengers started to disembark. Once they were all off the bus, Xiamen locked the door and set his alarm. He reclined his seat and laid back in it.

'Is this one of the places you visited last time?' Clara asked the woman that was beside her on the coach after they had passed the gatekeepers and walked into the park together.

'Yep.'

'So, what are the interesting things to see here?'

'I can't tell you that off the top of my head but, from what I have read about this park, a lot of things here are simply je ne sais quoi.'

Clara gave the woman a sharp look, trying to remember what the French idiom meant but she couldn't readily recall it.

'That's brilliant,' she said nonetheless as she continued to rack her brains for the meaning. Finally, she gave up and asked, 'Where are you from?'

'Jersey.'

'Jersey in the USA?'

'No, Jersey in the UK.'

'There's a Jersey in the UK?'

'Yep. Jersey is in the Channel Islands, which is part of the UK. Haven't you heard of it?'

'I haven't heard of Jersey, but the Channel Islands rings a bell. Where in the UK is it?'

'It's between Britain and north-western France. Although it was formally a French Normandy Isle, it's now the largest of all British Isles on the Channel waters. These days it's a lot more multicultural too; in fact, it's very much like London in that sense.'

'I see. Do they speak French or English then?'

'Both are official languages there, but English has dominated. You hardly find islanders there speaking French nowadays. You can find some among the older people though.'

'It must be an interesting place to live.'

'Of course. What about you? Where are you from?'

'I'm from East England. I was born in Beccles, that's where my parents are from. I live in Norwich now. Do you know it?'

'Oh yes! I've not been there though, I used to have a boyfriend who was an ardent supporter of Norwich City Football Club, he went to uni there.'

'Wow! It's a small world. I studied at the University of East Anglia too. Was he from there then?'

'Not at all. He is a Jersey Bean.'

'A what?'

'Oh, it's just a jargon we use to describe ourselves in Jersey.'

Clara looked at the Jersey woman with some bemusement and thought her somewhat funny. She wondered why the islanders in Jersey would call themselves beans. But she had never met anyone from there until now. She made a mental note to research the place.

'This park is so beautiful!' the Jersey woman said, suddenly stopping in her tracks. Clara stopped walking too, looking puzzled as she watched her new acquaintance stick her index finger between her lips like a thinking-emoji and throw sweeping looks at the surroundings. Then she noticed her gaze was fixed at one spot and followed her look.

'Hmmm… you know I am not so sure I will be coming this way again anytime soon, if at all. I want to make the most of it and take it all in this time. This section of the park we are on now is the Jade Flower Islet. It has most of the interesting bits. I wouldn't mind going up that hill if you're up for it.'

'Sure, let us go. I'm Clara Jerkins by the way.'

'I'm Sarah De Gruchy. It's nice to meet you Clara. I've got a visitor's information booklet about the park in my bag from last time if you want to check it out at any point.'

'That's good to know thank you. I am sure it will come in handy as we go along.'

They walked towards the north bank up a slope and went by Tibetan-style temples. Sarah consulted her tourist brochure and told Clara their names as they passed the Falun, ShengJue and PuAn temples. They walked further along the bank and across a bridge. They then came to a network of five pavilions that were interconnected by zigzagging stone bridges and fitted with pointed roof-tops and curved eaves.

'I think we are now in the Five-Dragon Pavilions,' Sarah announced.

'Oh wow, I guess that's the five dragons in the water there… amazing!' Clara pointed.

'Yep, sounds right.'

'Gosh! They sure don't look cheerful. Why is the one in the middle the largest?'

'Maybe they implied she is the mother. Let me see what this book says about them.' Sarah skimmed over the table of contents of her brochure. 'Oh, there's nothing about them here,' she said after a moment. 'But it does have a feature about the Nine-Dragon wall over there. I saw it the last time I was here. It was my favourite piece in the park actually. I can tell you a lot about it if you want to take a closer look. Would you like to?'

'Sure, why not.'

Getting to the wall, Clara was awestruck as her eyes took everything in. Pleased with herself, Sarah quickly offered some more information.

'This spirit wall represents the nine sons of the dragon king, a legend which is considered to be the most powerful deity in Chinese myth. These large dragons are also duplicated on the other side. Come on, let's go around to see them. Of all the ancient nine-dragon screens in China, this one is the only one that has got dragons on both sides. There are 635 dragon paintings on this wall, inclusive of the 18 larger ones. I was so fascinated by them the last time that I tried counting them.'

'Did you really?'

'Not quite. I got up to 200 then had to stop because of my stomach cramp. I did have fun doing it though.'

'What is it with the Chinese and dragons anyway? They iconise them like crazy!'

'I guess it's because of what they represent in their belief. The Egyptians did that with the Sphinx too.'

'The Sphinx?'

'It's some superstitious stone statue with the body of a lion and the head of a man that the ancient Egyptians idolised.'

'Oh yeah? I guess it's different strokes for different folks then.'

'Yep, it is!'

'I think what they did on this wall is pure vivid creativeness. It's amazing how they made these twirling dragons playful.'

'Yep, it's mind-blowing. Devising the dragons to play with pearls amongst the clouds doesn't portray them as ferocious. This is much better than making them breathe out fire.'

'I agree. It's very impressive indeed.'

'Yep, it's clearly an evidence of ancient creativity! Also, let's not forget this was done long ago.'

'That's true indeed. Uhm... ok Sarah, let's move on.'

'Sure, where do you reckon we should go next?'

'How about going into that big building with the white thing at the top?'

'Hmmm, I was thinking of maybe taking you into that Little-Western Paradise Pavilion over there. I went in there last time. The place is the largest square pavilion-style hall in the whole of China. I would love to show you the beautiful panorama of the Sumeru Mountain, it has a Bodhisattva sitting at its peak and Lohans sitting around the base. But let's go to the one you chose first. We can see the Bodhisattva and his Lohans later.'

'Okay great,' Clara replied and they started walking. 'How do you know all these weird names? What do Bodhisattva and Lohans even mean?'

'The Bodhisattva is a heavenly Buddhist, and the Lohans are his disciples. I've learnt everything from the visitor's booklets of course! I got hold of a few since I've been here,' Sarah said as they went across a bridge.

The bridge led them to a hilly island at the centre of the park. Going past a bell tower and a drum tower, they went through a colourful gate and entered a huge temple which was composed of several halls.

'Woah! This place is huge! What is it called?'

'One sec, I am looking for it. Aha! It's Yong'an Temple.'

'Wow! It's a massive temple indeed!'

'Hold on, I'll read you the description. It says here this is the largest Buddhist monastery in Beihai Park. It's also referred to as the temple of everlasting peace. The Qing Dynasty emperors used the main temple as a place of worship, and the adjoining halls for their political and social meetings. That's the summary.'

'This was a worship and political meeting place? No wonder it's so huge', Clara marvelled, glancing around. 'Hmm... well, it doesn't really look interesting now to me. Let's move on now, no point wasting time.'

'Alright, let's get out of here.'

After leaving the temple, they went through some courtyards and came to a square building with a cone-shaped roof. They went inside. Sarah consulted her brochure and told Clara the place was a Tibetan sanctuary called ShanYin Pavilion, also known as the Pavilion of Benevolent Voice. Strolling further on, they admired the image of the reposing Buddha in the blue glazed tiles and fed their eyes on the artefacts in the place.

They left the pavilion and walked down the north bank. Reaching the lakeside, Sarah held up her hand, motioning for Clara to stop.

'Do you fancy going up there?'

'Up where?'

'That long corridor. I think we can get a broad view of the park from there.'

'Er, I'm not a fan of heights… I don't fancy climbing to be honest.'

'Come on, it's only two-storeys high. We could see far and wide into the park from up there, instead of wandering too far out. Remember we don't have much time to kill here,' Sarah said with a giggle and she started walking away.

'No, Sarah, I'm not so sure about…' Clara started to say but stop short, seeing Sarah had already walked off. She hesitated for a second then followed her.

A few minutes later, the ladies were walking along the top level of the corridor enjoying a view of the park.

'There's much to see from here. Amazing! You were right indeed.' Clara praised the view.

'I told you didn't I? Next time I tell you something believe me. Look over there!' Sarah pointed.

'Where?'

'Over there, the pointy white tower on top of the hill.'

Clara turned to look. In the close distance was a towering domed structure with a bronze crown that reached into the sky. She could just about make out the engravings on it; there was a sun, moon and flame; little bells hung around it like the jingle bells on Santa's sleigh. 'What is that?'

'Hold on a moment, I'll check.' Sarah glanced down at her pamphlet. 'It's called White Pagoda.'

'What is it?'

'It is a Buddhist shrine.'

'Uh-huh? What's it about?'

'The White Pagoda Buddhist stupa is actually the official symbol of Beihai Park. It's situated at the centre and highest point of the park with a grand height of 131 feet. It was built in the year of 1651 to honour the visit of the chief lama and ruler of Tibet, and to reflect China's faith in Buddhism. The Pagoda contains a repository that stores relics... this includes monk mantles, alms bowls, urns of cremated ashes and religious scrolls.'

'Jeez! That sounds fetish. I didn't know such things were associated with Buddhism.'

'Haven't you ever seen statues of Buddhas before?'

'Not until I got here.'

'That's a surprise. A Buddhist temple is the best place to see graven Buddha images of all kinds, from figurines to large effigies. They come in different postures and significance. There's even a 420-foot tall Buddha statue at the Spring Temple in Henan!'

'Oh yeah? That must be imposing.'

'Indeed, it must be.'

'This White Pagoda is extraordinarily white!'

'Yep, it says here the stones that were used to build it were whitened in concentrated lime.'

'Ah! No wonder it's gleaming!' Clara said, still fixating on the Pagoda.

Sarah quickly rummaged in her bag and got out a Yashica film camera. She took a photo of Clara and took some of the White Pagoda. She asked Clara to take photos of her posing against the backdrop of the Pagoda. She took a few panoramic pictures of other sceneries as Clara looked on. After a couple of more wide shots, she returned the camera to her bag.

'I've took some really brilliant photos since arriving here. I hope they come out nice when I print them!'

'It beats me how the Chinese were able to erect all these structures back then, at a time when the world didn't have all the modern scaffolding technology like today,' Clara said, turning to Sarah.

'It's the same with the Egyptians you know. I've been to Cairo and went to Giza to see the Great Pyramids there. Those pyramids were built long before Jesus Christ was born and they are still standing to this day! How the Egyptians managed it is baffling.'

'Wow! You've been to Egypt too? You sure have been around the world girl!'

'Not really. I haven't gone anywhere else apart from there and now here. I only went to Egypt because my husband and I went there for our honeymoon.'

'I see,' Clara said. She turned her eyes on another object of interest and pointed to it. 'Is there some info in your booklet about that God-like thing on a stone, behind the white terrace over there?'

Sarah looked at what Clara was pointing at. Stood behind the white terrace was a bronze Deity holding a plate. The stone pillar beneath was beautifully decorated with a helical dragon. 'Hmmm... it says here that's the Bronze Dew Plate.'

'Is there anything more about it?'

'Yep. Emperor Qianlong of the Qing Dynasty used the dew that was collected in the plate to cook his medicine.'

'For real? Was he a herbalist too?'

'Who knows? The Chinese are known for their traditional medicine therapy.'

'I guess it works for them. What's that huge vessel standing at the front of the hall?' Clara asked, pointing at a green vase with decorative paintings of a dragon and a sea horse.

'Aha... that vessel has a funny story to it!'

'What story?'

'It's so funny. I gathered it belonged to an emperor called Kublai Khan. He used it for storing his wine.'

'What? Did he have to store his wine out in the open?'

'Why not, if he loved booze that much.'

'He must have been one of those ones who cherished drunken sessions.'

'Could be! Maybe the Drunken Master movie was produced to glorify him,' Sarah said laughing.

'Who was in it?'

'Jackie Chan and co.'

'Okay Sarah, can we get off this corridor now?'

'Alright. Come let's go to that garden over there?' Sarah pointed towards a walled enclosure at the southeast part of the park. 'That's the Circular City. Perhaps we can check out how the plants feel to touch.'

'Hmmm... that's too far away. And there is the bridge to cross too. Perhaps we should look at something a bit closer.'

'Such as what?'

'I don't know, something else that isn't as far,' Clara said as she looked around for an inspiration.

'Come on, don't be a killjoy. Don't you like flowers or what? Of all the things on this park, they are the only things that are truly nature's own. Let me see what this booklet says about the garden and tell you, I'm sure it will be interesting.' Sarah riffled through the pages of the pamphlet. 'Listen... The Circular City garden has numerous herbs of brightly coloured flower heads from the old-world Chrysanthemum, that are native to China. There is an exquisite rockery of alpines and a variety of lilies, including the white lotus. Most remarkable are the pine and cypress trees, believed to have been around for a thousand years. Did you hear that? The trees there are even older than Methuselah.'

'Who's Methuselah?'

'Methuselah was the oldest man in the Bible. He was 969. I think trees older than that must really have tough barks. Let's go have a closer look.'

'No, it's too far away. We should go to a place that's either close to here or nearer to the exit, so it will be quicker for us to make it to the coach when we need to head back. Do you think we will make it back in time if we go that way?'

'Of course we will. The driver won't leave without us. I saw that happen last time I went on the tour. One couple had delayed coming back from one of the stops and the driver never left till they returned to the bus. Believe you me, it was a walk of shame for them as they made their way through the aisle to their seats! Everyone gave them a disapproving look, including myself,' Sarah replied with a giggle.

'All the same, let's not go there. Look!' Clara pointed towards some shady trees on the west of the Islet. 'Those umbrella trees over there seem quite ancient. Let's go there and check them out.'

Sarah looked at the cluster of shady trees. 'Yep. Not a bad idea. They look nice... they do look like they have been around for ages. I like how they form canopies like marquees.'

'They might be even older than those other ones you called Methuselah.'

'I didn't say any tree is called Methuselah, I merely compared the trees to his age. But let's see what this booklet has about the trees.' Sarah quickly riffled through the pages of the brochure. 'Hmmm... Jade Flower Islet shady trees are remarkable due to their beautiful blooming branches. The trees inspired a famous odic poem which was written by Emperor Qianlong of the Qing dynasty.'

'Wow! The shady trees supplied the muse for the emperor's poetry? How lovely. Is the poem in that book?'

'Maybe, let me see.' Sarah flicked through the pages once more. 'No, this book doesn't have it. But it says a stone plaque is situated near the Qionghua Hill that features the title and verse of the poem in the Emperor's own handwriting.'

'Yay! There is a poem, that's great.'

'What now? 'Do you want us to try our luck reading a poem that was written in Chinese calligraphs?'

'Er, not really. I think we should go to the shady trees. I suppose they are worth checking out plus they are even closer.'

'You are such a chicken. I already told you the driver won't leave us behind. He is responsible for his passengers and won't dare leave without one. Come on, let's go over there together, or else I can just go alone and you can go to see the marquee trees if you like.'

'No way! We stay together. Let's get going.' Clara promptly took Sarah by the hand and ushered her towards the stairs to make their way down. 'We have to be quick. I wouldn't want to do the walk of shame. And for your information, I am no chicken, okay?'

'I believe you, girl,' Sarah said, giggling.

Chapter Three

Several minutes before the stipulated departure time, the passengers started coming into the coach in their groups. Xiamen welcomed them on, offering smiles and greetings from the driver's seat as they boarded. When Clara came through the door, his smile broadened as he spoke to her.

'Did you find it enjoyable?'

'Yes, it was lovely! Thank you for asking,' Clara replied with a small smile.

When all the passengers had taken their seats, Xiamen shut the door and rolled the coach into motion. He turned on the tannoy.

'Welcome back on board everyone. Next I'll be taking you to the centre of the city to Tiananmen Square. The square is, without a doubt, one of Beijing's most popular tourist attractions. It's officially ranked the largest city square in the world. I can't remember how large it is exactly, but you can easily get that information in the Guinness Book of Records. All of the important cultural events in Beijing are held at Tiananmen Square. Apart from that, the place contains some major memorials including a monument to the People's Heroes, the Great Hall of the People and the National Museum of China. Also situated there is the mausoleum of Mao Zedong, who in 1949 proclaimed China as a People's Republic at the same square.'

Xiamen took a brief pause to let the passengers digest the information, then he continued. 'Our stop at Tiananmen Square will be four-and-a-half hours. That should give you enough time to take a walk around the square and another great tourist place next door, the

Forbidden City. The Forbidden City is one of the most visited places in the world. Not only does it have one of the largest and best-preserved collections of ancient wooden structures on earth, it also highlights the wisdom of Chinese art and architectures. There's approximately 980 buildings spread over 180 acres, including the magnificent former Chinese political complex. It's so easy to get lost so you might want to buy a map at the gate if you don't want to lose your way back to the coach and be going around in circles. Does anyone have any questions?'

'Yeah! Is it possible to skip the Forbidden City?' The question was from the dapper man in a fedora.

'That's up to you. I'm taking you to Tiananmen Square. You don't have to wander over to the Forbidden City if you don't wish to.'

'OK I don't think I'll bother then.'

'You won't be able to cover the grounds in Tiananmen Square in four-and-half hours Even if you stick around anyway,' Xiamen enthused.

'Excuse me?' the woman beside the dapper man called his attention. 'I am curious, why do you want to avoid the Forbidden City?'

'I don't fancy seeing any building made of wood, let alone loads all in one place. You don't really want to be fooled by all that pep talk of the glitz of ancient timber. They could easily blaze up like firewood at the slightest ignite from a smouldering cigarette butt and roast everything within.'

'D'you anticipate a fire starting?'

'You can never know. Better to be prepared than sorry.'

'You have a point, maybe I should avoid going there too and just stick with you.'

'You're very welcome to be my company at Tiananmen Square if you would like to.' He flashed her an encouraging smile.

She smiled back. 'I'd like that, thank you.'

'The pleasure is mine,' he said pinching the brim of his fedora tipping it to her courteously. 'My name is Geoffrey. What's yours?'

'Leilani.'

'Lovely name. It's a pleasure to make your acquaintance Leilani.'

'It's a pleasure too. Are you Australian?'

'No, I just live there. I'm originally from New Caledonia.'

'Where's New Caledonia?'

'It's on the Pacific Ocean to the east of Australia and to the north of New Zealand.'

'I never heard of it before.'

'Yeah, most people haven't. I guess by your accent you are from the United States, isn't that so?'

'Well, yes, I live in San Francisco now, though I was born in Hawaii.'

'Hawaii! That's interesting. Do you go back there sometimes?'

'Yup, every December. I spend my Christmases there.'

'After The Forbidden City, we will be going to Gulou and Zhonglou, also known as the Drum and Bell Towers,' Xiamen's voice suddenly broke in and the coach occupants went quiet once more. The towers used to serve as the city's official timekeeper, pretty much like church bells ringing when they mark the hour. In the days before the skyscraper era, the towers were the highest buildings and the viewpoints for sighting an enemy far off. These days, the architectures are good points for tourists who like to see the city from a bird's-eye view. After we leave the Drum and Bell Towers, I'll take you to Dongcheng District and Wangfujing so you can have a wander down the busiest pedestrian shopping street. There you'll find traders selling all kinds of stuff and street food all the way along. I must warn you now, some of my past passengers have had spontaneous bowel runs and blow offs when they returned to the bus after trying some snacks on the street, so be mindful of what you eat there. From Wangfujing, we'll then head straight to our final stop to begin our Great Wall tour. I myself will show you around for that part. Is everyone happy with that?'

The passengers cheered their approval and talked amongst themselves.

Back at Xtopher Hotel, a man carrying a Gladstone bag had just walked through the automatic doors and was heading for the reception. Reaching the front desk, he stopped before Violet. 'Good afternoon… I am looking for Sarah De Gruchy. I believe she is lodging here, are you able to confirm that for me?'

Violet's brow creased with a suspicious look. 'I beg your pardon?'

'My name is Andrew De Gruchy, Sarah is my wife. I got the address of this hotel to come for her as we will be travelling back home together.'

The frown on Violet's face instantly gave way to a smile. 'Dear me! Welcome to Xtopher Hotel Mr De Gruchy! Give me a moment and I'll check if we have your wife here.' She looked over the register. 'We do have her here.'

'That's great! Let her know that I'm here please.'

'Give me a minute.' Violet lifted the intercom receiver and placed a call to Sarah's room. After a moment, she returned the receiver and looked through the key receptacle. 'Hmm, I didn't get any answer. Her room key isn't here either, so I have no idea whether she's in or out.'

'Okay no problem, I can go knock on the door. Can I have her room number please?'

Violet swiftly considered his request. 'I am sorry but it's against our policy to let a visitor up without checking with our guest first. If you take a seat over there and give me a moment, I'll have someone check her room.'

Andrew's face fell but he said nothing further. He went to sit in one of the seats in the lobby, keeping his bag on the floor beside him. Violet placed another call.

Up at the penthouse, Silver was just heading for the lift doors when the phone rang. He detoured and went to answer it. 'Yeah Violet, what's up?'

'Where are you Silver?'

'Where do you think? I am speaking to you through the phone in our suite, isn't that the number you called?'

'Dear me, sorry, that was a dumb question. Can you please knock on room 33 on your way down to see if you get any answer? There's a gentleman here looking for the lady.'

'Alright, will do. See you in a bit.'

'Great, thank you! See you soon.'

A few minutes later, Silver stepped out of the lift and came up to the reception desk. 'There's no one there. I think the guest is out,' he said to Violet.

'Then she must've taken the key along with her. That's not good.'

'Yea, she could easily lose it.'

'That gentleman there was asking for her. He says he's her husband.'

Silver turned towards Andrew and fluffed his hair with his fingers as he scrutinised him. He turned to Violet. 'Do you think she might be among the lot that went on the tour to the Great Wall by any chance?'

'Now that you mentioned it, I think she could be. I'll check.' Violet consulted the list of guests booked for the tour that day. 'You are right. She's on the list.'

'Right, well she's going to be away until this evening.'

'Surely he won't want to wait here until then. We can't have him sitting here all day.'

'Of course not. What's his wife's name?'

'Sarah De Gruchy.'

'I'll go have a word with him.' Silver walked up to Andrew who looked up as he approached. He greeted Andrew and carried on after Andrew responded.

'I understand you're looking for a guest at this hotel. Sarah De Gruchy, I believe?'

'That's right.'

'She's actually away on a day tour and should be back by six this evening.'

'I see. I suppose I Could wait here for her?'

'I am sorry that I have to tell you this, but our hotel doesn't approve of loitering unfortunately.'

'Thanks for letting me know. Is it possible to reach her with a message?'

'I'm afraid we have no way of contacting her.'

'Alright. Could I leave my bag at the reception while I go into town for some sight-seeing?'

'Let me come back to you on that. I won't be a moment.' Silver then left Andrew's side to have a word with Violet.

Chapter Four

When they got to Dongcheng, Xiamen parked In Woo Li Bay which was close to the famous Wangfujing Pedestrian walkway. He'd given his passengers 45 minutes to take a wander down the Wangfujing shopping street, deciding not to leave the coach himself during the interval. Still sitting at the wheel, he greeted the passengers as they returned to the bus in small groups. After everyone was seated, Xiamen started the engine and rolled the coach into motion. Driving away from Dongcheng, he drove through the connecting roads to the bypass and was soon speeding along towards the Great Wall site at Mutianyu.

Xiamen's coach sped past a couple of the 916 Express buses that plied the Beijing–Huairou route. These buses ran on a continuous loop from Beijing's Dongzhimen Bus Stop to the Huairou District, leaving every couple of minutes. They were therefore the most convenient and cost-effective public transport to the Mutianyu Great Wall site; visitors who preferred to take an independent trip frequently use them.

Xiamen suddenly drove up behind stationary traffic. The vehicles ahead had been forced to a halt. An emergency traffic tow van was towing a broken-down bus away from the road. The broken bus was one of the non-express 916 buses that also plied the route. Stranded passengers from the bus were moving between the vehicles, asking one driver to another for a ride. Some of the obliging drivers were letting them on and causing further blockages. The road was soon free again and Xiamen drove along with the moving traffic.

A short while later, Xiamen drove his coach up against another crawl. The coach ahead of his was driving below the limit. He repeatedly tapped his horn to urge it on but the bus simply crawled on, forcing him to drive behind it until there was an opening to overtake. He stepped on the throttle. Speeding past and spotting the occupants, Xiamen realised that it was one of the special charter buses that transported elderly visitors directly from Dongzhimen Wai Station to the Mutianyu Great Wall site. He waved at the driver apologetically then he accelerated, putting a good distance between them.

After driving for an hour or so, Xiamen's coach reached the transit hub at Huairou Beidajie. The hub was brimmed with crowds of people, most of them visitors waiting for the direct bus to the Great Wall site. Some street traders were hawking souvenirs whilst pockets of unlicensed drivers and transport syndicates were hustling for passengers. Xiamen drove past the crowded centre and headed towards Mutianyu. The road was swarming with vehicles shuttling passengers to and from the Mutianyu Great Wall site. Xiamen reached for the tannoy switch and turned it on.

'May I have your attention everyone! We're now heading for the Mutianyu Great Wall site which is about 70 km northeast from Beijing's city centre. But before we get there, I'll tell you some interesting history about it. If you didn't know this before, hear it from me now that the Great Wall of China is one of the oldest wonders of the world! The wall is simply the longest man-made structure that exists. It was originally created in the seventh century BC as a defence fort to fend off invaders, authorised by China's first emperor. Successive emperors later on built additional extensions to the wall for territorial defence and to control immigration and exports. In those days, the Great Wall was secured with watchtowers at strategic vantage points. From there the guards were able to easily spot encroachers from afar and raze them down like sitting ducks. As of today, the Great Wall spans westward from the east coast across China's northern interior, traversing through the plains, ridges and deserts of its provinces and municipalities. It's a total length of about 7,300 kilometres, or around 4,500 miles if you prefer. They say it might take you around 18 months to walk the full length of the Great Wall if you set out every day, so if you have the time to spare and wouldn't mind spending it on trekking, you might want to add that to your bucket list.'

The passengers burst into resounding responses. Xiamen didn't let them talk for long before he cut in.

'If you dig into the seat pocket in front of you, there are some pamphlets in there with some more information.'

Some of the guests pulled out the pamphlets in unison and Xiamen continued.

'There are two separate maps of the Great Wall. The one with the larger map shows you the entire extension of the wall and all the regions in China it passes across. The smaller map shows a bit more detail of the wall's pathway through Beijing. These include the provinces of Badaling, Simatai, Jinshanling, Juyongguan and Mutianyu. As you know, our tour is on the Great Wall section in Mutianyu. Even though I could've taken you to other sections of the Great Wall that can be more easily reached from Beijing, the scenic location in Mutianyu is more supercalifragilisticexpialidocious!'

The passengers abruptly cut in with a round of applause. The coach was strewn with cheers and giggles.

One passenger even whistled in appreciation. Xiamen waited for the cheers to quieten before he resumed talking.

'Thanks a lot, you're all amazing! As I was saying, I believe the Mutianyu Great Wall site is more special than the others. I'll tell you why. First of all, the wall's site in Mutianyu has been masterfully restored for visitors' enjoyment! This particular section of wall was built on a hill and is the most adventurous to walk too. If you like to hike, the zigzagging paths and steep ridges will challenge you. If you'd rather a lazy venture, there're mechanical vehicles that'll take you up and down the hill as well. This site is often less rowdy than the other Great Wall sites in Beijing, so we can enjoy the adventure without the presence of a crowd.'

The passengers' cut in, talking excitedly amongst themselves. Xiamen could tell they were pleased with this extra knowledge. He gave them a moment then carried on.

'We've now reached Mutianyu. There's a big aqueduct at the roundabout coming up. If you haven't seen an aqueduct before, it's not an overpass for vehicles like it appears. It's actually an overhead river. The channel bridge takes the water over the road, so the torrent is flowing above rather than below us. This type of water duct is ancient technology. Only a few still stand in the world today. Look! There is the overhead canal, moving billion gallons of water to the agricultural lands and other arid parts! Amazing, isn't it? I encourage you to take a photo of it for your memorabilia if you like to keep memoirs.' Xiamen turned off his microphone.

The passengers fixed their gazes on the aqueduct as they drove past it whilst some of them with cameras, including Sarah, quickly took snapshots.

'Phew! I took a couple of shots, not sure how they will come out though. I'll cherish them forever,' Sarah said as she returned her camera to her bag.

'I never heard an artificial river going over a road,' Clara said, still fixing a backward glance at the aqueduct. 'It's really amazing.'

'Yep... it is. I went to see the Citadel of Cairo Aqueduct when I was in Egypt, although it was no longer functioning. The old structure still stands and I took some pictures there too. I would have loved some shots of me with this one in the backdrop.'

'Why not? We can come back here after and I will do it for you.'

'I'm not sure there will be time for that. Thank you anyway.'

Xiamen soon reached their destination and pulled up in the designated parking area. 'We're here everyone! Welcome to the Great Wall site in Mutianyu!'

The passengers cheered with a resounding applause. Xiamen opened the coach door with a beaming smile. He talked to the passengers as they disembarked.

'This is our final destination and where we'll be spending the rest of the day. I promise you we're all going to have fun here. As I said, I'll be leading a group walk so you're all welcome to join me! You're free to wander off on your own if you like but try to get back to the coach by 4PM exactly. For your information, that large building there is the Tourist Service Centre. There's a cash machine that accepts foreign cards if you need some more renminbi, and toilets that you'll find very pleasing to use. For now, if everyone could just follow me I'll start the tour.'

A few minutes later, Xiamen had led the group to the right flank of the Tourist Service building where there was an exhibition hall. The hall displayed an array of photos of the Mutianyu Great Wall that had been shot at various points through history. An English-speaking Chinese woman was reading commentaries from a teleprompter, relaying histories of the Great Wall in general and Mutianyu in particular.

Xiamen led the group out of the exhibition hall and into the box office where he assisted with getting their entrance tickets. He then took them along the long road of shops and restaurants that led to the shuttle bus terminal.

'We're now going to the ferry bus station where we'll be boarding the shuttle bus. The bus will take us to the starting point of the Mutianyu Great Wall. If you'd like a snack or a bottle of water, I'd advise you to buy them now while we're on this side. Everything is more expensive at the Great Wall area. Once we've crossed to the other side, please beware of the hawkers! Some might try to rip you off with inflated prices so make sure you haggle. If a hawker is selling something that catches your eye and you really want to buy it, offer them half of the asking price. That'll definitely show them you can't be cheated easily and they'll offer you the best price!' Xiamen said with a laugh.

The group laughed with him. Some of them took his advice and proceeded to buy bottles of water. After a four-minute walk, Xiamen and the group reached the shuttle terminal and boarded a bus. The bus took five minutes to get to the starting point. After they had all alighted, Xiamen led them on talking.

'The wall here extends between two and three kilometres in length. It's the longest fully restored section of China's Great Wall that is open to visitors. If you've got strong legs and a good balance then feel free to go on an adventurous climb on your own now. Though mind you, the purpose of coming here is not to climb the wall but to see the wonder and enjoy the attractions here. For instance, you can see the watchtowers I mentioned earlier. The wall here mostly stands over ridged grounds and hills, surrounded by beautiful sceneries of forest on both sides. If you'd like to see the scenery that's beyond, do take advantage of the watchtowers. You'll definitely enjoy great panoramic views from up there. There are 23 restored watchtowers here in total. They spread along the top of the wall at short intervals, starting from that tower there to the last one at that end which is the highest one.' Xiamen stopped walking; he faced the group and asked if anyone had any questions.

'Can we go up the watchtowers?' Jake, the Canadian boy, asked.

'Of course. Most of them are accessible. You can go up in either a cable car or chairlift. That's a chairlift going up to a watchtower now over there.' Xiamen made a gesture with his hand.

'Isn't that a sledge?' Blake queried, not looking exactly at where Xiamen was showing.

'That one you're looking at is actually a toboggan. It's only for going down. The one I was referring to is over there.'

'Look over there, Blake!' Jake cut in, nudging Blake's head to the right.

'Oho, I see it now!'

'Dad, can we go up the watchtower now?'

'Not right now Jake. Maybe later,' his father resolved.

'But I want to go up too, Dad. How about Jake and I go?'

'Of course not. You can't go unaccompanied,' said their mother.

'Actually, I think they can. They're up to the recommended height. I'm sure they'd be allowed to go on the lower ones on their own,' Xiamen offered.

'I will go with them,' their father put in.

'Thanks Dad!' the boys chorused.

'Take that stone path, it leads to the chairlift station. You can use the chairlift. But if you'd prefer cable car, go further up the path. Whichever you prefer, the fee is the same.'

'Okay, thanks,' their father replied and turned to the boys' mother. 'Are you coming along, Debbie?'

'No, Justin, I'd rather stay with the group,' she replied.

'Alright. Come on boys, let's go.'

'Just a second!' Xiamen stopped them as they begin to walk off. 'It's cheaper to buy a return ride for one or the other, the cable car or a chairlift. If you don't wish to pay more, don't use different rides for going up and down. Especially the toboggan. That will cost you more. The handlers may sometimes want to entice you to use the toboggan for the ride down, so make sure you clarify what you want when buying the pass for the ride,' Xiamen advised.

'Will do, thanks a lot for the tips,' Justin said and he walked away with his boys.

Xiamen asked the group if anyone else was interested in going up the watchtowers. Some members simultaneously chorused that they would, including Sarah. She gave Clara a persuasive look but Clara shook her head in refusal. 'Chicken,' she mouthed, smiling. Clara nodded back with a grin. Xiamen gave some directives to the subgroup wishing to go up the watchtowers, then he released them. After they had gone, he threw his next question to the remaining group.

'So, is anyone here brave enough to climb the wall with me?' Seeing their hesitant looks, he said, 'It's really not that hard to do. I don't mean to take you to the summit. I'm just inviting you to do a simple traditional climb. There's nothing more prideful and memorable to boast about after you leave here. Wouldn't you like to brag to your friends that you climbed the Great Wall of China in Beijing? I think that'll impress them. This may be your once-in-a-lifetime opportunity, so why not make the best of it? We'll walk up along the stone steps to the eighth or tenth watchtower like we're doing a mountain hike. It'll take us roughly 30 to 40 minutes to get to the tenth watchtower. So, I reckon we should be up and back in an hour-and-half. Are we good to go?' The group cheered their assent and Xiamen led them on.

Andrew De Gruchy had left the hotel shortly after he was advised against waiting in the lounge. He was able to leave his bag with the receptionist and he also took the city guide map she'd offered him before leaving. Not having anywhere in mind of where to go next, he decided to feed his eyes on the beautiful city. What better to do than take a wander into Beijing; not that he'd been to China before.

Andrew had often thought about the growing Chinese industrialisation and its impact on world economy, and often mused over how the rest of the world had become so dependent on China-made products. How the Asian giant managed to produce so many products for the world at competitive prices, compared to other countries, fascinated him. He secretly nursed the thought of a global problem rising from China shutting down its exports abroad. Taking a wander around the Asian city was a real delight. Consulting the map, he pinpoint his current location and drew out his intended route with his finger. He crossed the street and walked towards the metro station.

A short while later, Andrew arrived at Haidian District and took a short walk to the East Gate entrance of Summer Palace. The huge gate had an impressive gable-roof with protective overhanging eaves and colourfully decorated beams. He took a moment to admire the plaque above the gate; it had nine artistically detailed dragons positioned around it and bore the Chinese hanzi "Yi He Yuan". A bronze lion and a lioness sat on white marble pedestals flanking either side of the gate, as if they were guarding it. Three grand doors were installed in the middle with two smaller doors on each side. The stone-carved stairway at the entrance was decorated with a pair of cloud dragons playing with a ball. After a bit of marvelling at the exquisite gate, Andrew bought an entry ticket and walked into the grounds.

The Summer Palace was an imperial paradise of islands that converged luscious gardens, lakes and buildings across an extraordinary 717 acres to create stunning natural and artificial grand designs. The engineering of Kunming Lake was a grand job in particular; it was dug in the midst of the grounds and the excavated soil was used to form the 200-feet-high Longevity Hill. The making of the lake and the hill led to further ingenious constructions of splendid stream bed and green forest on Longevity Hill.

Being a lover of nature and art, Andrew respected the Chinese for two things; how much they valued their ancestral antiques and how penchant they were for preserving them. He had read about the magnificent masterpieces of Chinese maestros at the Summer Palace and often considered visiting it one day if there was an opportunity. Today was his lucky day!

Andrew had two places of interest in mind that he wanted to see in the Summer Palace. The first one was the old administrative palace, also known as The Hall of Benevolence and Longevity. He was particularly intrigued by what he'd learnt whilst reading about the historic military expeditions carried out at the Summer Palace. British troops had looted the hall in 1860 and burned it down, and it was also vandalised again by the Eight-Nation Alliance forces in 1900. Andrew found the hall pretty easy to locate; it was the first building facing him when he walked through the gate. Happy with his luck, he went in.

Passing some sculpted incense burners at the entrance of the hall, Andrew paused in the courtyard to survey a bronze Kylin mythical beast; the sculpted object had the head of a dragon, horns of a deer, hoofs of a bull and tail of a lion. There were bronze phoenixes positioned in the middle of the courtyard and dragon statues positioned to one side.

Also outstanding in the courtyard were five exceptional-looking decorative engraved stones that bore the Chinese letters "Fengxuwulao". Andrew was captivated by the many old furnishings around the main hall. The centre piece was an exquisitely carved ancient throne on a raised platform which was ornamented with nine dragons and flanked by peacock-feather fans. Glimpsing the original fixtures in the hall that were once used for court sessions, he went over to inspect them. He admired an intricately carved wooden frame adorned with nine lions and a glass screen engraved with Chinese letters, including a crafted silk work of one hundred bats with the calligraphs of a Chinese Empress called Cixi. Andrew gallivanted to the north end of the hall where he saw an underground cistern, which he learnt was the Well of Extending Life.

Leaving the Hall of Benevolence and Longevity, Andrew walked towards the Hall of Joyful Longevity which was just beside Kunming Lake. Close to the lake at the front of the hall was a railed stone platform that led to a jetty. Also at the front of the hall were bronze sculptures of a crane, a vase and a deer. Going inside the main hall, he saw a staged carved sandalwood throne behind a folding screen. The throne was flanked on both sides by a pair of peacock-feather fans and two porcelain plates. an old colourful chandelier hung from the ceiling and glossy bronze incense furnaces positioned in each of the four corners of the hall. Also there, was a broad dining table, which Andrew gathered was once used to serve Empress Cixi an epicurean buffet of dishes. Andrew gadded further to the east and west sides of the hall, feeding his eyes on Empress Cixi's former dressing and sleeping chambers before making his way out of there.

Andrew next entered the Chángláng Long Corridor. Pausing at the entrance, he read the description and learnt it was 728 metres long. A mental rough conversion gave him an approximation of 2388 feet. Marvelling at the stretch, he strolled on. It wasn't long into the marathon walk than he was momentarily overcame by amazement. The walls, beams, and ceilings were decorated with thousands of colourful plaques, canvases and Su-style paintings. Some plaques bore hanzi inscriptions and there were many abstract paintings which Andrew couldn't work out. He had never seen so much literary and fine art in one place. He found the ensemble of exhibitions in the long gallery overwhelming as he looked from one work of art to another.

The long corridor led Andrew straight into Shizhang Pavilion, a rather small courtyard which he didn't find appealing. Without lingering, he went outside. Now standing at the front of Shizhang Pavilion, Andrew hesitated, contemplating where to go next. Finally deciding, he headed towards the lakeside.

On the west bank of Kunming Lake, Andrew walked up to a boat-shaped ark that was set on a base of marble stone. The lakeside boat measured 36-metre long and it housed a two-storey pavilion. Andrew got on the boat and went up to the higher deck. He slowly walked about on the tinted marbled floor, taking his time to glance over every detail. He saw the imitation paddle wheels on the sides of the boat and the colourful glinting glass panes on the windows. Also catching his eye were the fitted large convex mirrors that showed off panoramic views of the lake. Dragon-faced gargoyles were attached to the four points of the tiled roof to direct rainwater away from the decks. Finally, Andrew returned his look to the stationary paddle wheels and stifled a grin as he thought, the builders must have been crazy to have built a dragon boat this splendid just to ground it. He turned around to look at his other object of interest and momentarily held his breath.

Flaunting a length of 150 and a width of 8 metres, the monstrous Seventeen-Arch Bridge stood like a giant dragon in the undulating waves of Kunming Lake. This bridge was made of whitened marble stone and was the largest of thirty bridges in the Summer Palace; it was built to link the east bank to a separate island that stood apart in the lake. As per the name, the bridge was constructed with seventeen arches underneath to create passageways for boats. The highest point for bigger boats was the central ninth arch; it was flanked on both sides by eight arches of descending dimensions. The balustrades along the bridge were lined from end-to-end with over five hundred lion sculptures of distinctive designs. Each end of the bridge was anchored into the ground beside the willow trees planted close to the lakeside, and they were ornamented with fretworks of Kylin-like beasts.

Looking from the top deck of the Marble Boat, Andrew soaked up the spectacular scenery; the stunning sight blew his imagination away. The bridge looked nothing like what he'd previously seen on a postcard. He had never thought the day would come where he would have this experience, yet there he was, witnessing it with his own eyes! Viewing the real thing now gave him great joy. He itched to take pictures and wished Sarah hadn't taken his camera with her. Seeing the other visitors gallivanting on the bridge, he looked at his wristwatch and guessed he still had some time to kill. He hurried off the Marble Boat with his heart bent on exploring the bridge.

Chapter Five

'We're here ladies and gentlemen!' Xiamen announced as he drew the coach to a stop at the front of the hotel. Rising from his seat, he turned to face the passengers. 'May I have your attention everyone. Before you go, I'd just like to mention that giving tips is popular culture in China. So if you've appreciated my services today, you're very much welcome to leave me a little tip. I have some tour favours to give yoou too.' He showed them a stack of printed compliment cards. 'These have traditional Chinese words of wisdom that bear advice and truths of life, not like the typical British humour in Christmas crackers.' He got off the bus and stood to one side.

The passengers started to disembark and they exchanged pleasantries with Xiamen as he handed out the complimentary souvenirs. Some of them gave him tips and he thanked them. Pockets of passengers who didn't lodge at Xtopher Hotel dispersed in different directions whilst the hotel's guests made their way into the reception. When the coach was empty, Xiamen got back on and drove it round the back to park up for the day.

Meanwhile in the hotel reception, Andrew was back in the lounge with his Gladstone bag plucked down on his lap. After arriving there ten minutes prior, he had learned Sarah still wasn't back, but Violet had assured him the coach was to arrive at any moment and encouraged him to wait in the lounge for her this time. Seeing the guests filing in, Andrew scanned their faces expectantly. The guests in the lead walked to the reception desk and queued up. Violet greeted them with welcoming smiles, retrieving their keys from the receptacle for them. Clara and Sarah were in the middle of the crowd walking into the reception.

'What a day! I'm knackered! I could do with a nap.' Clara said tiredly.

'Me too. Nothing would be more pleasing now than falling like a log on my bed and crashing out. It's really been a long and tiring day!'

'Indeed! All that walking was very tiring.'

'Absolutely! I felt a bit dizzy going up in the chairlift as well. I regretted getting on it but the view up there was worth it.'

'It was brave of you to climb up the hill to join us right after getting off the chairlift.'

'Yep, I know. I like to be adventurous.'

'Definitely. I have seen that in you. So, what room are you in?'

'Room 33.'

'Really?'

'Yep. Why are you surprised?'

'I'm in room 35.'

'Really?'

'Now you sound surprised,' Clara teased.

'Wow! I wouldn't have guessed that you were just next door to me. It's a wonderful coincidence.'

'It surprises me too. This world is ever so small.'

'Yep. So, Clara, what do you plan to—'

'Sarah!'

The voice of Andrew suddenly cut across the hall, drawing attention. Some people threw cursory glances at him as Sarah stopped dead in her tracks with a popeyed expression. Sarah's abrupt standstill forced Clara to also pull to a halt; she looked from Sarah to the stranger bewilderedly. Andrew, now standing beside the chair and clasping his fingers around the handle of his Gladstone, flaunted an apologetic look. The remaining guests went past and joined the queue for their keys, some of them stealing glances at the unfolding drama.

'Who's that?' Clara asked quietly.

'My husband!' Sarah muttered, scarcely moving her lips.

'Didn't you know he was coming?'

'No I didn't.'

'Is there a problem?'

'Yep, a big one. I better go and have a word. Don't wait for me. I'll knock on your door later.'

Sarah walked over to Andrew with a hardened expression. Andrew's face crumpled into a pleading look as she approached, but Sarah's cold stare didn't at all alter. 'Come with me!' she said to him with a steely voice. She turned and walked towards the exit as Andrew humbly followed her. Going past Clara, Sarah gave her a slight nod and continued forwards.

Clara remained rooted in contemplation, staring until the couple turned the corner into the passageway to the restaurant and she lost sight of them. She shrugged and joined the queue to collect her key. Later that night, Clara was sitting in her room snacking on some shortbread and a glass of fruit drink when a tap sounded on the door. Guessing who it was, she got up from the armchair and opened the door.

'Hey Clara, would it be a bother if I were to crash here tonight? No hard feelings if you can't accommodate me.'

'Good to see you again Sarah. I don't mind if you want to sleep here. There's plenty of room. Come in and make yourself comfortable.' Clara let her in.

'Sorry I had to leave you impromptu last time. Andrew surprised the heck out of me.'

'Is that your husband's name?'

'Yep.'

'I have actually been thinking about you since you left with him. What is going on?'

'I suppose I can tell you. Especially after leaving like that. Let's sit down. It's a long story and might take some time.'

'Would you like some shortbread and fruit juice?' Clara asked as she moved her glass and biscuit from the stool beside the chair for Sarah to take the seat.

'I'll have some shortbread and some water would be great please.'

'Okay. Here, help yourself to the biscuits. I will get you some water.'

'Thank you,' Sarah said as she sat on the armchair.

Clara took out a bottle of water from the fridge and passed it to Sarah. She poised herself on the bed and stared straight at her. 'So, what's going on?'

'I married Andrew four months ago. Although we'd dated for two years before we tied the knot, I really didn't know him as well as I thought. He kept a secret from me, and I only found out about it last month...' Sarah momentarily fell silent.

Clara shifted with impatience and looked on at Sarah expectantly, but Sarah just continued to stare at the items in her hands. Clara decided to give her a moment and started licking off the particles of biscuit that were trapped between her teeth. After a brief silence, she changed the subject.

'Come on girl! don't just keep staring at the snack. Have a drink and eat, you'll feel better.'

Sarah took a helping of shortbread and placed the packet on the coffee stool. She nibbled on the biscuit and drank some water. Finishing the bottle, she placed it on the stool and looked at Clara. 'Sorry for breaking off like that. It's all been too much for me, I've not been able to come to terms with it. Talking about it still makes me feel so angry!' She fell quiet again looking tense.

'Don't bottle it all up, it helps to talk about things.'

'I found out that Andrew had a secret child before he met me,' Sarah said and paused again.

'No, don't stall again Sarah. What happened?' Clara didn't muffle her impatience.

'The whole thing was a scandal.'

'What do you mean?'

'So, Andrew has an older brother who is married with a five-year-old daughter. Last month, it turned out that the girl is actually Andrew's. I was caught up in the whole drama when it came out. His brother went into a murderous rage and wanted to kill us all.'

'I don't understand.'

'I mean Andrew had slept with his brother's wife and got her pregnant. His brother found out about it and went mad with rage. He wanted to kill the wife, the child, Andrew, even me! Can you imagine that he wanted me dead too? I did nothing to him and he came after me as well. The wife and child had to be put into a safe haven. The police arrested the brother with a hacking knife outside our door. He was charged with intent to commit harm with a deadly weapon. They only released him after he signed a restraining order against Andrew and me.'

Clara gawked open mouthed at Sarah.

'Yep. It's shocking, I know.' Sarah said in response to Clara's stunned look.

'Oh my God! Sarah, that really is scandalous!'

'Yep. I'm completely blameless in the situation yet I'm now having to suffer because of it. I am so mad with Andrew for putting me in the middle of the mess… I would have killed him myself if I didn't love him so much… and on top of it all, I am pregnant too…' Sarah suddenly began to sob.

More shocked by the latter revelation, Clara looked at her new friend bewilderedly. She swiftly racked her brains for the best words to console her. It made sense to give her a moment so she waited for her to pull herself together. Sarah composed herself and continued.

'It isn't entirely Andrew's fault, even though he was a dick for sleeping with his brother's wife. Andrew told me they had a series of flings six years ago when he occupied a room in his brother's flat. His brother frequently worked nightshifts and the wife often complained to him about her loneliness. He swears that it was she who came onto him and wouldn't leave him alone, and he'd always hated himself after for doing it.'

'What was he thinking? Sleeping with his brother's wife in his own house? Didn't they think of using protection?'

'Andrew told me he'd often used a condom, but there were a few times he didn't have them, and she would promise him not to worry about it that she was safe. He said he had trusted her to be wise, but that wasn't the case.'

'Wise huh? She wouldn't think of getting it on with her brother-in-law if she was the least wise.'

'Yep. The nympho had the hots for Andrew and just couldn't keep her claws off him. Now look what shit has come out of it.'

'So, how did the whole thing blow open?'

'From what I gathered, Andrew's brother and his wife were trying for another child but it wasn't happening naturally. They'd gone for fertility checks and the brother was diagnosed as infertile. The news was like a blast from a double-barrelled gun when it hit his brother. He was devastated to learn he couldn't naturally father a child and even the one he'd always thought was his, wasn't at all. After he learned the child was Andrew's, his sanity crumbled and he went mad with fury.'

'Oh dear... I imagine his ego was bruised. Was a DNA test taken?'

'Andrew denied having any intercourse with his brother's wife at first, even after she had confessed everything. But he did a DNA test eventually after I pleaded with him. When the results came out, shit really hit the fan. The brother came after us with a weapon.'

'What a story!'

'Yep. It's all so fucked up. I am now suffering with trauma because of it all. I blame Andrew for not handling things better. Ugh! I hate him so much right now!'

'What are you going to do now Sarah?'

'I came to Beijing to be far away from all the mess and to clear my head. I needed to think without being close to Andrew. He has been pestering me with apologies. I told him I don't want to be with him anymore but he hasn't left me alone. That was why I left. Now he has come here to continue with his fake pleas. He is such a damn hypocrite!'

'What does he want you to do?'

'He wants me to give our marriage a chance.'

'Would you prefer if he wasn't sorry and just moved on?'

'What do you mean?'

'You are carrying his baby. He would be more of a dick if he didn't at least try to make amends with you.'

'What are you saying now?'

'I am saying it might be that Andrew is genuinely sorry. Perhaps he is beating himself up for his past actions, they can't be changed now. Have you considered how he might be feeling about himself?'

'Excuse me, who's side are you on now?'

'Of course I am on your side. But we need to really appreciate the whole thing objectively. Maybe if the brother could have had another child with his wife, nobody would have ever found out otherwise... the truth would have stayed buried. Now the truth is suddenly out of the bag, better to deal with it now. Come on Sarah, cut your husband some slack. He might have been a dick for what he did, but that was before you knew him. Remember the little girl is just as blameless as you and equally caught up in the mess. Have you even considered how confusing it must be for her to learn that her uncle is her father and not the man she had been calling daddy? It is neither her fault nor yours, and it's not entirely your husband's. Don't you have any empathy for anyone else's trauma but your own? Believe me, you aren't the only one strung up by emotional distress. Everyone in the quadrangle is just as strewn with stress as you. Do you understand that?'

Sarah moved her lips as if to say something, but she stopped herself and stared into space with a conflicted look. Clara regarded Sarah closely and gave her a moment to mull. After a silence, she questioned her.

'Where is your husband now?'

'I left him in my room to have it for the night. He said he won't leave Beijing without me but he might as well return home tomorrow. I'm not going back with him. He'll have to sort his own accommodation if he chooses to stay on longer … not at this hotel either. I came here because I don't want to sleep in the same room as him. You sure you don't mind me roosting here?'

'Of course I don't mind you sleeping here. But seriously, I can see you still care for him. Why would you vacate your room if there was no love there? You could have just marched him out of the hotel there and then, couldn't you?'

'That would have been a mean thing to do. He came all the way here because of me.'

'So you do care? You said you didn't want to be with him anymore, but your actions don't line up with your words. Didn't he make any provisions for his own sleeping arrangements?'

'Well, he said he didn't. He had pleaded with my sister to give him my travel itinerary. She gave it to him without asking me first or even telling me about it after. Argh! I am mad at her for doing that. She will be answering to me when I get back to Jersey that's for sure.'

'So, he knew all about your accommodation here and came to take advantage of that?'

'I think he knew I wouldn't have the guts to shut the door in his face. He's hoping to use the last days of my holiday to talk things through and to convince me to travel back with him.'

'In that case, I think that you should reconsider your stand.'

'What?' Sarah frowned.

'Your husband wouldn't have bothered to fly all the way here if he didn't truly love you. Not all men can humble themselves like that! My ex is far from the type, he's a jerk who will never apologise for his wrongdoings.

If you want my honest advice, give your husband a chance. Try not to punish him for mistakes in his past. You are carrying his baby, at least try for the baby's sake.'

Clara observed Sarah's frown swiftly metamorphosed into a thoughtful look and took the opportunity to drive home her point. 'It's likely that Andrew never had a meaningful relationship with his brother's wife. I presume it was just series of rumpy-pumpy brushes. It's not like he knew any better that the child was his, you were all equally in the dark. The baby you're carrying and the other girl are going to be family. Do you not realise that you're technically now her step mum? If I were you, I would resolve the situation in their best interest. What are you really mad about?'

'I don't know. Maybe I just wanted things to be perfect. I was angry because this came between us. It's all just a big mess.'

'I get that. But let it go Sarah. Your husband is here now and in your room. You didn't imagine he would make a gesture as big as travelling across the world to make amends. If I were you, I would stop torturing him because you are actually the one causing more pain now.'

'What?' Sarah looked surprised.

'You heard me right. Like I said before, your husband must be feeling low and he probably hates himself for his mistakes. Try to see beyond the past and focus on the future. Don't you think everyone deserves another chance? Imagine Andrew was your brother. If his wife wouldn't forgive and accept him back, would you be happy with the wife? Would you like any woman to treat your brother that way? Moreover, since your own baby is on the way, don't you think it deserves to be born into a nuclear family especially as the father is pleading for it?

Just put yourself in the shoes of others and you'll understand what I'm telling you.'

'Wow. How did you learn to talk like this? You've made me feel guilty now.'

'Sarah, you know damn well that you still love your husband. I think you came to Beijing to run away from yourself. You needed to be far away in your attempt to get over the feelings you have for him. True or false?'

Sarah's sudden stark look of admission said it all. 'That's what I thought. Running away won't kill your feelings for him. At the end of the day, when you lie back in bed to sleep you'll remember that you didn't forgive him. Wouldn't you like to teach your baby about forgiveness? Or are you going to tell him or her that you couldn't forgive their father because of something that occurred before he met you? Your child and the girl are going to want their daddy and there is nothing that you can do about that. Better get used to it. Unless, there is no iota of conscience in that heart of yours.'

'Okay. I get it. Stop talking now. Let me think.'

'Sure, take your time. You should probably sleep on it. I'm sure by morning you'll have a clearer head. I'll get the bed ready for us to sleep.'

Clara got up and made the bed. She took the spare pillows out of the wardrobe and laid them on the bed. After that she changed into her pj's and excused herself to go brush her teeth. By the time she came out, Sarah was on her feet looking anxious.

'Humm... I've changed my mind. I will sleep in my room. Thank you for the moral lectures. You certainly knocked some sense into my head. You are too much, girl. Thank you really.'

'Don't mention it, I only helped you see things from a different angle.'

'Yep, I know. I will see you tomorrow. What time do you go down for breakfast?'

'Probably between nine and ten.'

'I'll see you in the restaurant then. Thank you for being so supportive. Have a good sleep.' Sarah moved to the door.

'Wait Sarah! Let me give you a hug before you go.'

'Oooh, that's very nice of you. Thank you dear.'

They embraced briefly before Sarah left. Clara locked the door after her. She stripped out of her sleeping clothes and crawled into bed in her birthday suit. It wasn't long before she fell fast asleep.

Chapter Six

Xiamen returned to the penthouse straight after the tour had finished, exhausted from all the driving and talking. he'd crashed as soon as his head hit the pillow, not stirring until the next morning. Getting up at 8:30, he immediately knew from the silence in the suite that his parents were already out. He felt a hunger pang and poured himself a quick breakfast, took a shower and got ready for work.

A short while later, Xiamen was in the lift going down to the reception when the doors slid open and Clara stood facing him.

'Oh, you again!' Clara exclaimed as she stepped into the lift.

'I'm afraid so... good morning,' Xiamen replied, flaunting a grin.

Clara turned her head to face him. 'A good morning to you too. Is it just a sheer coincidence that I meet you at the lift again, or are we running on the same schedule?'

'Could be one or other or both. Whatever it is, I'm glad to be in the company of a pretty lady.'

'Thank you, I am flattered,' Clara said smiling. 'You really made the tour for us yesterday, you were good fun.'

'It's what I do, I try to give it my best.'

'How long have you been a tour guide?'

'Going on two years now.'

'You are brilliant at the job... you're very good indeed.'

'Thank you, Clara Jerkins... er, sorry, I didn't mean to call you by your name like that. I'd memorised it from your bus ticket yesterday.'

'Oh really? Do you memorise every passenger's name when they show you their tickets?'

'Not generally. I was thinking about the name after I saw it on the ticket and I liked the sound of it. It kinda struck me like the title of an interesting book and made me very curious as to what the inside pages were like, so it's been stuck in my head like a must-read novel. To tell the truth I've been carrying the thought of you in my head around ever since. You don't mind me wondering about you like that, do you?'

'Ha-ha! You are funny. I guess you can amuse yourself however you choose after all... Oh my! We haven't pressed a button yet.'

'That's right, I'll get it.' Xiamen pressed the button. 'Done, off we go!' The lift doors closed and descended. 'It's a pleasure to meet you Clara Jerkins. I'm Xiamen Christopher.' He stretched his hand out for a handshake.

'Nice to meet you too, Xiamen Christopher.'

They shook hands. Xiamen continued to hold on to her hand until she pulled it from his.

'So, is Jerkins your maiden or married name?'

'Excuse me? Aren't you being rather too forward?'

'Pardon me lady. I don't mean to come across as forward, it's not in my nature to be brash. It's just that my mind won't be at ease until I know that what I'm hoping for is true.'

'And what would that be?'

'I'm hoping that you're not a Mrs Somebody to tell you the truth. Could you now put me out of my misery please before my curiosity suffocates the life out of me?'

'Well, Mr Xiamen Christopher, if it will give your mind any comfort, for the record I have never been married. So, now that you know, do you want to propose to me, huh?'

'Ha-ha! You're funny. I don't mean it like that.'

The lift doors opened. Clara stepped out. Xiamen followed and kept up with her. They walked down the corridor towards the reception.

'I suppose you're going for breakfast, right?' he asked her.

'Yes. What about you, where are you going?'

'Nowhere precisely, just walking with you. Do you like it here?'

'Yes, Beijing is a pleasant city.'

'I mean, do you like it here in the hotel?'

'I haven't seen anything to complain about yet.'

'Very well then. Should you find anything here unpleasant, don't hesitate to let me know. I'll personally sort it.'

'Thank you. I'll remember that.'

Violet was attending to a guest when Xiamen and Clara walked up to the reception lobby. Without pausing at the desk, Xiamen greeted his mother from afar and gestured that he would be back; he carried on walking with Clara before his mother could even respond. Violet glanced after them briefly before returning her attention to the guest. Clara looked at him with a puzzled expression.

'Are you going out?'

'No.'

'But you are going towards the exit.'

'No.'

'Where are you going to then?'

'I'm going with you to the restaurant. I'd like to assist you with your breakfast if you'd welcome my company as a waiter. Do you mind?'

Stifling a smile, Clara gave him a peeking-glance out of the corner of her eye and said nothing. They walked the rest of the way in silence. In the restaurant, Xiamen led Clara to a table and pulled out a chair for her. After she sat down, he stood by her like a server.

'So, what would her ladyship like to have for breakfast?'

'Is there anything else on offer apart from a full English?'

'Good question. There're some cereals but I reckon the hot food would be much more satisfying. How hungry are you?'

'As hungry as a horse.'

'I recommend you go for the fry-up then. Perhaps I can bring you a selection. What would you like?'

'Before I answer that, I have one question.'

'Yes?'

'Do you intend to join me for breakfast, or are you going to serve me and then disappear?'

'Well, it depends.'

'On what?'

'I'd like to join you but only if you'd permit that. I wouldn't want to act a nuisance and hover around you if you'd prefer to be alone. My plan was to serve you and make sure you have everything you need before I left.'

'You can join me.'

'That's great! With all pleasure. So, tell me, what would you like to have?'

'I may as well sample the lot. Give me the full package.'

'Okay hungry horse, one of everything coming up. I'll be back with your order soon.' Xiamen went off.

At the buffet table, Xiamen took a plate from the stack and started filling it up. He hadn't got halfway into dishing the food when Clara suddenly appeared beside him with a plate in her hand.

'Hey… my humble server, what would you like to have in your plate?'

'Hey, what're you doing here?'

'Getting you your own breakfast,' she said with a slight giggle.

'But I'm the one doing the serving not you.'

'Yes, for me, as I understood. I don't remember having the discussion about you serving yourself, or did we?'

'I'm here at your service, so I'm doing the serving, not you.'

'Serve me, and I will do likewise.'

'Come on now Miss Jerkins, go back to your seat and let me take care of the serving.'

'I can't agree to that.'

'Why not?'

'Because what's good for the geese is good for the gander.'

'Good one. But you don't have to serve me too.'

'Since I agreed to you to serve me, you better let me do likewise for you too, or we can just swap plates now and do our own serving. What would you prefer?'

'Feel free to serve me in that case, thank you for choosing to do it.'

'My pleasure. So, what would you like on your plate?'

'I'll have the full package as well. What's good for the geese is good for the gander, right?'

'Touché!'

'So, how much beans would the geese like on her plate?'

'Three spoons are just about right. What about you?'

'I'd rather skip the beans.'

'Didn't you just say you wanted the full course?'

'Yeah, I did, but now I think I'd rather skip the beans.'

'So, no beans. What else?'

'I prefer to have just the toast, you can leave out the fried bread as well as the mushroom and pudding.'

'Okay, clear. Would you like to add anything else?'

'Yes, make it two toasts for me please.'

'So, apart from the ones you didn't want, you'd like two toast and one of everything else, right?'

'Yes.'

'Don't you eat much?'

'I ate some cereal earlier.'

After piling up their plates, they made their way back to the table, sat down and started to tuck in.

'Clara! There you are!'

Clara lifted her head and spotted Sarah walking towards her table with Andrew following closely behind. 'Hi Sarah, good to see you again!'

'Good to see you too,' Sarah replied before shooting Xiamen a questionable look. She turned back to Clara. 'Hmmm… what's going on here? Why are you having breakfast with our coach driver?'

'You mean Xiamen.'

'Of course I remember his name. Well I'm surprised to see you here having breakfast together. Since I've been in this hotel, I have not seen the coach driver or his parents in this restaurant at all, let alone eating with a guest.'

'Excuse me, it's not correct that I don't eat here. It's probably because you hadn't taken notice, and I'd prefer it if you referred to me by my name please,' Xiamen chipped in with a scowl.

'Sorry, I will. So what is going on between you two?'

'Chillax Sarah! Nothing is going on. Xiamen and I are just having breakfast.'

'Oh really? But that isn't what I see here. You two seem pretty into each other. Or am I mistaken?'

'Ahem! Please pardon my wife. She can be a nosy cat sometimes,' Andrew threw in, pinching Sarah's wrist gently.

'—Of course, I should mind my business. I can't help myself sorry. This is Andrew, my husband. Honey, this is Clara from East England, the one I told you I was with yesterday.'

'It's so good to meet you, Clara,' Andrew offered.

'Good to meet you too, Andrew.'

'I don't know much about Xiamen, but I know his name means gate of China, his parents own this hotel and that he drives passengers on the tour bus and talks so—'

'It's a pleasure to meet you Xiamen,' Andrew cut in.

'My pleasure too,' Xiamen said.

'Hey guys, why not join us on this table. We can carry on getting to know each other,' Clara enthused.

'Awesome!' Sarah concurred.

'You sit down babe, I will go get us some food.' Andrew said and pulled out a chair for her.

'Thanks honey.'

Andrew went to the buffet as Sarah sat down and made herself comfortable. Placing her elbows on the table, Sarah rested her chin between her knuckles and looked from Clara to Xiamen meaningfully. The probing stare from Sarah disconcerted Xiamen and Clara. They stopped eating and stared right back at her.

'Why are both of you looking at me like that? Oh, just never mind... it's none of my business anyway. In other light, Clara, I can't thank you enough for last night. To think my sister had tried to talk me into forgiving Andrew for weeks? It only took you a couple of minutes to help me see the light. Andrew would like to thank you too.'

'That won't be necessary. I only stated the obvious. You just needed a neutral person's perspective, I was just in the right place at the right time.'

'All the same, I still think you're indescribably amazing, simply je ne sais quoi.'

Clara's mind pricked up as she mentally deciphered the idiom's meaning. 'That's sweet of you Sarah... thank you.'

Andrew returned with a full plate and placed it in front of Sarah. 'That's yours darling. I will go get mine.' He went off again.

Sarah picked up the cutlery on her side and went straight for the sausages and bacon. By the time Andrew returned with his own plate of food, Sarah had devoured the whole portion of meat.

'Honey, I'd like some more bacon and sausage please,' Sarah said through a mouthful before Andrew could sit down.

'Of course. Here, have mine. I will go get more for myself. Is there anything else you'd like me to get you?'

'A cup of tea will be lovely please,' Sarah said as she transferred the meat with her fork from Andrew's plate to hers.

'No problem, I will get that for you. Does anyone else want a cup of tea?' Andrew asked, looking between Clara and Xiamen.

'I'd rather have mine after eating,' Clara replied.

'Same with me... I'll get ours later so don't bother, but thank you for asking,' Xiamen added.

Andrew soon returned with the tea plus more bacon and sausages. He transferred some to his first plate and gave the rest to Sarah who accepted it with a grin. She emptied the contents on to her plate and carried on eating quickly. Andrew noticed Xiamen and Clara exchange glances as he sat down to eat; he smiled at them and made a hand gesture to tell them Sarah was pregnant.

Sarah spotted his action. 'He is right of course. I am eating for two! I'm over two months gone now!'

A short while later, they had all finished their breakfasts and were sipping on their teas. Sarah wiped her mouth with a tissue, tossed it on her plate and rubbed her belly.

'O my, I think I might've eaten too much. I feel like a pregnant duck... quack-quack!'

'That's actually ironic. An expecting duck with a full tummy!' Clara teased.

'An irony indeed,' Xiamen added.

'Don't worry about it babe. The little one will absorb everything before you know it,' Andrew said sleekly.

'Anybody fancy a walk along the city's Hutongs?' Xiamen broke in with the question.

'What is that?' Andrew asked.

'Hutongs... they're narrow streets lined with traditional courtyard residences, known as siheyuan. Many neighbourhoods in Beijing were formed by joining one siheyuan to another. I can take you to Xicheng District which has a concentration of historic siheyuans.'

'And what is so special about the siheyuans?' asked Sarah.

'It's a true taste of the urban culture here, a contrast from the typical tourist sites you might see. The residences have a range of different layouts and social classes living in them. Some of them are substandard and are without even the basic convenience amenities, while others have tastefully and well-laid out beautiful gardens and Modern facilities. The build of a gate into a siheyuan will easily tell you which class of family it belongs to. For example, siheyuans with modest gates would have lower-class residents, the ones with moderate gates would be for middle-class and the extravagant gates would have upper-class families.'

'That doesn't sound that interesting,' Clara countered.

'Oh it does to me, I'd love to see the siheyuans,' Sarah threw in.

'Me too. It wouldn't be a bad idea to go see those discriminatory housing setups of old Beijing,' Andrew agreed with enthusiasm.

'Here's what you might find interesting,' Xiamen said, looking directly at Clara. 'How about after the hutongs I take you to Wangfujing? I don't think you had time to explore the shopping street properly yesterday. We could go there again. It'll be a perfect opportunity for you to stroll through the street and pick up a bargain to take home. Perhaps I can take you to a Jumping Chicken joint too. What do you say?'

'Jumping Chicken is frog meat, isn't it?' Andrew asked before Clara could reply.

'Yes, that's it. Have any of you ever tried it?'

'Ew! I wouldn't eat such a thing!' Clara said with a terrified grimace.

'Come on, it can't be that bad. The Chinese wouldn't eat it otherwise,' Sarah enthused.

'Well, I wasn't suggesting that you try the cuisine. I was more hoping to take you to see the way it's prepared from scratch, so you may witness how they go from pond to plate. People point at the one they want and it's netted and prepared right before their very eyes.'

'Oh yeah? I've seen lobsters done that way back home,' Clara said.

'Me too,' Andrew added.

'How is it prepared?' Sarah asked.

'The cuisine is served either lightly fried in minced cutlets or cooked in a thick curry.'

'Sounds like something delicious. I wouldn't mind having a try.'

'Ew! Sarah no!' Clara moaned with a look of horror.

'That's definitely not a good idea, darling!' her husband piped.

'Of course, I was only kidding. It's bad enough that I snore as you tell me, so, I wouldn't want to add croaking to it.'

'Well, your snoring already sounds like a bullfrog.'

'It does?'

'I am afraid so. But don't worry, it's for better or for worse… I will tolerate it till death do us part!'

They all laughed. Sarah threw her crumpled tissue at her husband who ducked. The tissue dropped to the floor. He picked it and tossed it on his own plate.

'So, Do you guys want to go downtown?' Xiamen asked the question.

'I do,' Sarah put in first.

Xiamen looked from Clara to Andrew expectantly. 'Guys?'

'Sure, why not. I'm up for it,' Andrew replied.

'The majority wins so count me in.'

'Alright, great! I want all of us to be fully immersed so we'll start by taking the metro to the hutongs in Xicheng. We can go from there to Wangfujing and take a wander along the pedestrian street to check out a jumping chicken joint. And since we all like to drink tea, I can also take you guys to a famous tea spot to try out some Asian tea flavours.'

'Mmmmm... the tea part sounds promising!' Sarah expressed.

'I am looking forward to the tea too,' Clara added.

'Let's go then,' Andrew said and stood up.

The others got to their feet. They walked out of the restaurant and left the hotel. Xiamen led them to the metro station to start the day's adventure.

Chapter Seven

Xiamen took the group to visit more interesting places, in addition to those he'd originally promised that morning. He made sure it was a fun-filled day. He and Clara got better acquainted during the outing and they ignited a relationship pretty quickly. By late afternoon they were walking hand in hand around town like high school sweethearts. When Xiamen found out that Sarah and Andrew would be leaving for Jersey the next day, he treated them to a special meal at a gondola diner. To end their day out, Xiamen took the group to the Guanghe Theatre in Qianmen to see a romantic opera.

The group returned to the hotel in the evening for dinner and drinks together in the restaurant. Sarah and Andrew had an early flight to catch so they said their goodbyes once they'd eaten. Xiamen and Clara continued drinking into the night and were merrily tipsy by the time the restaurant closed. Clara didn't offer any resistance when Xiamen asked her to accompany him to the penthouse. She followed him sheepishly from the lift to his bedroom.

Once behind closed doors, the new lovebirds wasted no time. The aftermath of the evening's drinking set to work and threw them into a drunken make out. They started kissing like two fighting gouramis before hurriedly taking off their clothes and taking the passion to the bed. Her sensuality and his virility matched compatibly, so much so that they spilled out several wet sessions during their intense fusion. Their exhaustion and tipsiness eventually doused them into deep slumbers.

After a passionate night, they slept in Xiamen's bed until it had past midday. It was a sharp knock on the door that made Clara wake up suddenly. Her eyes shot to the door as someone turned the knob. She had a mental recollection of Xiamen turning the key in the lock after they'd entered the room the previous night. The knock sounded again. She tapped Xiamen on the shoulder and he stirred.

'There's someone at the door.'

'Huh?' Xiamen muttered.

'I think someone is trying to get in.'

Xiamen lifted his head against the headboard and glanced at the door. Nothing happened. He turned to Clara.

'They must have gone away,' she said.

'That's probably my Dad coming to find out why no one has seen my face today.'

'Do you have work today?'

'No, but I don't usually stay locked inside my room like this.'

'Oops, we have slept in a bit late.'

'We sure have.'

'So, what now?'

'Better get up I suppose.'

'Then what?'

'I guess that's down to us huh?'

'What about your parents, do you think they will like me?'

'They'll love you.'

'Be serious now... will they really?'

'I don't see why not.'

'You think so?'

'I know so... They'll love you because they love me. It's a pretty straightforward logic.'

'Let's get up then. I better get back to my room to freshen up.'

'Yeah, that's a great idea. But come here first.' Xiamen reached for her.

'Now, huh? What's on your mind bad boy?' She edged closer to him.

'I think the femme fatale may already know.'

'You naughty boy,' Clara said with a giggle before planting her lips on his.

Suddenly, a knock rapped on the door once more and Silver's voice called from the other side. The pair immediately stopped kissing and stared at the door breathing hard. Clara instinctively pulled the covers over her exposed breasts and looked searchingly at Xiamen.

'Are you alright in there Xiamen?' his father called out again.

'I'm alright Dad, I'll be getting up in a minute.'

'All right. I was just checking you are okay.'

Later, Xiamen and Clara came out of the bedroom and Silver was surprised to see them together. He wasn't aware that Xiamen had returned with a girl the previous night since he hadn't warned them first like he usually did when he intended to. He threw a brief accusing look at his son before turning his attention to the visitor. Xiamen formally introduced his new acquaintance and his father gathered Clara was English. She kindled Silver's interest and he proceeded to grill her with many questions about her life and family. In twenty minutes, Silver learnt more about her than Xiamen had managed to gather himself in their short time together. Clara's chat with Silver gave her an opportunity to learn more about the host family too. After she left, Xiamen talked to his father about her.

'I think I'm falling in love Dad.'

'So soon? Haven't you only just met her?'

'Yeah. But I know what I feel, and it's driving me crazy.'

'Better slow down the wheels son, speed can cause an accident when applied recklessly.'

'Dad, I know the rules of driving of course. But with her beside me, I'm not sure I can avoid being reckless.'

'Better be sure she wants to drive along with you in that fast car of yours.'

'Maybe she will, or maybe she won't. I'm out of my mind absolutely, I feel like flying over the moon.'

'It takes two to have a romance to the moon, we better hope she likes to be an astronaut too.'

'Even if she doesn't, I'll enjoy the moment while it lasts.'

'Well, good luck with that. She seems like a nice person though… I hope it works out.'

In the next few days, Xiamen and Clara couldn't stay apart from each other; their union grew tighter and stronger with each passing moment. Xiamen took Clara around Beijing, showing her more beautiful places and treating her to the very best the city could offer. Clara spent most of her time with Xiamen when he wasn't working; she would even follow him to work too when it was permitted. She practically hung around in the penthouse for the rest of her stay, only using her hotel room scarcely.

Clara warmed her way into the hearts of Xiamen's parents too. Violet especially got on well with her; she was impressed with her knack for housework. Clara had cleaned the penthouse suite and had even volunteered to clean some rooms in the hotel to save her the housekeepers' cost. Violet taught her to cook some Asian dishes and they shared several meals together. Eventually, Clara's holiday drew to an end and it was time for her to go. The Christophers were all emotional about her leaving Beijing. Each of them had taken a liken to her in their own separate way and reacted differently to her departure.

After Clara had gone, Xiamen couldn't bear her absence and he simply lost himself in missing her. They made an effort to snatch as many calls together as the time difference would allow. Xiamen used the penthouse or reception telephone whilst Clara was only able to communicate when she was at work. To make matters worse, the office phone wasn't even on Clara's desk so they could never have an intimate conversation out of earshot. Clara sometimes used pay phones to speak to him but the toll for Beijing–Norwich wasn't cheap. The lovebirds eventually resorted to using fax messages for more privacy but they found it unsatisfactory for their tweeting. They wanted more.

Within the course of a month, Xiamen and Clara arranged to meet again at the earliest opportunity. Xiamen briefed his parents of his intentions to travel to England for two weeks. Violet and Silver were surprised and tried to talk him out of it because of his work at the hotel, but Xiamen's mind was made up. Though they were not pleased with his sudden travel plans, they found a replacement driver to cover the time he'd be away and his mother purchased a return ticket on his behalf. Before long, Xiamen packed his bag and left for England.

Chapter Eight

By the age of twenty-six, Clara Jerkins had established a career working as an admin clerk in the Government Department for Education. She had joined the civil service three years ago after completing her studies in Public Administration. Clara rented a place in a block of flats that were well situated in the heart of Norwich. Although the one bed apartment wasn't spacious, she had commensurately stacked it with everything that was sufficient for her needs. She loved nature's flora and kept potted plants on all her windowsills, dedicatedly looking after them like her pets.

Three days before Xiamen's arrival, Clara fully stocked her kitchen and thoroughly cleaned her flat. She made some space for his stuff so he could feel at home and looked into some possible places they could visit. She was so anxious of his coming that she fretted with impatience as the clock approached the final countdown. Finally, the day came and she drove to the airport to wait for him.

Xiamen's KLM flight from Beijing landed at Schiphol airport in Amsterdam after an overnight direct flight of ten hours. After getting off the plane, he made his way to the small airbus zone to board a connecting flight to Norwich airport. Clara would be waiting for him there. He yearned to have her in his arms again. He wanted to make love to her. He couldn't wait!

It wasn't until mid-afternoon that Xiamen arrived in Norwich. His connecting flight was scheduled to leave at eleven o'clock so he had a bit of a wait before departure. Upon arriving at Norwich, Clara was waiting in the arrival lounge to greet him. They straightaway reunited with a tight embrace, kissing in full glare of others.

Clara couldn't keep her hand off Xiamen; she fondled him as they walked to her car and kept making passes at him during the drive to her flat. Later, she led him into her apartment and took him straight into her bedroom. She pushed him on the bed and straddled him.

'Honey, welcome to my little home of no regrets. I have a surprise for you.'

'Oh yeah? Should I close my eyes?'

'No. It isn't that kind.'

'What's the surprise then?'

'I have taken two weeks off work to be with you full time whilst you are here. I'll be doing some grinds with you for most of the time, so this bed will be our bouncy castle for the next couple of days. Any objections?'

'Not at all! I like your style, most femme fatale.'

Clara giggled. 'I'm going to make you beg for calling me that!'

'Oh dear, has my loud mouth landed me in trouble already?'

'Surely you will be punished, mister big mouth.'

'Ooh! Mercy me.'

'So what would you like to eat? You must be hungry, aren't you?'

'Oh yes I'm hungry, but it's you that I really wanna chew up.'

'You mean you want me like, right now?'

'Yes sugar... I want you right now like crazy. I've been starving for you.'

'Come here baby.'

Clara clasped Xiamen's cheeks and dipped her chin towards his. Her hair fell obstructively on his face; he lifted it out of the way and smoothened it back on to her head. She went for his lips again. They kissed intensely, their desires flushing through their bodies like a rapid running river. They gave in to their Feral hormones and hurriedly ripped off their clothes.

Xiamen and Clara spent the following days indoors. He found Clara's home wholesome, despite its small size, and he particularly liked the cosy feel of her bed'; the gel memory foam mattress on it was supplely comfy.

Clara treated Xiamen to his favourite meal requests, opting to cook at home so she could show off her culinary skills. She refused to accept his money when he offered his bank card on their outings too; it wasn't in her book to let a guest pay in her hospitality. Xiamen was bowled over by Clara's openness and kindness. She cleaned up after him without fussing over the mess left after he'd shaved his beard or brushed his teeth. She even washed and ironed all his clothes and underwear. Her caring acts mesmerised Xiamen and took him back to childhood with his mother. He'd never had a girlfriend look after him like Clara did. On top of that, his desire for her drove him crazy. She made him feel so good, so alive and so natural; so much so that he was hooked on her.

On the second week of the visit, Clara took Xiamen for a bit of sight-seeing. She explained that Norwich wasn't a great place for architectural monuments, especially compared to Beijing, but promised to take him to see some outstanding ones.

The first place she chose was Norwich Castle as it was in walking distance from her apartment. As they approached, the striking thing Xiamen noticed about Norwich Castle was its gleaming white wall; he thought it looked like a snow igloo on a hill. He caught sight of the debris of the old wall that had once stood as a stockade around the top of the hill. He took a swift glance over the buildings and looked at the keep for a moment before he turned to Clara.

'I reckon this place used to be a palace.'

'Yes, that was what it was before. They made a section of it into a museum and left the keep intact, so the museum and the keep are the main attractions here.'

'I see. Where do we start from?' Xiamen asked.

'I've got admission tickets for both places. Which would you like us to go first?'

'I'm not that keen on the museum. Let's tour the keep.'

'Okay. But, for your information, the museum is a good place to see some historical relics that are natural to Anglo Saxon and the old Northwick. This castle was listed as a recognised Ancient Monument because of the specimens that are stored here.'

'I don't doubt that. Have you been in the museum before then?'

'No.'

'So you don't know what's in there?'

'To be honest, I don't. But I gathered the museum has various displays of chinaware and silverware, plus other archaeological specimens and art collections. I think there may be other more interesting stuff in there too if we go in and see for ourselves.'

'Of course there will be other stuff in there. All museums have their own peculiar bits and pieces, this one won't be any different. I think the keep will be more fun to tour so I'd like us to go there first.'

'Come on then.' Clara led the way.

At the main entrance of the keep, they came across a memorial plaque that told the story of a man called Robert

Kett but they didn't stop to read it. Xiamen admired the exquisitely crafted blind arcades at the exterior and thought the walls were faced in medieval stone. In order to gain access to the keep, they walked to the eastern side and went up a stone stairway to a mezzanine on the first floor before descending down the keep stairs.

The ground floor was filled with canvas displays of the castle's history. There were miniature castle models and try-on costumes for visitors to indulge. Xiamen tried on a King-William-the-Conqueror costume for fun and talked loudly in a phoney archaic English. Clara was amused and laughed at him. A few other visitors were amused too as they watched Xiamen fool around.

Clara and Xiamen continued their exploring and headed down to the cellar. They wandered into a prison dungeon and looked around. The grim communal cell was able to fit a dozen or more prisoners and still had the straw beds where the inmates once slept in. The pair shortly moved out of the gaol and went up on the first floor to the royal quarters.

The archway leading to the royal quarters was lined with pictorial tapestries and tableaus. They moved into the built-in chambers in each section of the royal quarters and fed their eyes on the old vestiges that hadn't been dismantled. The king's chapel still had the old medieval capitals on the entablatures too.

After spending a couple of hours in the keep, Clara took Xiamen to the museum too. They spent a few more hours there before they called it quits and left the site.

The following day, Clara took Xiamen to another site also close to her house. They walked along Chapelfield Road and accessed the grounds through the pedestrian gate at the southwest entrance.

'Wow! Chapelfield Gardens! There're loads of trees here! I didn't think there'd be something like this in a small city like Norwich,' Xiamen said, looking around in amazement.

'That's right! I have gathered some information about the gardens so I can tell you something about it too. Not that I will be as good as a tour guide as you, but I will do my best. Let's walk this way, I will tell you what I've learnt as we go.' Clara led the way.

'As you can see, the landscape and walkways are dominated by beautiful trees. These tree avenues here have retained their mid-eighteenth century-layout since the gardens first opened to the public in 1880. Before the park was commissioned as a public site, it underwent several historic phases. First of all, the place was originally a religious centre for priests and they used the monastery in the old St Mary's Chapel as a praying sanctuary. It is on record that the Queen's cavalry fought the Spanish fleet in 1588 and used the grounds here for their jousting and archery training. A portion of the grounds was set aside as a mass burial site for victims of the buboes during the Great Plague. That old, dilapidated wall over there was built around the thirteenth century as a perimeter to surround the city. But that's all that is left of the old medieval wall now. Today, this garden anchors all the main social events in the city. That large building over there with the pagoda is the Theatre Royal. It hosts most of the big cultural events in Norwich, including fairs and festivals. The timber stage over there is used for anchoring live performances. There is a playground for children to play on that side. As we walk around, you will notice that the grounds are triangular and accessible from all sides via the surrounding roads. Apart from the well-spread bushy branches of trees that line along the walkways, the lawns, shrubs and flowers that spread across the park are well-pruned. The city council takes charge of maintaining everything in the park. That's all I can remember for now. Thanks for listening.'

Xiamen gave Clara a round of applause. 'Well! Very impressive... well done babe!'

'Thank you. I am glad I managed to remember that much off the top of my head. It was interesting to learn the history about the park for myself too. I'd never really considered it before now.'

'You were amazing. Come, let's go to that timber stage and have a seat.'

'Why? We are supposed to be walking around not sitting?'

'We will, but let's sit, just for a minute.' They walked on the snaking pavement that led straight to the bandstand and sat on the edge of the platform.

'Are you hungry?' Xiamen asked.

'Not quite yet, why do you ask?'

'I see a restaurant over the road, how about we go have a look at the menu?'

'No need for that, I've got food for us at home.'

'But it's nice to eat out too. I'd like to give you a special treat as you've been so generous.'

'Maybe later then, but somewhere else.'

'Alright then.'

'Tell you what, you know some trees here are incredibly old.'

'Is that so?'

'Yes, though not as old as Methuselah.'

'Methu what?'

'I meant they are not as old as the ones in Beihai Park. I gathered some trees along the promenades are a variety of species and ages, mostly of 19th and 20th century origin. The oldest are the elm trees, I read that the first elms were planted in 1746 to be precise.'

'For real?'

'Yes.'

'Can you show me one?'

'That I cannot. I don't know what an elm tree looks like to be honest, but it shouldn't be too difficult. I think we'll be able to spot one if we try. We might find some clues on the bark if we look carefully. Old age doesn't hide well after all.'

'That sounds probable.'

'Come on, let's go then. I bet I'll beat you to it and find the first one.'

'No way!'

'Game on then!' They left the band stand.

Two days before Xiamen's holiday was to come to an end, Clara took him to visit the Norwich Cathedral; a gigantic cloister set on 44 acres that was famous for being the second-largest monastery in England. Not a bad place to show off Norwich's architectural monuments. She warned him that she hadn't been to the cathedral before and couldn't tell him much about it in advance. Xiamen wasn't enthusiastic about the place and preferred they not go into the duomo, so they walked around on the close. Clara noticed he was withdrawn and repeatedly asked him if he was okay. Though he assured her he was, she didn't see his countenance brighten. When they got back to Clara's, the moment of truth came when Xiamen finally dropped the bombshell.

'I don't wish to go back to Beijing.'

'What?' Clara asked with a startled expression.

'I want to stay here in England with you.'

'But your home is in Beijing. What about your job there?'

'I've been thinking about it and have concluded it's time I moved on with my life. It's true my home and work are in Beijing, but you don't live in Beijing. You're here so I want to be here too.'

'What you are saying is serious. Are you sure about this?'

'I've never been this sure.'

'You know this involves planning, right? It will be a sudden change for you and your parents, and me too.'

'I know that. Are you not okay with it?'

'It's not a problem for me. What about your parents? Are you sure they will be okay with it?'

'It isn't up to my parents. As I said, I've been thinking about it and thought it over enough. I want to be with you always and forever. I mean every day for the rest of my life. But I've got to ask you first. Would you grant me the privilege of spending my life with you?'

'Are you proposing to me?'

'Kind of.'

'Your technique is very crude.'

'Pardon?'

'First of all, you are not on your knee… and secondly you don't have a ring.'

'Ah, I'm sorry. I hadn't planned it well despite thinking over it continually. It seems I may be in a rush, but the circumstance forces me to do it this way. In less than two days, I'll return to Beijing. I didn't have it in mind to stay, but now that I'm here I don't wish to go back. So I need to know.'

Sliding out of the bed, Xiamen knelt down facing her and clasped his palms like a praying mantis. He looked earnestly into her eyes.

'Will you marry me, Clara Jerkins?'

Looking amused, Clara promptly went down too, kneeling in front of him.

'So, when would you want me to marry you? Now, or later?'

'I beg your pardon?'

'I am ready, I can marry you here and now.'

'Are you kidding me?'

She gave him a steadfast look. 'Do I look like I am?'

Xiamen locked eyes with her. 'But there's no ring, and no witnesses.'

'That's your fault for being a terrible wedding planner.'

'My apologies then. I love you with all my heart Clara Jerkins. Will you marry me?'

'I love you too Xiamen Christopher…I would very much like to be your wife.'

'I request permission to kiss the bride.'

'Permission granted.'

It may have been a mock wedding, but they knew in that moment as they kissed that there was no going back. Their lovemaking that night was markedly different! The following day, Xiamen went with Clara to a jewellery shop and he bought her an engagement ring. He called his parents and told them the news.

Xiamen's father didn't quibble over the development, but his mother engaged him in a long argument as they went back and forth debating it. She tried to counsel him and pleaded with him to at least return back to work to give them time to adjust before he left for good but Xiamen wouldn't agree. He chose to follow his heart. He told his parents he would let them know when the wedding was once they'd fixed a date.

Clara phoned up her father and informed him about her new relationship status. He rejoiced at the news and asked when he would be meeting her fiancé. The meeting was fixed and the couple went to Beccles the following Sunday. Mr Barnaby Jerkins and Cecelia, Clara's stepmother, treated them to a roast dinner and a rose cocktail. Barnaby had a chance to talk with Xiamen and asked him a few random questions. He was quite impressed by Xiamen's broad knowledge on philosophy and remarked that Xiamen should reconsider going back to teaching one day.

Xiamen settled in with Clara quickly. Their relationship tightened and blossomed like a flower in spring; the pair couldn't be happier with each other. Xiamen shortly found work at a taxi service company. He and Clara got married six months later. His parents came from Beijing to give their blessing and support at the wedding.

Xiamen and Clara eventually had their first child, Elisabeth, in 1987 after three years of marital bliss. They had another child, a boy, when Elisabeth was five and they named him Simon. Xiamen and his wife bought a house in Attleborough and made it their family home. They went to Beijing from time to time on holiday to visit his parents; his parents travelled occasionally to Norwich to visit them too.

Twenty years after Xiamen had relocated to Norwich, his parents retired from running the hotel and sold it off to another entrepreneur. They did not include the penthouse in the sale deal; they kept it for themselves and continued to live there as their forever home. The ex-hoteliers often travelled around the world on getaways, enjoying their retirement.

On the third weekend of December 2004, Xiamen's parents travelled to Sumatra in Sri Lanka for a two-week holiday to memorialise their fiftieth wedding anniversary.

Xiamen called his mum shortly after they arrived to wish them a happy anniversary. He passed the phone to the rest of his family one by one so they could share their greetings.

The following Sunday, tragedy struck unexpectedly in Sumatra. A tsunami, caused by a magnitude 9.0 earthquake in the Indian Ocean, flowed ashore and submerged the surrounding coastal lands. The news of the tidal deluge soon hit the global media and escalated a gripping sense of foreboding for everyone in Xiamen's household.

Xiamen himself particularly followed the news with grappling trepidation. Eventually, it was assumed that his parents were caught in the disaster of the temblor waves because their bodies were never found. Devastated, Xiamen was never able to wrap his head around the mystery of his parents' whereabouts, even after everything had calmed. Wherever their bodies were washed off to was unknown, so Xiamen's family grieved with no bodies for a formal funeral. Xiamen took some time to grieve his loss.

Chapter Nine

Eight years after the Sri Lanka tsunami, the members of the Christopher family had advanced prosperously. Xiamen had his own cab and freelanced as a taxi driver. Clara had moved up in the ranks at her workplace to a management position. Their son Simon was in his final year of study at Norwich University of the Arts and Elisabeth was an accountant in a forensic auditing firm. They all still lived together in their Attleborough home.

It had just passed into the early hours of Monday morning in the Christopher household. Elisabeth had been sitting up in bed, her mouth hanging wide open as she wailed. Her disturbing cries were so loud that they stirred the sleeping house; all of the family got up and approached her bedroom to investigate.

'What's the matter, Elisa? Why are you screaming?' her mother asked as she arrived.

'Mum... my gums aah swollen... it's so painful I can't sleep,' Elisabeth groaned talking with her jaw hanging down.

'Let me have a look, open wider.'

'Aah.' Elisabeth widened her mouth.

'Goodness me, it does look sore!'

'Let me see.' Xiamen joined them and leaned in to look. 'Ugh... what do you have there, Elisa? How did it get like that?'

'I don't know, Dad. I have been having some sensitivity in my gums for the past two days. It wasn't painful or anything so I didn't worry about it... I thought it would pass like always. It got so bad I woke up and couldn't get back to sleep.'

'Whatever it is, it's got your gums inflamed and pooh! They smell rather badly.'

'No need to be so blunt, honey. Don't mind him Elisa. I think you have a gum infection from the look of it. I will clean it for you... let me fetch some cotton wool and peroxide and I'll be back in a minute,' Clara chipped in before giving Xiamen an admonishing look and leaving the room.

'Let me see,' Simon's voice cut in as he walked towards the bed.

Xiamen turned to him. 'Go back to bed Si. Your Mum is handling it,'

'I was asking Elisabeth, Dad,' Simon replied defiantly.

'It's okay, Simon. Do what Dad says, Mum will see to it in a minute.'

'I just want to see what it looks like, why can't I?'

'Didn't you hear what Dad said? It smells, so leave me alone. Go away both of you.'

'I don't care if it smells, I just want to see and learn how it looks, that's all.'

'Er, Elisa, maybe you should oblige your brother. And sorry I said it smells,' Xiamen enthused.

'Okay, apology accepted.' Elisabeth gestured to Simon opening her mouth.

'Heck! The blood vessels of your gums appear swollen. They're so red, must be very painful. I think you best have some painkillers. I've got some if you'd like me to get it for you.'

'Oh please.' Elisabeth turned away waving Simon off.

'I didn't know we have a secret dentist in the house.' Clara returned looking at Simon critically.

'I was only observing her mouth, Mum.'

'So what's your diagnosis, doctor?'

'I'll Google it to learn what it is now that I've seen what it looks like.'

'How very thoughtful of you, but give way now please so I can attend to your sister.'

'She is all yours Mum. I will go check on Wikihow to see if it has some information about it. Perhaps I could find out what first aid is best,' Simon moved out of Clara's way and disappeared out of the room.

'Don't go searching on the internet now, Si. Go back to bed, it's late. You hear me!' Xiamen called out after him.

'Loud and clear, Dad!' Simon shouted back.

Xiamen turned to his wife and daughter. 'I will leave you ladies to it. And please, Elisa, try not to scream anymore. I don't want to think our house is on fire again.' He patted his daughter' on the arm before leaving.

The pain in Elizabeth's gums persisted till the next morning. She couldn't go to work. She called in sick and made a call to the dentist to ask for an emergency appointment. Luckily, they were able to see her later that morning. Elizabeth couldn't focus on driving so her dad offered to take her. After they arrived at the surgery, Xiamen waited in the lounge whilst Elisabeth was seen by one of the dentists on duty.

The dentist examined Elisabeth's mouth and leaned back into his chair. 'You have a periodontal infection that has progressed to gingivitis. That's what has caused the inflammation on your gums.'

'What's a periodontal infection?'

'It's a disease that attacks the gum and bone under the teeth. Do you have any guess as to what might have caused it?'

'No,' Elisabeth replied shaking her head.

The dentist looked into her mouth again with the concave mirror. After a moment, he leaned back looking concerned. 'You have lots of tiny gaps between your teeth that trap food particles. The micro food deposits have been corrupted with plaque, and that has caused the infection. I'm guessing you may be a fan of chocolate?

'Uhm... kind of. But I do try and give my teeth a good scrub with my electric toothbrush.'

'How long have you had the toothbrush for?'

'I've been using it close to a year now.'

'Have you been using the same brush head for more than six months?'

'Longer than that I think... mine has a fixed head.'

'Well we do recommend replacing the heads every six months. In your case, you can stop using that one anyway as I will give you a high-speed electric toothbrush today. This one is with hard bristles. We prescribe it for cases like this, it should help with cleaning your teeth thoroughly. It has a replaceable head, and comes with three spares, so make sure to change it every six months. For the infection, I will write you a prescription for some anti-inflammation tablets plus some specialised toothpaste and mouthwash. It might prove difficult brushing your teeth whilst the inflammation persists. You can use the mouthwash in the meantime if you find brushing too difficult. After the inflammation subsides, you should continue to use the toothpaste and mouthwash until you come for a follow up appointment. I will inspect the progress before we can sign you off. Don't rinse your mouth after brushing, it is better to leave the triclosan ingredient in the toothpaste to remain working. So we will book you in for another appointment in one week's time and again the week after so we can check on your progress. Are you okay with this arrangement?'

'Another two appointments in short time will be expensive. I doubt I can afford it to be honest.'

'Of course, I understand. As you have been to see us today, I can add you to a programme that will give you 70 per cent off the consultation fee every time you see us. However, it would only apply to this course of treatment.'

'Fair enough. That will do.'

'Do you have any other question you'd like to ask me today?'

'What is your name?'

The dentist looked with surprise at Elisabeth before he answered, 'Wilson Atkins.'

'I am guessing you're from Salford, right?'

'No, but a close guess. I am from Manchester.'

'Oooh, I thought you might be from Salford. I have a colleague at work that talks in the same accent as you.'

The dentist smiled. He signed the paperwork and passed it to Elisabeth. 'Here is your prescription. I will see you next week.'

'Sure. Thank you, Dr Atkins.'

'Thank you too for seeing us today, Miss Christopher. Enjoy the rest of your day.'

'You too. Bye for now,' she said and left the consulting room.

Elisabeth was a hardworking accountant with an innate knack for bookkeeping. She had developed an interest in mathematics early in life and this led her to study accountancy at the Cass Business School in London. By that time she was able to spot balance sheet errors in a glance; her quick analysis and delivery of accurate accounts impressed her tutors so much that they recommended her to several employers. It was no surprise she had many job offers after graduating. In the end she only had an eye for forensic auditing so she chose to work with a chartered firm. Though only twenty-five, she was already a member of the Association of Accounting Technicians. Her current nine-to-five job had a good pay package and a bonus overtime rate of 100 per cent. The downside was the demanding nature of her job didn't give her much freedom to socialise with people outside of work.

Other than being a hardcore worker for her firm, Elisabeth judiciously looked after her appearance. She exercised regularly and tried to keep her weight in check as much as possible. Given that her comfort pleasure was chocolate, she wasn't able to resist treats when they were readily available; to compensate this she jumped on the treadmill in her bedroom every morning before work, burning around five hundred calories in ninety minutes. On weekends, she would attend a health club to work out before ending the day in the spa. Her voluptuous figure was pleasing to behold and she felt confident in her own skin.

Elisabeth was a reserved person by nature. She'd kept much to herself during her teens through to her university years, only ever having one boyfriend, Ronald, who was a classmate of hers. Two years after their graduation, Ronald travelled to Turks and Caicos Islands to take up employment in his uncle's offshore investment firm. He kept in touch with Elisabeth for a few months before suddenly becoming quiet and unresponsive to her texts and emails; his phone line ceased to work and she couldn't find him on social media anymore. She eventually gathered, from a friend of a friend, that he was still very much active on the networking sites and concluded that he must have blocked her. She used a friend's account to snoop on Ronald's news feed posts and saw he'd posted some recent photos of himself and another woman with their newborn together. Elisabeth didn't understand why he wasn't man enough to let her know he was moving on before choosing to ghost her. The experience left her bitter. She took to eating chocolates for an escape and it became a habit.

After the first consultation, Elisabeth visited the dentist the following Wednesday and subsequently every week after for three weeks. Now on her lunch break, she was back there again for her fourth check-up.

'I see that your dental health has improved remarkably Miss Christopher. There is next to nothing left of the plaque. You have certainly been on top of it,' the dentist cheered as he sat back from inspecting her mouth.

'Yep, thanks to that power toothbrush I got from you, that did all the work. I love how squeaky-clean my teeth feel after too,' Elisabeth remarked.

'That's brilliant. I am glad the toothbrush worked for you. By the look of everything, you can stop using the toothpaste and mouthwash I prescribed, it's okay to resume with a standard one. And you no longer need to be seeing us weekly. I will place you on a quarterly repeat check-up. If things remain positive afterwards, you can stick to a yearly routine visit. Are you happy with that?'

'So I won't see you again for another quarter?'

'Pardon?'

'I thought I would see you again next… er, I mean, be here again next week… I didn't…' Elisabeth stopped her words, averted her eyes and began to twiddle her fingers.

The dentist stared surprisedly at Elisabeth. Wondering what could be going on in her mind, he took the opportunity and ran his eyes over her.

Elizabeth's rounded figure flaunted a stylish paisley dress with reddish-orange patterns. Her lustrous dark hair was styled in eye-covering bangs partly hiding her left eye. Her brows were lined with eye pencil and her lashes were tinged with mascara. Her full lips were complimented by a glossy red lipstick circle and her round cheeks were powdered with a rosy blush. Her sparkly drop earrings and nose stud, plus the glittering moondust on her long ruby red artificial nails, added suave to her debonair.

The dentist stared on at Elisabeth admiringly, like a bull appraising a heifer. 'So, Miss Christopher, you were going to say something?'

Elisabeth remained engrossed in twiddling her fingers in silence. The dentist gave her a few seconds before he spoke in a soft tone.

'if you would like to see me again next Wednesday, would you fancy we meet up for lunch somewhere else outside these walls?'

Elisabeth instantly shot up her head, giving the dentist a serious look. Decisively, she braced herself to turn down his offer. 'Well, I think it's nice of you to propose a lunch meet up, but…' She paused for a moment. 'Erm, okay. Sure, sounds great.' She mentally slapped her mouth, not believing her own words.

'That's good! Was there anywhere you'd like to go in particular?'

'You can pick a place and text me,' Elizabeth spoke rapidly as she fished a business card from her purse and offered it. 'Here. My work mobile is on there. I rarely use my private phone on weekdays when I'm at work.'

Whilst the dentist was skimming over the card, Elisabeth made an effort to muffle her panting. She jumped to her feet urging to rush out of there. The dentist looked up from the card.

'All good, I will do just that.'

Elisabeth shot a glance at her phone's clock. 'Well, I better get going then.'

'Very well then. So, that would be all for today then. Everything I said earlier still stands. We will see you back here in three months, and I will see you next week. You sure you're okay with the plan, AAT Elisabeth?'

Elisabeth instinctively smiled. He was referring to the title on her business card. She knew right then that he was bridging formality whilst still remaining formal. 'Sure, I will see you soon, Wilson Atkins, DDS. Have a nice day,' she said courtly and briskly exited the room before he could get over his surprise.

Driving back to work, Elisabeth spent the time thinking about her slip up before the dentist. She chided herself that it was a dumb move and could not understand her own behaviour. The dentist must have thought she fancied him as he was quick to make the lunch proposition. She counselled herself to abstain and resorted to respond with an apologetic decline when he eventually texted her the venue. She hadn't meant to give him the notion she was interested in him; it was never the type of thing she would do normally. She had never been the type to approach men let alone give them a green light. So why had she been so coy with the dentist? Maybe it was because his accent had reminded her of Reece's the moment she'd heard him talk.

Reece Walker was Elisabeth's co-worker from Salford whom she had a friendly relationship with. She loved Reece's accent and loved to banter with him whenever there was an opportunity, but that was as far as it went because Reece was already taken with a wife and little son. After her first appointment with the dentist, she liked his accent so much it kindled her curiosity. She had searched the internet to know more about him. She found out that he was in his early thirties, unmarried, and had a doctor degree in Dental Surgery. She stored the information in her mind without defining the purpose for it, but now it had become clear to her. She was abashed by her own behaviour.

After a couple of days, Elisabeth strangely started having mixed feelings about the lunch date. Her initial denial rescinded and she somewhat began to look forward to it whilst still counterbalancing the thought. Thus, her mind was entwined in the middle of a tug between do and don't.

The following Sunday, after completing her Pilates class in the gym, Elisabeth went into the changing room to prepare for the sauna. Stepping out and draped only in a white bath towel, she entered the steam room and laid herself on a bench. She shut her eyes and drifted inwards to experience the stimulation of her sweat glands. Before long, her skin was swimming in her sweat whilst her thoughts centred on the dentist. Later, Elisabeth was home in time for dinner. As the family were tucking into their desserts, she brought up the conversation.

'Mum, I have a lunch date on Wednesday.'

'Who with?' her mother asked.

'My dentist.'

'Your dentist?' Xiamen butted in.

'Yes, Dad. I have been seeing him every week for the past five weeks, remember?'

'Yes, of course. You were seeing him at the surgery, so what changed?'

'Well, I was, but it wasn't on anything personal. We are meeting outside the surgery this time.'

'Where're you going?'

'Honey, I think Elisa is trying to have a conversation with me, could you just listen and not butt in please?'

'Sorry, I thought it was an open conversation.'

'She did start the conversation with Mum to be honest, Dad,' Simon threw in.

'Good grief! Si, are you now Elisa's lawyer?'.

'Honey, Si was only pointing out the obvious,' Clara emphasised. 'Do be quiet now and let Elisa and me talk. It's a girlie talk so stay out of it.'

'Okay! Sorry for jumping in. Elisa, you can continue.'

'I am sorry, but I have changed my mind. I'd rather keep it away from prying ears. Mum, I will give you the gist later.'

'That's not fair, Elisa,' Simon complained.

Elisabeth looked at him in disbelief. 'Excuse me? What is it to you?

'I was interested, that's all'

'You should mind your business. I wasn't telling you.'

'Yes, I know. You were telling Mum without minding that we could hear you, then you changed your mind of a sudden! Why would you do that?'

'Seriously, Si? So what if I did? It is my business, not yours, so back off!'

'Hold down your swords kids. There's nothing to argue about here. However, Elisa, I agree with Si. It isn't fair that you suddenly changed your mind after arousing our interest. By the way, which of the dentist were you seeing at the surgery?'

'Dad, I'm not telling anymore now. Perhaps I will after the lunch date, if there's anything.'

'Of course, it's only a dull talk about a date with your dentist after all. Boring!'

'How dare you Si? You will never hear anything more about it from me I promise you!'

'So be it then, I'm no longer interested.'

'Fine! You can buzz off now… effing busybody!' Elisabeth retorted.

Xiamen held up his hands. 'Alright both of you, stop with the drama. Si, apologise to your sister now.'

'But, she called me an effing busybody, Dad! Doesn't she need to apologise for that?'

'You Si, are just being silly. Sorry Elisa, don't let him cause you to lose a strand of hair. We can talk about your dentist boyfriend later and keep the girls talk between us. Here's to girl power,' Clara raised her hand to Elisabeth for a palm clap.

Elisabeth bumped palms with her mum. 'Thanks Mum, but point of correction, he isn't my boyfriend,'

'Don't you mean he isn't yet?' her mum teased.

'It's apparent that you girls have connived to exclude us. I guess the rest of us will have to keep our ears on standby until the next public broadcast. By the way, that palm bumping wasn't it. Don't we do it better, Si?'

'Aye-aye, Dad!'

'Let's show them.' Xiamen raised a clasped fist to Simon who punched his father's knuckles with a grin spread across his face.

The following night, Xiamen and Clara were in bed and he asked her if she had gathered more information about Elisabeth's date, but she curtly told him to mind his business.

'Come on cherry baby, tell me what you know. I am curious about which dentist it is as I already have a suspicion.'

'Honey, back off. Don't be a nosey parker.'

'You know from my research, there's only one doctor who's unmarried in that surgery.'

'You're impossible. I can't believe you already went digging. You had better keep your snout out of Elisa's affair until she is sure of something concrete.'

'Aha! Is that what she said? So, there's nothing concrete as of yet?'

'Like I said, mind your business.'

'Why are you keeping it to yourself when I am going to know everything sooner or later?'

'Better wait until later, cos you won't be hearing anything from me until Elisa is ready to tell you herself.'

'Yeah, whatever!'

'Don't you sound like Si now, honey?'

'I sound like Si now? Never mind telling me then, I'm no longer interested. Good night!'

'Of course. Nice of you to throw a hissy fit when you don't get your way. Good night to you too!' Clara switched off the lamp on her bedside and turned away.

'Don't do that. Didn't we agree we won't sleep with our backs to each other no matter what?'

'I am not turning back, but you are welcome to watch the view of my behind until you fall asleep.'

'Ouch, that hurts. Don't be nasty. Come on now, reverse the move.'

'Do stop talking to me now please. I want to sleep.'

'Okay! I'm sorry. Now, reverse the move please.'

'Fine.' Clara turned back to Xiamen and shifted into his arm.

'That's my girl! I didn't mean to upset you my cherry baby. I love you. Do you hear me? I said …I… love… you,' Xiamen whispered the last sentence into her ear and started to lap it.

'Mmm… stop it… mmm… stop sticking your tongue in there… hee-hee-he… stop, I don't like it… oooh-oooh-okay! I love you too… leave my ear alone now please.'

Xiamen took his tongue out of his wife's ear and looked into her eyes. She lifted her head to his and kissed him longingly. Xiamen equally reciprocated, and they started making out passionately. Before long, they were breathing fast and hot with desire. They hurriedly undressed and delved into a world of their own.

Chapter Ten

It was early Wednesday morning and Elisabeth was jogging on her treadmill. Breathing heavily and huffing like a chainsaw, she was dripping with so much sweat that she had to wipe herself every so often with a towel. The digital display showed she had burned 415 cals, eighty-five off target. Checking the time, she summoned all of her remaining energy and picked up the pace to a run. Elisabeth needed to get off the machine by quarter to eight to shower and get dressed, eat breakfast then drive to work.

She successively went through her other routines and by 8:35, she was speeding her car down the carriageway. She had to be clocked in before nine, else the system would automatically record her late and register a surcharge.

Before long, Elisabeth arrived at her workplace and let herself into the office she shared with her immediate boss. She settled behind her desk and turned on her computer. As the PC booted, she took out two phones from her handbag. After putting one of them on silent she put it straight back in her bag. She powered up her work phone to find there was a new text from an unsaved number. She gathered from the contents who it was from and saved the number as DDS Wilson. Placing the phone on her desk, she looked up and rolled her eyes at Reece Walker as he breezed in.

'Good morning Elisabeth, shining bright in your east wing already?'

'Morning Reece. Clocking in at five minutes before nine? You were almost late boss. That's unlike you!'

'Gosh! I know… it's been a hectic morning,' Reece expressed as he settled in his chair. He loosened his necktie a shade and turned on his PC.

'What happened?' Elisabeth asked.

'My wife caught a stomach bug and couldn't take our boy to day-care, so I had to take him.' Then I had to drive the long way through to avoid the morning-rush hour traffic.'

'Couldn't your boy stay home with her?'

'Oh no, she hadn't wanted that. She is on an afternoon shift and is hoping to go to work later when her stomach calms down. Anyway, is there any news about the Rowland Brothers' account?

'I can tell you in a sec after I log in, my computer is loading up.'

'No worries, I will see for myself in a jiff.' He faced his computer. 'Mother of Christ! What a marvellous start to the day!' He leaned back into his chair with a flustered countenance.

'What's wrong, Mr Walker?'

'My PC is updating !'

'Patience Sir. The morning has only just started. You've got the whole day ahead of you,' Elisabeth expressed with a chuckle.

'Right. Have you logged in?'

'Not yet, I'll log on now.'

'Your PC isn't updating, is it?'

'Mine is up and running fine.'

'Great! Log in and check on the Rowlands' account please, I want to know if their internal auditors have reconciled the discrepancies we raised.'

'Yes Sir. I will get on it.' Elisabeth buried her face in her computer, pursing her lips to stifle her laughter. After a moment, she looked up. 'I don't see any feedback from them as of yet.'

'Christ! They've got to be kidding me!' Reece pouted.

'I think they may reply when they resume work later. It's still bedtime in New York now.'

'We sent them notice on Thursday. I would've thought three days were enough to sort out the discrepancy.'

'Let's give them the benefit of doubt and wait till the end of the day. If we don't hear back from them then, we can send them a reminder.'

'I should say send it right away, but yeah, let's do as you say. Aha! Elisabeth, you've got your lunch date today, right?'

'Aah... so you remembered! We are meeting at Bohemia gastropub, that's where he chose in the end.'

'That's not far from here. You can walk there. He must have chosen the venue for your convenience.'

'Yep, he must've, considering how far away it is from the practise.'

'So, you like the guy?'

'Erm... Yea I think so.'

'That's good. I am glad to hear that.'

'Don't get me wrong. I meant platonically. I hardly know him outside the surgery.'

'Sounds to me like you like him more than just platonically. Do you plan to see more of him after today?'

Elisabeth flushed. 'I don't know. I don't think I am keen to know him beyond platonic either. I intend to have lunch with him, that's all.'

'No need to get defensive now. You don't have to prove anything to me,' Reece remarked cheerily. 'By the way, Sam and Cooke Limited is ripe for peeling. You should start working on it after you finish with the Halford Milton account.'

'Will do. How is your little Josh doing? Is he still crying a lot?'

'Oh yeah, Josh is still wailing like a banshee and certainly not ready to quit. He is not happy teething. Maybe something else might be wrong with him. But we cannot know for sure since he can't yet talk, so I suppose that might be why he keeps crying out meaninglessly.'

'Aw! Don't mock your boy like that, Reece.'

'I only said it the way it is. Hey, my PC is up and beckoning, time for work. Give me a shout if you have any questions about the HM account,' Reece instructed and forthwith glued his eyes on his computer screen.

'Yes Sir!' Elisabeth replied and followed his example, knowing there would be no more unofficial chitchat until break time.

At lunch time, Elisabeth left the office building and headed towards the gastropub. She deliberately took a longer route and walked at a gentle pace. She planned to double the six-minute walk, in hope of making Wilson Atkins wait for a few. As she approached Bohemia Restaurant, she caught sight of him standing in the smoking porch. She faltered in her tracks and gasped, instantly caught by surprise. She wouldn't have thought he smoked.

Standing still, she watched Wilson contemplatively and swiftly deliberated within herself whether this would be a problem. She didn't have any preconceived prejudice against smoking so she couldn't readily surmise a judgement at that moment. Shrugging her shoulders, she resumed her walking.

Wilson wasn't looking her way so he didn't see her coming until she was right at his front and greeting him.

'Hey, Elisabeth,' he said with surprise.

'Yep! It's me.'

'But I was watching out for you on that side, I thought your workplace was closer from that way. Did you not come directly from the office?'

'Yes, I did. I just went the longer way to give my legs a stretch after I've been sat all morning.'

'Clever! I was here ten minutes early and thought to have a quick cig as you hadn't yet arrived. Well, I wasn't quick enough, you caught me right at it. This wasn't how I wanted you to find out about it, so please pardon me for surprising you like this. I guess now would be a good time to ask you your thoughts. Do you mind?' Wilson's eyes were pleading as he looked into hers for a response; his cigarette remained burning between his fingers.

Elisabeth eyed the side stream smoke from Wilson's cigarette. 'Uh-oh, it looks like your ciggy still needs your attention. Do what you have to do. I don't mind,' she enthused with a sarcastic tone.

'I'll get rid of it.' Wilson put out the cigarette and tossed it into the residuum bin. 'Let's go in. How much time do you have for your break?' he asked as he opened the door to let her through.

'I can have up to two hours, but I always do one-and-half.'

'Brilliant, we've got more than enough time then.'

Chapter Eleven

After her lunch with Wilson, Elisabeth returned to her workplace. She finished her work for the day and left the office. The memory of the date lingered during her drive home and was still fresh in her mind up to the time she was having a shower. Later, she wandered into the kitchen to join her Mum who was getting dinner ready.

'There you are, Elisa! How was your day at work?'

'Really, Mum? That isn't what you really want to know, is it?'

'Okay, you got me. I will cut to the chase. Tell me then, how was your date?'

'Well…Wilson is 32… he is from Manchester and he has two degrees in dentistry. He doesn't like onion and he is allergic to nuts, and he prefers cats to dogs. His parents, and his older brother and sister, live in Manchester. His Dad is a professor of medicine at the university and his mum is a nurse practitioner. Both of his siblings are general practitioners too!'

'Mmmmm! It's remarkable that He's from a medical family. So, any past exes to be aware of? Or kids?'

'I don't know. He didn't tell me of any.'

'Did you ask him?'

'I didn't. But he would have told me about it… wouldn't he?'

'Not generally on the first date.'

'Why not? Shouldn't stuff like that be mentioned, especially if kids are in the picture? I really should have asked him about it.' A cloud suddenly overcast Elisabeth's face.

'Don't worry about that now love. Not that it would matter if he had kids, or would it?'

'I don't know. I guess not.'

'Well just ask him next time. I suppose you will see him again, right?'

'Yes. He invited me to have dinner on Saturday and I agreed.'

'Looks like it's going well by the sounds of things. So what do you think? Do you like him?'

'It's too early for me to know that yet. I don't want to jump into anything. But… to answer your question, I think I do to be honest.'

'How do you know that?'

'He smokes, Mum! And I kind of didn't have a problem with it.'

'What? A dentist that smokes? Who would have thought?'

'That's exactly what I thought when I saw him doing it!'

'Pshaw! He couldn't keep it away on your first date? Well… it looks like it's in his blood! He must be hooked on it. That would be a deal braker were it me. But it's you, and I guess it's okay if you weren't put off by it.'

'I wasn't, Mum. You know he'd stalled because of my presence and asked for my opinion. I actually surprised myself when I said he could carry on.'

'Dear girl! I am surprised too. I wouldn't have thought that a dentist would enjoy something like a coffin nail. I hope he isn't carrying a chimney around as lungs? Hmm… okay, food is ready. Help me lay out the cutleries on the table for the family please.'

'I can help with that… let me do it, Elisa!' Simon's voice cut in suddenly as he entered the kitchen.

'Oi! Si?' Elisabeth blurted out.

'Yes Elisa?'

'Have you been eavesdropping?' she fired at him.

'Of course not. I didn't hear anything, I promise,' he replied with a smirk.

'Mum, has he been there all this time?'

Their mother turned to Simon with a serious look. 'Si, were you behind the wall?

'What does it even matter anyway? Mum, I can smell the aroma of tuna and sweetcorn, are we having jacket potato?'

Elizabeth glared at Simon furiously. 'Don't change the subject!'

'Oh come on sis, give me a break now. Chillax!'

'How dare you listen in on my conversation? Didn't I say you weren't going to hear a word of it? But you resort to perching on the wall like a housefly. You're such an effing nuisance!'

'That's enough Elisa, don't be nasty. And you Si, you didn't have to be a fly on the wall. You should be ashamed of yourself.'

'I've done nothing wrong for God's sake. It's not my fault I was in hearing range. I was only coming to the kitchen, I didn't mean to listen in. Should I be sorry about that?' Simon defended himself and proceeded to lay the table with cutlery.

Elisabeth hissed and stiffly took out plates from the cupboard. She placed them beside the cutlery, making sure to avoid body contact with Simon.

'Ni hao, family!' Xiamen greeted them, entering the kitchen. 'What's going on here? Another war? Elisabeth? Simon? Why are your swords drawn?

'Honey, there's no war here anymore so let it lie.'

'Ole! If you say so Mamito, no problemo,' Xiamen cheered at Clara. He sat in the head dining chair and turned to Elisabeth. 'So, Elisa, why are your shoulders still stiff? You best loosen them before they become permanently hunched. What was the aggro about anyway?'

'Si was playing spy on us, Dad.'

'What was he spying at?'

'He secretly listened in to my conversation as I was telling Mum about my lunch date.'

'Ah ha! So how did it go?'

'I am not saying anything now. Not with Simon here,' Elisabeth said sitting down.

'Too late, sister. I already know everything you told Mum,' Simon threw in, also sitting down.

'You two-faced fibster! Didn't you say you didn't before? You are disgusting!'

'Sorry, big sister, I don't recall I said that before. Well, you might as well tell Dad now cos I will if you don't.'

'Thank you, Si, but I prefer to hear from the horse's lips. Elisabeth, perhaps you can fill me in now since Si already heard everything.'

'Could you all just shush please... let's have dinner in some peace and quiet!' Clara instructed as she finished laying the food and took her seat.

'Sorry, our apologies dinner lady. Let's obey now everyone before she takes the food away,' Xiamen jested.

Clara flipped a dismissive hand at him thrusting out her lower lip in a disdainful grimace. She proceeded to dish food on to Simon's and Elisabeth's plates, then on to hers. After she finished, she stretched the serving spoon to Xiamen.

'Here Papito, help yourself. I am sure you won't have a problem with being your own server.' She waited for

Xiamen to take the spoon. When he didn't, she dropped it on his plate and started to eat her food.

Turning popeyed, Xiamen stared at Clara who simply ate on without a care. Simon and Elisabeth giggled as they watched their parents' comedic behaviour.

Chapter Twelve

The following Saturday, Elisabeth met Wilson again for dinner, and then again after that. It didn't take long before they spend their first night together at his. They subsequently lost themselves in each other, eventually pairing like lovey-dovey budgies. Their affair glided into blissful horizons as the weeks passed. As Elisabeth missed spending her weekends at home, she quickly progressed to spending weeknights at Wilson's as well.

Wilson also had a treadmill, so Elisabeth had no hindrance in keeping up her morning jog at his. Her office wasn't far from Wilson's either, so she often left her car at his and walked to work to save on expenses. After six months of being together, she had fully marked her territory at Wilson's house with some of her belongings.

One Saturday, Wilson took Elisabeth to Manchester. She met his parents and brother at a dinner hosted in their home; unfortunately, his sister was working a shift and so couldn't attend. Meeting Wilson's family gave Elisabeth a chance to learn Wilson hadn't brought anyone home in five years. He'd previously told her he'd had a bad break up but he never delved into details.

The following day, Wilson took Elisabeth to meet his sister's family; Suzanne, her three girls and her husband. Whilst there, Wilson went outside for a cigarette and the two ladies were in the kitchen alone. Suzanne filled Elisabeth in with the details about Wilson's previous break up.

'My brother had been engaged to a girl called Cedella. Cedella got pregnant, they got engaged and made all the wedding arrangements. Three days before their wedding there was a shock revelation.'

'What happened?' Elisabeth asked with raised brows.

'Cedella confessed to Wilson that he wasn't the baby's father and she didn't want to live a lie with him.'

'Oh my God! That's appalling!'

'Indeed, it was. The revelation broke Wilson's heart. He was a wrecked lovelorn for a while and he took to smoking like a chimney after the disgraceful breakup. He eventually picked himself up, but he hadn't stopped smoking since then,'' Suzanne concluded.

'I am so sorry that happened to him.' Elisabeth said with feeling. She was saddened by the information and understood why Wilson hadn't talked about it.

Elisabeth and Wilson left Manchester late Sunday afternoon and arrived back in Norwich in the night. Wilson pulled to a stop outside his place just after ten o'clock; they alighted from the car and trudged into his house sleepy and ready for bed. The following morning, Elisabeth left Wilson's house to go to work and went straight home after instead of returning to his. During dinner later that evening, she told her folks about her meeting with Wilson's family and declared her intention to bring him home to see them soon. Clara was pleased to invite him over for dinner too, but Xiamen suggested they should invite him over for a cup of tea first. Clara brushed off his suggestion and urged them to take a cue from the Manchester visit. Simon backed his mother, so it was agreed they'd hold a dinner for Wilson.

The next weekend, Elisabeth stayed at home to help her mother prepare the food. They remembered that Wilson didn't like onion or peanuts and planned the menu accordingly. That Saturday evening, at six o'clock on the dot, the doorbell chimed and the other members of Xiamen's household braced themselves to meet Wilson Atkins. Elisabeth went to open the door.

'Hi, babe,' she greeted him.

'How's it going my love?' Wilson stepped in, brushing his lips against hers in a light kiss.

'I'm great thanks. Let me take your coat.'

'Sure... hold this for me for a moment while I take it off.' He gave her a plastic shopping bag.

Elisabeth received the bag and felt it. 'What do you have here, babe?'

'It's just a couple of random gifts I got for your folks. Where's everyone?'

'They're in the sitting room and dying to meet you.'

'I am dying to meet them too.'

Wilson passed his coat to Elisabeth. She hung it on a coat rack next to the door and led him through the hallway to the lounge.

'Hello young man! It's nice to finally meet you.' Clara popped out of the kitchen and greeted Wilson.

'Good evening, Mrs Christopher, it's nice to meet you too,' Wilson offered his hand to her.

'We are glad to have you,' said Clara, shaking his hand.

Wilson looked from Clara to Elisabeth. 'Wow! The apple didn't fall far from the tree. The resemblance is remarkable!'

'She's my daughter of course!' Clara returned proudly, patting Elizabeth's shoulder.

The three of them walked into the sitting room to join the others.

Simon sprang from the three-seater sofa as soon as they entered. He extended his hand to Wilson for a handshake. 'I am Simon, it's nice to meet you, Dr Wilson Atkins.'

'Nice to meet you too. Just call me Wilson, I'm cool with that. Elisabeth tells me you are called Si at home, can I call you that too?'

'Yes of course. I don't mind at all,' he said, grinning.

'Great! I have a little surprise for you. I gathered you are a fan of Freddie Mercury, I am too!' Taking the bag from Elizabeth, he fished out an unopened CD pack and gave it to Simon. 'I've brought you a limited-edition CD that has all the best Queen songs.'

'Wow! Thank you. I didn't know you were a fan of Queen too.' Simon took the CD album and threw an accusing glance at Elizabeth.

'Well you know now, we'll have to catch up on our faves later... Mrs Christopher, I've got something for you too.' He took out a pretty plaid neck scarf and passed it to Clara.

'Oh... how nice of you. This is so lovely. Pink is my favourite, I just love it. Thank you,' she said, looking pleased as she felt the smoothness of the mohair muffler.

'You're welcome.' He turned to Xiamen who was sitting in the two-seater. 'And finally, for you Mr Christopher, I gathered reliably that Ciu Ciu wine has been the main favourite of your paternal pedigree, so I brought a bottle of premium Italian special for you Sir.' He moved over to him with the remaining gift.

'Interesting!' Xiamen said, Taking the bottle. 'I see that my daughter has been divulging my family secrets to you. Apparently, she'd only leaked the beneficial ones so I'm pleased. Thank you for this kindness. It's a pleasure to meet you finally.'

'It's my pleasure too Sir.'

'Please sit.'

'Thank you.'

Wilson made to sit in the armchair but Elisabeth nudged him towards the three-seater and sat down with him. Simon proceeded to perch on the armchair as Clara settled herself beside her husband.

'So, how's work and everything with you?' Xiamen asked.

'My work at the practise is pretty good. As for everything else, I can't complain.' Wilson replied.

'Dinner is ready and the table is all set, so come on through everyone,' Clara enthused.

'Let's go over and eat,' Elisabeth added, standing up and offering a hand to Wilson. 'I hope you are hungry?'

'You bet!' Wilson clasped her hand and rose to his feet. He went with her to the dining room and the others followed them.

'Here we are! Sit here.' Elisabeth ushered Wilson to one of the dining chairs and took the one next to his.

Xiamen and Simon proceeded to sit down. Clara retrieved the food from the oven and Elisabeth got up to help her. They brought the meal to the table and took their seats.

'Wilson, we have grilled sardines laid in tartar sauce for starters. For the main course, panned-fried lamb chops and tenderised chicken breast are on the menu. You can choose one or have a mix of both, there's enough to go round. They are served with oven-baked potatoes and stewed tomato sauce. There is salad on the side and vanilla rice pudding for dessert. Please help yourself.'

'Thank you for the menu overview, Mrs Christopher. The aroma is very enticing, I think I'll have a bit of everything.'

There's a bottle of sparkling Chardonnay in the fridge for you too, Elizabeth mentioned you like Jacob's Creek.'

'Splendid indeed! Thank you all for making this about me. I'm grateful for it,' Wilson appreciated. He groped Elisabeth's knee and gave it a gentle squeeze.

Elisabeth threw quick glances at her family members, but none of them seemed to be aware of Wilson's action. She continued to search their faces hoping they wouldn't notice before he took his hand off her knee. Wilson had a habit of groping her whenever she was sat within arm's reach. Elisabeth figured it was his non-verbal way of reassuring her, so she had never bothered to caution him about it. She didn't think he would dare to commit the act right in front of her parents and brother. They wouldn't think it decent of him. She contemplated to shake his hand off her knee before the others noticed. Suddenly, she didn't feel his hand there anymore. It slid into view and Wilson picked up his cutlery. She heaved a sigh of relief.

After dinner, Elisabeth drove Wilson home in her car. He'd booked a taxi on the way there as Elisabeth had planned to drive him home then stay over.

'Your folks are really nice. The food was so good!' Wilson admitted, patting his belly.

'I'm glad to hear that. My mum will be pleased. Did you enjoy the rest of the evening?'

'Every bit of it. Everything was made especially for me.'

'You were our special guest of course.'

'My gosh... I am gasping for a gasper after all that food.'

'What?'

'I mean that I am craving for a smoke. I could really do with one right now.'

'Of course, I bet you're itching to have one now, huh? Thanks for not stepping out for a quick one at my parents.'

'I needed to make a good first impression. Doing otherwise wouldn't have scored me good points.'

'Of course it wouldn't have. But don't worry, we'll be at yours in ten so you can have your stick.'

'Would you be kind enough to let me have a quick smoke now if I wind down and make sure I blow the fumes out?'

'Not in my car!'

'Come on, Be lenient. I won't stink up your car I promise.'

'Just drop it cos I aren't going to let you!'

'I hear you. I was only trying my luck.'

'You better not! Smoking is out of bounds in my car!'

'I know, you said that many times before. I won't push my luck.'

'Thank you.'

'Anyway, I have some special treats lined up for us this weekend that will mesmerise you.'

'What are you on about now?'

'You will never guess where I am taking you.'

'Where are we going?'

'I am not telling. Wait until the weekend. You will be blown away for sure.'

'Now I am curious. I want to know.'

'I'm not sharing.'

'Come on now, give me just a tiny clue, please.'

'Sorry, no clues, wait until the weekend.'

On the Saturday of the weekend, Wilson took Elisabeth to Gorleston-on-Sea. When they arrived, Elisabeth was baffled when he led her along the dock and she looked at the place with disapproval. It looked to her they were going on a boat ride; she silently chastised him for being out of his mind if he thought that was particularly special.

Her eyes widened when she saw what he was leading her to. Mooring on the water, at the head of the dock, with *The Queen of Hearts written across her body,* was a gleaming state-of-the-art yacht! Elisabeth admired the glazed metallic silvery body; it was the first thing that caught her eye. Her reflection on the shining boat stared back at her as if she was looking into a mirror.

'What... Wilson! Are we going on that?'

'You bet!' he boasted proudly.

'Oh my God! What is she?'

'She's a love boat that's specially designed to take lovebirds across the River Yare! The cabin below is the garden of Eden, wait until you see it... it's simply a Shangri-la! What do you think?'

'My gosh! She's beautiful!'

'Oh yes she is! I have reserved her for the two of us but we have a driver on board too, we can board in a minute.'

'But where are we going?'

'I will explain more about that when we are in the cabin. Come on, let's get on board.'

Elisabeth still stood, admiring the yacht. 'She's a shining beauty! How did you find her?'

'I will answer all your questions but let's get on board first. There are a lot of amazing treats in the cabin that I want to show you. Come on!' Wilson climbed on and offered a hand to help Elisabeth.

After leaving the dock, Elisabeth found that the cabin below held the biggest surprise. It was designed in the style of a Kama Sutra chamber and featured a full collection of erotic objects at their disposal, from sensual massage tools to more kinky stuff. The exotic design of the bed looked like it was taken right out of a photo of Mark Anthony and Queen Cleopatra's love nest. Even the self-service drinks and snacks were spiced with aphrodisiacs for their pleasure.

Elisabeth and Wilson shut themselves inside for solid few hours and engaged in some role-play, exploring the carnal toys one by one. The couple used the opportunity to explore each other's feral side. Eventually they rose to enjoy the outside views whilst indulging a bottle of Champagne.

Following their pleasurable ride on the yacht, Wilson took Elisabeth to dinner at a Mexican restaurant that evening. He had booked it for a special Mariachi performance especially. The singers treated the whole dining room to a rendition. Whilst they were having dessert, Elisabeth was taken aback when the Mariachi's last song became about her. Her face creased in confusion and she threw a suspicious look at Wilson. At that moment, Wilson went down on one knee and opened a jewellery box as the Mariachi continued singing.

'*Congratulations Elisabeth*
Wilson is popping the question
Don't leave him on his knee, you queen of his heart
Don't leave him on his knee, you light of his life
Don't leave him on his knee, you apple of his eye
Don't leave him on his knee, you sugar in his tea
Don't leave him on his knee
Don't leave him on his knee...'

'Yes!' screamed Elisabeth.

Wilson slipped a ring on her finger and Elisabeth kissed him. A burst of applause filled the restaurant as the other diners joined in on their celebration.

After the restaurant, Elisabeth stayed at Wilson's for the rest of the working week. By the weekend, she returned home and broke the wonderful news to her mother. She even showed her father and Simon the engagement ring. She went back to Wilson's the following day and continued to live at his, only going home briefly every week or so for a catch up.

Elisabeth and Wilson's engagement further tightened their love. They subsequently became head over heels and slept in each other's arms every night. As their union grew tighter, stronger and more intimate they relished their relationship and basked in their fondness for each other. Eventually, Elisabeth moved in with her fiancé officially and settled in his house. Wilson totally warmed up to his wife-to-be; she was his dream come true and he treated her lovingly.

Elisabeth fell pregnant in the second year of their engagement. They fixed a date for their wedding sooner than they had anticipated and got married on March 7th, 2014. Following their wedding in Norwich, Elisabeth and Wilson jetted off to China for their honeymoon. They boarded a Malaysian airline from Heathrow Airport to Kuala Lumpur. The honeymooners took a connecting flight from Kuala Lumpur to Beijing.

A few hours after the scheduled departure, it was broadcast across worldwide news that Malaysian Boeing 777 flight had gone off radar. It went missing with over 200 passengers and crew on board.

It seemed like a hoax to Xiamen and Clara when the news hit the global news terrain. As the days turned into weeks and the weeks became months, the missing plane didn't resurface. it became starkly clear to the Christophers that the airbus could really be lost forever. The impact of the realisation gave the Christopher family a bitter chill, forcing each one of them into a melancholic apprehension.

Clara and Xiamen joined forces with Wilson's parents and other British families who had lost loved ones on the plane to raise their concerns to the home office, insisting they look into the whereabouts of the missing aircraft. Eventually, they were made to understand that the plane may have gone missing whilst flying over the Indian Ocean; apparently it wasn't feasible to carry out a search for the plane because there was no accurate location to search.

That bit of information only got Xiamen infuriated. The last thing he wanted to hear was that once again, the Indian Ocean was involved in the mysterious disappearance of his daughter's and son-in-law's bodies. Xiamen's family grieved Elisabeth with no body for a formal funeral. The same fate he had previously experienced with his parents hit again.

Chapter Thirteen

Two years after Elisabeth's mysterious disappearance, another incident whirred like an ill wind and blew Xiamen's household into further despair.

That day, Xiamen was driving two passengers to Great Yarmouth when his private mobile phone rang. The personalised ringtone told him that was his wife calling. She never called him on that number when he was on the job as she knew his work phone was connected to handsfree. He thought she might have made a mistake and waited for her to call his work phone, but she didn't call back.

After Xiamen dropped off the passengers, he returned his wife's call. The ringer buzzed repeatedly but Clara didn't pick up. He tried again, then again for a third and fourth time. Still getting the same result, Xiamen wondered why she had rung ten minutes before but was not answering her phone. Baffled, he tossed the phone on the dashboard and reversed his cab. Xiamen had no sooner started driving back to Norwich than the customised ringtone for Simon went off on his work mobile. He instinctively became anxious.

'Si, what is it?'

'Something's wrong with Mum, Dad!'

'What?'

'She's unconscious and not responding, I want to call an ambulance!'

'Slow down Si. Where's she? Aren't you supposed to be at school?'

'I came home early because the teacher called in sick at the last minute. I found Mum lying on the kitchen floor. I've tried to revive her but she won't budge!'

'Oh my God! Is she breathing?'

'Yes, but she looks really pale!'

'I am on my way now. Call the ambulance after I ring off and keep me updated if they get there before I do. Okay Si?'

'Okay Dad.'

'And, Si?'

'Yes?'

'Stay calm, okay'

'I am trying, Dad.'

The paramedics arrived and took Clara to the hospital before Xiamen could reach home; he changed his route immediately and arrived not long after them. Xiamen entered the emergency ward and joined Simon in the family lounge. He gathered Clara had been admitted and was still comatose. He and Simon sat there waiting, tense with worry as the medical team attended to Clara.

The team didn't administer immediate medical treatment because they needed to wait until the next day for the conclusive test results. Clara didn't come round that day either, so Xiamen and Simon went home to sleep. The following morning, Xiamen was back at the hospital whilst Simon went to school. Xiamen met the doctor and learnt of his wife's condition.

'Mr Christopher, the blood test result has shown presence of malignant tumours in your wife's body. We used CT scans to locate the abnormal cells in her colon. We are presently looking into what might have caused it and will be performing further tests on her blood to see if the cells have spread beyond there. We don't have a prognosis at the moment unfortunately, so I can't tell you anything actual until we understand what is really going on.'

'I don't understand what you are saying, doctor.'

'We think your wife has undiagnosed colon cancer which has spread within her intestine.'

'But, she was perfectly okay this morning. She didn't complain of anything. I don't get it. How is this possible?'

'I am indeed sorry about your wife's condition Mr Christopher. I am sorry to tell you this, it doesn't look good for your wife. But we are going to do everything that is possible to save her.'

Xiamen's thoughts momentarily welled into a deluge of confusion flooding his mind like a burst dam. He sat in shock, quietly pleading to God to help.

Clara came out of the coma the following day, pale and weak, and only able to talk scarcely just above a whisper. The hospital gathered more facts about her situation from the medical tests and advised that she remained in admission. Her treatment was promptly started.

Within two weeks of commencing chemotherapy, she started to deteriorate; her skin sprouted pustules that spread all over. In a desperate attempt to save her, her bowels were removed to stop the cancer spreading, and she could only eat parenteral food thereafter. Unfortunately, trying to save Clara's life was to no avail; she shortly passed away in hospital. She was gone before the chemo had even had a chance to take effect.

The event of Clara's death landed like a shot-put on Xiamen and Simon; the two of them shared the grief equally and they buried Clara with sorrowful hearts. The father and son's relationship became estranged after

Clara's passing as they sought out different ways of dealing with their shared grief.

Losing Clara didn't make any sense to Xiamen. The impact left him with a yawning wound that burrowed deep into his heart. Everything had happened too fast to allow him to grasp the situation meaningfully. How could his wife be hale and hearty one day and a frail dying person the next? She was his soulmate and suddenly she was no more!

Although Xiamen continued his cabby business, Clara's absence extinguished his happiness. He became a sad soulless man who was functioning but not living. His melancholy radicalised the way he viewed life; it refashioned his thought process and made him become a fatalist with a mentality of "whatever will be, will be". His mental state slowly deteriorated into a psychological anhedonia and subconsciously gravitated towards a dark depression that was sheathed in the pit of his mind. He lost the ability to be happy and couldn't do anything about it.

Chapter Fourteen

Simon was twenty-seven when they buried his mother. The memory of her death remained fresh in his mind as he was never able to get rid of the mental image of her poorly frame when she laid dying on the hospital bed. He took account of the black events that had occurred in his family and was overwrought by a painful agony. Why were his grandparents washed off? Why did his pregnant sister disappear into oblivion? Plus, his mother had deteriorated into a living corpse before his eyes too? Simon couldn't understand it all. He carried on with his life and became furious eventually.

A burning anger from the depth of hell crept into Simon's mind. Not only did the anger incensed his thoughts, it also burnt the life out of his contentment and prejudiced the way he viewed everything. From that point forwards, hateful thoughts towards life's unfairness brimmed his mind.

That same year, Simon finished his Master of Arts in Sports degree. He moved to Scotland to work as a coach in a university sports complex. The job often permitted him to travel to various places for competitions. In order to escape from the emotional pain that lingered in his heart, Simon adopted a precarious lifestyle and began to engage in adrenalin-fuelled sports. He joined an enduring group of sportsmen with a defiant disregard for danger or its consequences. The daredevils engaged in perilous sporting events together and these activities helped Simon release the burning anger in his heart.

Two years after his mother's demise, Simon was off to partake in another adventure. He enlisted to participate in a mountain-climbing competition which took place on one of the rocky highlands in the Himalayas. The cliff-climb challenge kicked off by sunrise. Simon and the other amateur mountaineers started their ascent on the rock in attempt to do the 100 ft climb to the top in record time. Six hours after the start time, Simon was halfway up and in fifth position when an avalanche suddenly occurred. Although it was only a minor rockfall, it sent most of the climbers reeling down. The rock slide caused the main anchor to unscrew, letting loose the carabiner that attached Simon to the rock. He tried frantically to retain himself on his harness, but his pitons lost their grip and came off with the loose rocks. Simon went crashing fifty feet down on the craggy base and landed bang on his back.

Thankfully, Simon didn't lose his life but he sustained colossal injuries. He was taken in an air ambulance to a hospital in Kathmandu where his injuries were examined and medicated. His insurance company covered Simon and he was later flown to the Norwich University Teaching Hospital in England. He was ventilated and in poor physical shape.

The hospital in Norwich received Simon as a quadriplegic; he was paralysed from the neck down. All voluntary body actions from his neck to toes were lost. His spinal cord was damaged. On top of that, he had respiratory problems caused by a damaged medulla oblongata and needed a ventilator to support his breathing. Due to his irreversible, life-changing condition, Simon could not sit up or use any of his limbs; he wasn't able to utter a word, not even a grunt or a cough. They found that his mental faculty wasn't affected and he could still hear, read and feel touches on his face.

When Xiamen saw his son's condition, it broke his remaining spirit and he wept. The unfortunate incident shattered him; he was just as mentally broken as his physically broken son. He stopped working temporarily after Simon was discharged from hospital so he could look after him at home.

Putting his life on hold to be a full-time carer for his son changed Xiamen's lifestyle; it wasn't an easy responsibility. He didn't find it easy, but he was motivated by love. With sheer determination, he willed himself on. He supported Simon in every way possible and even attended support groups to learn more about coping. For six months, Xiamen committed himself to the task as best he could until he couldn't cope anymore. Not only did the responsibility drain him physically, but it almost stirred his mental health into a tipping point of insanity. He decisively gave up and sought for external help before he lost his mind.

Chapter Fifteen

Xiamen subsequently looked for suitable accommodation for his son, eventually choosing the Tender Care Nursing Home in Bungay. He rehoused Simon there and visited him once every two weeks.

Buoying on with life as a lone pirate made Xiamen uneasy. He became apprehensive of the three-bedroom house. The house spooked him, haunting his mind like a burial ground. He developed an uncanny premonition of death hanging over his head, believing in his heart it was his turn next.

Xiamen had taken on full responsibility for the house mortgage after his wife's passing. Though Clara's life insurance had helped to reduce the interest, he had still worked extra hours to compensate. Simon's care package was now presenting a new financial problem; the cost per week was even more than Xiamen's monthly mortgage. Thankfully, he was swiftly able to obtain support from the National Health Service to cover some of the cost. All in all, Xiamen didn't struggle financially but he worked even harder to keep himself distracted from his melancholy.

Xiamen never used to drive his cab at night before; now he was working nearly seventeen hours a day. He would often get home close to midnight to sleep. He would rise by six o'clock each morning, take a few minutes to get ready and would be gone from the house before 7:30. He devised this strategy to keep out of there for as long as possible, so the place was often left in a state of abandonment.

After the death of his wife, Xiamen had initially employed someone to clean the house once a week. He maintained the housekeeper's services when Simon was in his care too. After Simon was rehoused, Xiamen dismissed the domestic help and took up the task of doing the house chores every Sunday when he didn't go to work. He'd kidded himself that he needed to save the money, but after two months of doing it he lost interest and even started going to work on Sundays. As a result, the surfaces of furnishings in the house had become casualties of incidental dust.

One Friday morning, Xiamen picked up two passengers from Norwich train station. They requested to be taken to St Edmunds Church in Southwold. He gathered from the men's conversation that they were industrialists. Sometime through the journey, one of them asked Xiamen if they could smoke. Xiamen politely refused and wondered why he'd ask when the "NO SMOKING" sign in his cab was conspicuous. He had no sooner turned down the man's request than he heard him further demand.

'Ok fella, pull over briefly and leave the meter running. We would like to have a quick smoke before we continue.'

Xiamen didn't buy into the man's request at first. He contemplated briefly, wondering if the men could be robbers. They wouldn't get far if they carjacked him or get a bountiful reward if they turned out his pockets and went through his cab with a fine-tooth comb. Without further ado, Xiamen found a free strip on the road to park up and the men alighted to have their smoke.

Xiamen watched both men in his wing mirror as they lit their cigarettes and start to puff. He thought it strange what they were doing. Ordinarily, taking a cab from Norwich to Southwold wasn't a cheap journey. It took roughly a little less or more than an hour, depending on the traffic. Taximeters were programmed to charge more for out-of-zone trips too. He imagined there wouldn't be many that would tell a commuting taxi driver to pull over for a cigarette break with the meter running. They must certainly have deep pockets to be this prodigal.

As if to collaborate Xiamen's thought, the men lit up their second sticks before long. They carried on puffing and chatting mindlessly without any urgency. After seven minutes, they finished up and got back into the cab. Xiamen continued the drive. He rolled down his window for some air. The men's re-entrance into the cab brought a sudden stench of cigarette smoke. Xiamen immediately regretted pulling over for them to smoke but after he saw the reading on his taximeter, his lips curled into a grin.

Chapter Sixteen

Xiamen headed straight back to Norwich after he'd dropped the binge-smoking passengers. He decided to take his cab for a wash at Arthur and Gors, a Car wash owned by two Armenia brothers. Xiamen loved to have his car valeted there because the washers did a great job. Their skilful manual wash left both the exterior and interior of his cab looking thoroughly clean. The car wash had two separate lounges for their customers to wait in, a small bar and a hookah saloon. Xiamen went into the bar, bought himself an energy drink and perched on a bar stool to drink it.

Just then, Harrison Powell entered the bar and approached the counter. 'Hey Xiamen!' he hailed, walking up to him.

Xiamen looked his way and responded, 'Hello Harrison, you alright?'

'Yeah, I couldn't be better, bruv. How are you holding up?'

'So-so. I'm not complaining.'

'I heard about what happened to your son. Spencer told me all about it. I am deeply sorry. He did mention that you were taking time off to tend to your son too. I didn't know you had returned to work. That explains why Spencer isn't calling me up now like he was. So how's your son doing now?'

'I've put him in a nursing home.'

'How is he?'

'He's just hanging in there. Nothing he can do really.'

'So sorry, bruv. I can't imagine how it must make you feel.'

'Yea. It's the life the universe presented to me. I'll never understand or be able to explain it.'

'I feel you, bruv.'

'Did you want a drink?'

'Yeah, I was coming for a quick one when I saw you.'

'Have it on me then.'

'Thanks bruv. I owe you one next time.'

'No problem.'

Harrison ordered a bottle of beer and settled on a neighbouring bar stool. He sipped his drink and looked Xiamen in the eye. 'So, how are you coping with everything?'

'What do you mean?'

'I mean with all the bad stuff that has happened to your family?'

'I'm coping as good as anyone who's been through same.'

'It must be pretty hard to deal with.'

'Yeah, the world is full of unexpected occurrences… anything can happen to anyone at any time and place.'

'I agree. It's the randomness of the universe of course.'

'We're all at its mercy. No one can truly be safe from it's long arm. The universe authors and finishes everyone's destiny.'

'You know I also lost a child two months ago.'

'You did?' I didn't know you had any children.'

'Well, I didn't. We were expecting one, but my wife miscarried.'

'What?'

'She was seven months gone, the baby was formed and everything. Then she lost him.'

'I'm sorry to hear that.'

'Yeah. It was very painful for us. She almost lost her life too. The baby went still inside her womb and she didn't know until she fell sick. It was at the hospital we found out she was carrying a decomposing foetus. The stillborn was evacuated to save her life. After the whole thing, they warned us to take a break from trying. We'd already been trying to conceive for many years before all this so we're at a loss as to what to do now.'

'So sorry to hear that.'

'My wife fell into depression after that. Now she eats anti-depressant like candy.'

'That's something at least if it's helping her. Maybe the pill is what I need too.'

'You don't want to go that way bruv. Trust me, those pills don't work.'

'They don't? How do you know?'

'I have tried them before.'

'You mean you went on anti-depressants after the stillbirth too?'

'No. It was way before that. I had some during my first few years of marriage when I encountered an issue that made me fall into depression. I was getting the medication from my doctor. Then he prompted me to join a support group and I found one doing group therapy. During one of the sessions, the coordinator told us about a natural remedy for depression. He didn't directly recommend it, but he planted the idea in my head.'

'What did he say?'

'Well, I can't really say why I did it, but I took the coordinator's word to heart at the time and I started researching what he said. Much of the info I gathered corroborated with his, so I decided to give it a try. My very first trial of the stuff convinced me.'

'What did you try?'

'I am talking about Mary Jane.'

'She's a woman?'

'More than that. She's a goddess!'

'What?' Xiamen gave him a sidelong glance.

'She's the goddess of the greens. A green goddess with pure and curative powers of herbal remedy.'

'What are you talking about?'

Harrison gestured with two fingers over his lips like he was puffing a cigar and lowered his voice. 'I mean weed!'

'What?' Xiamen looked popeyed.

'I am talking about cannabis. I am not joking bruv. I haven't let go since after I tried it. I use it every now and then when I feel down.'

Xiamen's initial look of surprise turned into a dubious stare; he observed Harrison without uttering a word. Harrison drank up his beer. When the bottle was empty, he placed it on the countertop and stood up.

'Honestly bruv, what I told you isn't just my theory. I assure you that weed is a natural self-medication that you can take to boost your low spirits. It has no side effect. I know the stuff works because it worked wonders for me. But you know, everyone is different. One person's treasure is another's trash as they say. If you ever want to try the stuff, I know where you can get it. Heaven helps those who help themselves. You don't have to prolong your internal suffering when you can do something about it. Consider that food for thought. Well, I better go and see if my cab is ready. I guess I will see you around bruv.'

Harrison left the bar as Xiamen keenly stared after him. He found his car looking sparkly clean, but all the doors were still left open; the guy who washed it hadn't yet finished the job. Harrison took out some money from his wallet and approached him.

'Nice work Futa! I'm impressed as always.'

Futa straightened up from returning a foot mat to the car and closed the door. 'Good evening, master,' he said. 'I have wash your car very well. It is shining like white snow and very clean! Let me show you a test.' He drew a finger along the car's body and it made a sleek squeaky noise. 'You see what I mean?' He beamed a proud smile.

'Ha-ha, of course. I can see that clearly. Great job.'

'You are my good customer, so I always clean your car with my talent.'

'That's kind of you.'

'Next time you come, I will clean your boot for you. I was not able to do it today because of the lock.'

'I know. I will leave it open next time.'

'Okay master, that is fine. Your car is almost ready. I will return the other mats, then you can drive it away.'

'Alright, I will hang by while you do that.'

Futa went to the platform where the mats were drying. He brought the three remaining mats and placed them onto the hood of the car, placing each one back into position one by one. After he had finished, he straightened up and wiped the hood. 'Master, I finished now. Your car is ready to go.'

'Very good Futa, thank you.'

'No problem, master.'

'Here, Futa, have this. Keep the change too.' He handed the money to him.

'Thank you very much master.'

'No worries. Thank you too for doing a good job. Goodbye Futa.' Harrison got into his car.

'See you next time master.' Futa hurried away as Harrison drove off.

Xiamen had remained sitting, staring into space as he chewed on the mental food Harrison had fed him. He resigned it was just nonsense and cast the thought aside. He finished his drink and left the bar to collect his car. He approached the washing bay and met the guy who was washing his car still on the job.

'Hey Davit! How long before you finish?'

'Give me five minutes Sir. I am almost done. I just need to finish cleaning the dashboard.'

'Alright, take ten and be done by then, okay?'

'I will try Sir.'

'Alright. I'll be back,' Xiamen said and started to retrace his steps.

'Big master!'

Someone called after Xiamen. He turned and saw Futa waving at him by the car he was washing. 'Hey Futa, what's up? You didn't wash my car today?' Xiamen threw at him from his distance.

'No, my friend Davit is washing it for you... he is a talented washer as me! But next time I will wash your car for you!' Futa hauled back.

'I guess you all are talented! Alright, Futa, I'll catch you later!' Xiamen started to walk.

'Excuse me big master, can I get anything small for my lunch today?'

'Nothing today Futa. I'll see to that when you wash my car next time!' Xiamen hurried back into the bar before Futa could chip in another word.

The workers at the car wash usually rounded off their work before 7PM as the water pumps automatically shut off just after that time. There were up to eight guys that came around to work there daily. Apart from Futa, who was African, the other Seven were Armenians. Davit gravitated more towards Futa than the other Armenian guys because they shared a special relationship. After finishing his work for the day, Davit went into the storeroom to keep a vacuum cleaner. He met Futa there putting away a container of cleaning stuff.

'Hey Futa, when are you leaving?'

'I am going after I put away these things.'

'Maybe you like to join me for a smoke? I have some sensi.'

'Yes my friend. I am not in a rush anyway.'

'Okay, we can go right after I put away this hoover.'

Futa and Davit walked out of the premises. They headed towards the back and took a lane that led to a small woodland, chatting as they went.

'How much in tips did you get today?' Futa asked the question.

'Thirty-five.'

'Woah! That's plenty!'

'I know. What about you?'

'I don't know, I've not counted it yet. I will do that after we sit.'

'Your big master friend give me only two today.'

'That's something at least.'

'Didn't he give you more than that when you wash his car last time?'

'Yes. He likes my country that's why.'

'How do you know that?'

'Once when he was here, he asked me where I from. I said my father land is Futa Jallon. He didn't know where it is so I tell him it is a plateau in the Republic of Guinea. He said he never hear of it. He come here another time after that and he tell me he see Futa Jallon on a Google map of West Africa and pictures of the highland on Google Earth. He said it is a beautiful place that he like to visit there one day. After that, he called me Futa Jallon every time he come here.'

'So it was he that gave you the name?'

'Yes. He likes to shout the name when he sees me. Other people hear it and start to call me that too. I think they like the name.'

'That's true. Some don't know you as Kofi.'

'Yes. I myself sometimes forget that's my real name. I like Futa better than Kofi.'

'Me too.'

'How many rolls do you have?'

'Three. We will have one each and can kiss the third one together.'

'Nice. Next time, I will bring the sensi.'

'That is what you say every time but you never do.'

'I know, but this time I swear.'

'You swear before and do nothing. So maybe just give me the money and I will buy the smoke and bring it for next time.'

'Believe me this time, brada... I will supply the sensi next time.'

'So, tomorrow?'

'Yes, tomorrow. I promise.'

'I will believe when I see it.'

They walked up to a fallen tree and climbed over it. Davit lowered himself on the trunk, whilst Futa opted for the forked branch. He sat on it and rummaged in his pocket for his cash. Davit took out his wrap of weed and started to gently crush the coarse greens with his fingers. He placed the wrap on the trunk and fished out a cardboard case of rolling papers. He took one of the blanks, left the cardboard case on the trunk and transferred some of the weed into it. He began to skilfully roll it into a joint. Futa finished counting his money and slipped it back into his pocket. He joined Davit on the trunk, picked a blank and started rolling his own joint.

'So, Futa, how much is your tips?'

'Only sixty.'

'Wow! That's more than what I got today.'

'But you get more than that many times.'

'Yes, I know, but you yourself get more tips than anyone else. I think the customers like to dish you money.'

'It's because I have the skills.'

'What skills?'

'I ask them for lunch money with some style, and they give me something sometimes even when I don't wash for them.'

'What? Man that's begging! I can't beg like that. I'm not a beggar.'

'I don't ask them because I am a beggar. I do it only because I am trying my luck. Sometimes when the customers are in good spirits, they dish me small money just because I ask. I think people who cannot beg are too proud.'

'I don't think I am proud. I would be ashamed and hate myself if I don't get money after begging for it. I prefer to work and wait for tips.' Davit finished rolling his joint and frisked through his pockets. 'Dam it, I have lost my lighter.'

Futa fished his from his pocket. 'Here, use mine.'

Taking Futa's lighter, Davit lit his joint and started to relish the fumes. Futa lit his joint too and began to emulate Davit's slow and steady drags. Before long, the psychoactive vapours inspired their cerebrum hemispheres. They soon fell quiet and went into deep concentration. Their thoughts escaped into the mental honeycombs that had suddenly erupted in their minds. Each of them started seeing things with their mind's eye. Futa's imagination took him back to his country where he'd become the president and was being chauffeured in the presidential bulletproof jeep. Davit saw himself in an action movie realm where he was playing his favourite action hero and blasting away an assault gun at the bad guys.

Chapter Seventeen

The following morning, a gleaming white taxi drove up Madeline Avenue. The taxi stopped by the kerb opposite number 25 where a woman was stood waiting. The driver of the taxi looked at her expectantly. The woman then crossed the street and walked to the rear passenger side. She hesitated by the door for a moment before she opened it. She got into the backseat and slammed the door with a bang that caused the driver to grit his teeth.

'Where may I take you, madam?'

'Were you not briefed?'

'No, I wasn't.'

'I did give the telephonist my journey details when I phoned up.'

'You might've, but the taxi switchboard operator doesn't give me that information. I only see where to collect you from on my dispatcher log, as I'm the closest cabby to your location.'

'All right, take me to Lonsdale Conference Centre please.'

The driver removed his foot from the brake and slowly rolled the car into motion. 'Would you like me to take you to the west or south entrance?'

'To the south gate please,' the passenger affirmed as the cab gathered speed. She nestled into the seat and sank into her thoughts.

'Do you live in that house madam?'

The driver's voice cut into the passenger's thoughts like a waspish wasp. 'I am sorry, what did you say?' she blurted out.

'Do you live in that house where I collected you?' The driver dared to ask again.

The woman impulsively ignored the driver's question, mentally rebuking him for not minding his business. Within an instant, she thought he might have a reason for asking and reconsidered. 'No, am lodging in the Airbnb apartment there temporarily.'

'Aha! I thought you might be a personal guest of the ship captain that owns the house.'

'Do you know him well?'

'Yeah, the captain is a well-known VIP. I've done some errands for him a few times. But… uhm, I don't see much of him. He is hardly ever around due to his work.'

'His house is quite a big one but I haven't seen anyone else about. Doesn't he have any family? I mean children.'

'Children, hah? The captain is too committed to the sea. I don't think he ever had time for a family or a typical relationship. He sure isn't the settling type that's for sure'

'I see,' said the passenger in a bland tone. She leaned back into the seat, looking downcast.

Watching the passenger from his rear-view mirror, Xiamen realised his gossip hadn't gone down well with her. He wondered if the captain was in town and she might have eyes for him. He suddenly had an insight to rectify his mistake.

'I heard there was a special woman in the captain's life once upon a time. He loved her to bits, but it turned out that she was a scammer. She helped herself to bundles of his cash and made off with her accomplice who was some conman posing as a passenger on his ship. They deserted the ship together in Puerto Rico.'

Xiamen surveyed her again and saw her expression perk up. Encouraged by that, he continued to spin his yarns about the captain's love life. By the time they reached her destination, he had filled her ears with his version of the captain's lovelorn experience. He stepped on the brake and pulled to a stop.

'We're here madam, this is the south gate. That will be twelve sixty-five please.'

The passenger fished out her debit card from her purse and handed it to him. 'You can round it up to twenty pounds, I'd like to leave you the rest as a tip if you don't mind.'

'Bless you madam, that's very kind of you. Thank you.' He debited her card and gave it back.

'goodbye,' the passenger said and promptly exited the cab, shutting the door with a slam.

'Once more rattled by the bang, Xiamen gritted his teeth. Quirking his lips into an ironic smile, he mused with dark humour as he watched the woman walk away. *The kind lady might have eyes for the captain after all. No point dashing her hopes or spoiling things for the chieftain. I hope he gets lucky with her.*

The dispatcher panel on the dashboard suddenly dinged with information from the taxi switchboard operator. Xiamen had been allocated to pick up a passenger from 44 St Stephens Street. He promptly steered away from Grapes Hill and headed towards the city centre.

The passenger was a rather lanky, dapper-looking man, dressed in a double-breasted olive jacket over a bright red shirt and black trousers. He had a lush leather messenger bag across his shoulder and a bulging House of Fraser shopping bag in his hand, containing evidence of a spree in Chapelfield Mall. Something about the man made Xiamen give him a second look. The gentleman requested that he was taken to St Crispins Road. He seemed somewhat in a dreamy state, like he was stoned. After he'd settled himself in the back seat, Xiamen reversed and drove to the requested destination. Not long after, the man's phone rang and Xiamen overheard his conversation.

'Hello Jeff, what's up?' There was a pause as the man listened to the person at the other end. 'Well, that's great! I am happy to hear that.' He paused again. 'Yeah, I know, Mary Jane takes care of a depressed mood like nothing else... she is a goddess for sure. I am glad she has helped you too... Yeah, sure, no worries. Just let me know if anything changes otherwise.' There was another pause, then the man bade the caller farewell and rang off.

The phone conversation stirred Xiamen's thoughts and his mind went back to the stuff Harrison had fed him earlier. It was the second time he'd heard about Mary Jane in the space of a few hours. He suddenly felt apprehensive about the coincidence and was tempted to break into a conversation with the passenger. He spied at him through his mirror. The man was leaning back into the seat and closing his eyes like he didn't want to be disturbed. Xiamen repeatedly watched out for an opening, but the man's impassive remoteness didn't shift. Xiamen thought he'd better let him be and drove the rest of the way in silence, dwelling on his own thoughts.

After Xiamen dropped off the dreamy man, his dispatcher panel shortly displayed the location of his next client. He drove to Norwich central bus station and met a middle-aged couple with their teenage son and daughter waiting. The mother gave Xiamen the address of a hotel in Great Yarmouth and he opened the boot for them to keep their bags. The father sat in the front passenger seat whilst the rest of his family settled themselves in the back. Xiamen began their journey.

'Are you looking forward to having some fun Celine?' the father piped in a falsetto voice, Turning backwards to face his daughter.

'Yes Dad, I researched a few places on the internet I'd like to check... er, I mean I'd like us to check out'

'I saw you were looking at the theatre plays, I certainly won't be joining you for that one I'll tell you that now.'

'Come on Jack, be a sport. There's a good show on this week. They will be doing a Mamma Mia tribute! I want us all to see it.'

'I'm not keen on that sort of thing, sorry.'

'You are such a bore Jack, boo!'

'What's Mamma Mia?'

'Do you really not know, Ross?'

'No, Jolene, I don't. I take it you do?'

'Of course I do, am surprised you don't.'

'Tell me then.'

'It's a musical show based on covers of Abba songs.'

'Abba? That rings a bell, but I can't remember any of the songs now. Jog my memory, will you?'

'Celine, you do it,' Jack quickly cut in.

Mumma Mia! Here I go again, my my, how can I resist you. Mamma Mia! does it show again, my my, just how much I've missed you?'

'Good one Celine, but it doesn't help.'

'Try this one Ross. 'Money Money Money, must be funny in the rich man's world —! Money Money Money, always sunny in the rich man's world. Aha-aha-aah-aah, all the things I could do if—'

'Okay! Mum stop, Dad's got it!' Jack butted in, cupping his ears.

'Yeah-yeah, I got it alright. It's the band that did the Dancing Queen song, isn't it?'

'Yep, that's the one Dad,' Celine concurred.

'Dancing Queen is my favourite, I know every word by heart. I can sing that now if you like.'

'No please!!!' screamed the others.

'You're all so very rude!' Jolene reproached them.

'I gathered Great Yarmouth has got some fun entertainments in the small town. They say it's like Disneyland and Las Vegas in a bowl.'

'I'd say it's more like Disney and Vegas in a teacup,' Jolene chipped in.

'Is Vegas like Disneyland, Dad?' asked Jack.

'In some sort yes, but I'd say it's more of a fun place for adults.'

'Do you mean Las Vegas doesn't have any fun places for teens like me?'

'Not quite, but most of the hotels and casinos there are age-restricted.'

'I would like to go on holiday to Las Vegas someday.'. Dad, can we?' Celine threw in.

'Not until you turn eighteen,' her mother retorted.

'That's only two years away for Celine, I'll only be sixteen then. Does that mean I can't go?'

'Ahem! Let's focus on this trip guys. I have a surprise treat lined up. I actually booked a canoeing tour for us.'

'What? It's freaking cold now Ross. Who goes canoeing in this weather?'

'Me! I'd love to go. Will they let us fish dad?'

'I think so, but I don't know for sure.'

'I won't go out on any river in the cold!' Celine said, pouting.

'We don't have to go with them Celine. Jack and Ross can go when we go to the show.'

'Oh no, it won't be the same if Jack and I go alone. The canoeing is supposed to be a family treat.'

'Thank you Ross for the good intention, but we won't be joining you and Jack for that excursion. Does the boat even have a motor?'

'No, the one I booked is a big canoe with dual paddle stations.'

'And who did you suppose would be the other paddler?'

'You.'

'Well then, Jack can be your assistant.'

'I am fine with that Dad, I will row the boat with you.'

'No, Jack, I can't manage it with you alone. You can't keep at anything for long. All of us will have to go.'

'I am not going, I mean it Ross!'

'Neither will I!' Celine concurred.

'Come on girls, I need you to cooperate'

'You can't be serious Ross. How could you book a canoeing trip without asking Celine and me first? We are not going so deal with it.'

'Be reasonable now Jolene. I'm sorry I didn't ask first. I meant it to be a surprise.'

'Well, we don't appreciate the surprise, sorry.'

'I understand, but I have already booked a big boat for us. It will be a wasted effort if we all don't go so reconsider.'

'I am not going.'

'I'm with Mum on that.'

'Come on two of you, please.'

'Drop it Ross.'

'But I can't just go with Jack alone.'

'We are not going so drop it.'

The argument over the canoe trip continued between Jolene and Ross as he tried to persuade her unsuccessfully.

Celine and Jack joined in too, each buttressing their respective stands. They all argued noisily with disregard for the peace and quiet of the cab. Xiamen's palms clenched the steering tighter than usual. His ears had taken in more than they could bear. He put on his invisible noise cancellation earplugs and mentally redirected his listening to his own thoughts.

It takes a lot of effort to run a taxi, the driving is only the start. Putting up with passengers who yammer too much in my ear can be especially tiresome, too much information thank you very much! How can these people on board not care that their constant yakking might offend me? Anyway, they aren't the only unmindful passengers that I've had inside my car. The ones that engage in conniving conversations on their phones really make me boil. Some even cheat on their partners and dare to come in my taxi with their lovers, shameless and without remorse. Then they'll be insulting their spouses behind their backs! How can some men call their partners fat cows and women call their men boring pigs? If I were a cabby vigilante of some sort I could just as well punish the culpable passengers. But there'd be no gain for me in that. Perhaps I could become a small-time blackmailer and milk money from those foolish enough to spill their mouths in my company. Now that's an idea! But that could come with nasty surprises too...

Xiamen reached some traffic held up at the crossing that linked the north and south of Great Yarmouth. The bridge stood in the canal that vessels passed to the cargo port in Gorleston-on-sea. It featured a metal structure with dual platforms which were operated by a bascule lifting mechanism. The traffic lights at the bridgeheads had turned red for motorists and the automated traffic barriers had swung down, keeping the long string of vehicles in check as the platforms lifted to let an oncoming ship cross. From where Xiamen's car tarried, it was possible to see the ongoing bascule platforms going up.

The ship came into view and passed the crossing. The platforms were lowered and the traffic soon started going again. Xiamen drove on, feeling inwardly pleased for another opportunity to witness the seesaw action of the bascule platforms. He was fascinated by the mechanics and was always delighted whenever he had an opportunity to witness the spectacle. A sudden burst of raised voices roused him from his peace. His fingers gripped the steering harder as he silently vented.

Can these noisy bunch jus hush and suck it in? I'm not their personal chauffeur! They must think it's their right to talk freely in my cab. But this isn't a considerate conversation for crying out loud. What about my right to peace and quiet? What if I switched on some heavy metal music at full blast? They wouldn't be able to hear themselves for sure. What then? They'd ask to be let out and I'll lose income? Not fair... I hope legislation will come in to enforce silence as a rule one day, like it is on trains and buses. Why are taxi's any different, huh?

Out of the corner of his eye, Xiamen threw a pouty glance at the man in the passenger seat beside him as he started another line of discussion. Not only did the man's constant yakking piss Xiamen off, his falsetto voice equally irritated him. The man was the most talkative of the group and spearheaded the flow of conversation. He must have infected the rest of the family with his verbal diarrhoea. Xiamen continued to moan inwardly as he listened to the chatty passengers talking over themselves to have a say; the vicious circle of discussion just went on and on.

Despite his irritation, Xiamen maintained calm and drove like the professional cabby he was. In his many years of experience, he'd heard and seen enough to know that this family, although unconcerned about his peace of quiet, were innocent; their disturbance was just a tiny part of the unpleasantries in the trade.

Drawing close to the family's destination, Xiamen slowed down the cab and brought it to a halt outside the hotel. He announced the fare and went to open the boot for their baggage. The man got out first and followed him.

'Whose is this? Is this yours Jack?' Celine asked, holding up a wallet.

'It's not mine.'

'Mum, a wallet has been left here.'

'Show it to the driver, maybe someone has left it behind,' her mother advised.

'Excuse me, I found this on the back seat. I think someone might have lost it,' Celine said to Xiamen.

'Oh, it could belong to the last passenger I took before you. thank you for your sincerity.'

'You're welcome,' Celine said, handing the wallet over.

Jolene gave Xiamen some cash for the fair and told him to keep the change. Xiamen mumbled his thanks and jumped back into the cab. Placing the wallet on his dash, he revised the car and drove off. The drive back to Norwich was filled with the welcome sound of silence. He was glad to be rid of that noisy lot.

Chapter Eighteen

Shortly after Xiamen arrived back in Norwich, the dispatcher log on his dash started blinking for his next pick up. The display showed the potential passenger's location on Magdalen Street. Six minutes later he was there to pick up a woman going to Barn Road. After dropping her off, he remembered the wallet sitting on the dashboard and pulled to a stop.

Opening the wallet, Xiamen saw a couple of neatly arranged £20 notes. He fished out a driver's licence and immediately recognised the dreamy passenger in the photo. Flicking through the wallet, he found a stash of identical business cards in one section. He drew one and studied it closely. *Adam Griffin... Ph D in Counselling and psychotherapy... 18 Woodley House, St Crispins Road. Ah... I wouldn't have thought he was a shrink.* He took out his mobile phone and called the number on the card. The ringer rang for a few seconds then played a greeting message. He left a message requesting a call-back. He returned the card back to the wallet and kept it in his glove compartment. Xiamen got back on the road and drove to a fast-food place for a snack.

'Hey Xiamen, not you again!' Harrison called out as Xiamen stepped into the fast-food joint.

'Hello Harrison, so we meet again. I guess you just happen to be looking for food at the same time that I am, and in the same place too.' He joined Harrison at the counter.

'It appears so. Have this one on me. I owe you one from last time as I recall.'

'Ha-ha. You'd said that, but you needn't bother really.'

'Oh, come on, just make your order and don't worry about paying.'

'Alright, thanks.'

Xiamen ordered himself a chicken burger and a milkshake. He and Harrison took their takeaway bags and strolled out. They said their goodbyes and Harrison started walking away.

'Just a moment, Harrison!'

Harrison stopped and turned around. 'Yes?'

'I have a question. Do you have a minute?'

Harrison took a couple steps back and replied. 'I am all ears.'

Xiamen swiftly glanced around and lowered his tone. 'It's about that Mary Jane goddess you told me about last time.'

Harrison shifted even closer. 'Do you want to try the stuff?'

'Not really… I just want a bit more info about it. I suppose that it's illegal to be in possession of it. How do you use it without getting into trouble?'

'It isn't so difficult. You just have to be careful and keep it a secret from anyone who will rat on you. My wife for instance, she doesn't have a clue I use the stuff.'

'But you told me without fear. I could've reported you.'

'Yeah, you could, but that won't prove anything. You will need evidence. I won't be prosecuted due to hearsay. Anyway, I know you are going through stuff and you might benefit from it, that's why I sold you the idea. You have been thinking about it, haven't you?'

'To be honest, it did cross my mind a few times after you told me about it the other day. I wouldn't want to be implicated in something I don't really understand.'

'Look bruv, you called me back. So what do you want to know?'

'Where do you use it?'

'What do you mean?'

'I mean where do you smoke the stuff? I just want to know in case I want to have a go. So, where can it be done?'

'Right, I will only tell you this now. Anytime you are up for it, find me and I will take you.'

'Where?'

'I can't tell you more, sorry. There's no rocket science about it to be honest. You can actually do it alone, it's pretty much like puffing a cigarette. Have you ever smoked a cigarette?'

'Yes, a long time ago in my uni days. But it wasn't a thing long-term.'

'Alright then. When you get a roll, you light it up and drag in the smoke like you would on a cigarette. It's as easy as that.'

'But where do I do it. I can't just stand in the open can I?'

'No, you can't, but you can find an isolated place, like the woods or some back street. Or you can do it at home since no one lives there with you now.'

'And where do I get the stuff from?'

'I can help you with that of course. When you are ready, let me know and I will introduce you to a guy. I will have to vouch for you before any dealer will sell to you direct.'

'Okay, I get it. I'll let you know if I make up my mind.'

'Take your time, bruv. I'm not pushing you into it.'

'That's fine. Thanks for the chat. I'll see you around.'

'Sure, ta-ta bruv.' They dispersed.

The following day, Xiamen headed out early as usual for another busy morning. He received a call from Dr Griffin when he was out on his first call. He offered to take the wallet to him. After dropping off the passenger on board, he drove to St Crispins Road. He found a place to park near the office block, took the wallet and made his way to the building. Dr Griffin opened the door and greeted Xiamen with a broad smile. Xiamen peeked over his shoulder and glimpsed at a spacious and tastefully furnished office. The room contained a three-seater sofa and an armchair, both of which had small coffee stools beside them. Two identical black leather swivel chairs were positioned on either side of a matching leather-lined desk.

'It's nice of you to bring my wallet back, good man. I really appreciate it, thank you very much.'

'You're welcome. It's my responsibility to keep items lost in my cab safe.' Xiamen passed the wallet over.

Dr Griffin received his wallet and looked through it. He took out a £20 note and gave it to Xiamen.

'No thank you. I can't accept that.'

'Please do. I appreciate you bringing this to me instead of asking me to come for it. I presume you've had to be off work to do this. It's cool, take it.'

'Thank you again, but no. I won't accept it.'

Dr Griffin looked surprised and pleased. He returned the money to his wallet. 'You are amazing. Thank you for your selflessness. There are only a few like you these days.'

'That's alright,' Xiamen said.

'Thank you once again.' Dr Griffin slipped his wallet into his pocket and placed his hand on the door. 'That will be all then?'

'Uhm, not quite. I was wondering if I could speak to you about something.'

Dr Griffin lifted his brows slightly. 'What is it about?'

'Pardon me. When I peeked into your wallet to establish whose it was, I gathered from your business card you are into counselling. I thought I could ask you a personal question if you don't mind.'

'Sure, you can ask me.'

'Uhm, I feel embarrassed to say this, but I think I am going through depression.'

Dr Griffin's initial look of surprise instantly transformed into a look of curiosity. He glanced at his wristwatch. 'Do you have a moment to come in and talk about it?'

'Yes. How much is your consultation fee?'

'Don't worry about that. This time will be for free. I will tell you after if there's a need to see you again.'

'Thank you.'

'You're welcome.' Dr Griffin smiled as he stepped to one side to give Xiamen passage into the office. He offered Xiamen the seat by his desk and sat opposite him, letting some moments pass as he watch Xiamen check out his office.

Xiamen roved his eyes around the office interior, taking in the stunning exquisiteness of the carpet before lifting his look to the desk. The top of the desk featured a few miscellaneous items presented in an organised fashion. A picture frame of a smiling lady on a horse took dominant position. Beside that was the doctor's nameplate, followed by his diary and a ballpen holder with the pen tucked in. A telephone, a jotting pad, a CD album of Bob Marley and the day's newspaper also nestled on the table. Xiamen returned his glance from his inspection and met Dr Griffin's eyes.

'You have a very nice carpet.'

'Thank you, many have said so.'

'Is it Bohemian?'

'It's Arabian.'

'It looks lovely.'

'It is indeed. So my friend, introduce yourself and tell me about your issue.'

Xiamen introduced himself and delved right into his story. He talked in a low and agonised distant voice, like a man talking from a deep hole. He dwelled longer on his wife's untimely death, verging on tears as he told it. After twenty minutes, he'd unloaded a summary of the tragedies that had occurred to his family. He swallowed hard, looking sadly into space.

Dr Griffin maintained a straight face as he looked on at Xiamen steadily. He let a few seconds pass before leaning into his chair and responding. 'Your narrative is touching indeed. I understand how you feel. However, I can't really do anything to change the past, but I can help you in the aspect of your future. If you would like my help, then I will coach you on how to mindfully deal with all that has happened without dwelling on the feeling. You can process your feelings of sadness without sinking in it. Do you understand me?'

'Not quite,' Xiamen replied with a lost look.

'Here's my view. You are affected by all that has happened and have been living with the trauma without actually dealing with it. We will work towards a closure that will let you understand how to process the sadness you feel without dwelling on it. Does that make sense?'

'Kind of.'

'That's good enough for now. If you want me to work with you, my consultation fee is twenty-five for the first hour and fifteen for subsequent hours. I normally recommend two hours for the first session and there will be a break for ten minutes after every forty-five minutes interval for recalibration. I can book you in for an appointment if you want to see me again. Does that sound good?'

'Yes, thank you, it's been a long time coming'

'Okay, give me a moment and I will check my schedule. He skimmed over the pages of the diary on his desk and looked up. 'I can see you Monday next week. I have 12 or 4PM open.'

'I can do 12 PM.'

'Brilliant... I will see you then, Mr Christopher.'

'See you then.' Xiamen left.

After the weekend, Xiamen went back to see Dr Griffin. He welcomed Xiamen and promptly directed him to the three-seater sofa this time. He went to sit in the armchair opposite and picked up the jotter on the stool by his chair. He used a few seconds to scribble some notes before opening the conversation.

'Right, Mr Christopher, the first thing we'll do is establish some rapport between us. I would like us to be on first name terms. So, you may address me as Adam, and I will call you Xiamen. Is that okay?'

'Sure,' Xiamen said.

'Brilliant. Now, it is important that I know the details of your background. So, the first thing I'd like you to do is to tell me all about your early life, education, career, and hobbies. It is important you talk freely without holding back. I know you already told me some aspects of your story before, but I don't mind if you go over them again.

Speak freely and informally, it's okay to say anything here. I won't judge you.'

'Ok. Well, my parents were originally from East London, but I was born in Beijing. They used to teach here before they migrated... when they moved they changed careers and went into hotel management. They had two children, my sister and me. Marlene was born three years before me, but she died when I was five. I still have some vague memories of us playing and when she was sick lying in her bed. My mother told me later that my sister had sickle-cell disease. After my post-primary education, I proceeded to study at the University of Hong Kong and I graduated with first and second degrees in Contemporary Philosophy. My first job after school was as a teaching assistant at a college in Shanghai, but I didn't think it was for me. I quit and joined my parents in the hotel business, working as the guest chauffeur and tour guide. I met Clara when she was on holiday in Beijing... she was a lodger in our hotel and had travelled from England. I fell in love with her the moment I saw her and, fortunately for me, she fell for me too. After we hooked up, our relationship moved pretty quickly and we spent every moment together. I couldn't bear her absence when she returned home so I came here to visit her in Norwich. I never went back to Beijing after that, except to visit my parents later of course. I moved in with Clara, we got married and started a family. Then the first tragedy struck that stole the lives of my parents—'

'Hold on just one second now. Let me clarify some things before you continue. Tell me about your job as a chauffeur. Do you like driving people around?'

'Oh yeah I do. Driving is my hobby. I was very much interested in formula one race as a kid. I actually learnt to drive at sixteen and got a professional licence. I was even able to manoeuvre a truck by that age,' Xiamen said enthusiastically.

Adam made some notes, then asked, 'Out of curiosity, why did you choose to study philosophy?'

'Oh, that. I was fascinated by how the philosophers of old created knowledge through thinking… I thought I could be a philosopher and tried to project wisdom through thinking, but later understood it doesn't work like that in the real world. I realised that people can't always get past their emotions to carry out objective thinking, and that includes me. It was just not realistic to practise what I was trying to preach. So, I lost interest in the whole idea of philosophising.'

'I think that makes sense. Do you regret the time you spent studying the course?'

'I wouldn't say I regret it. I just didn't believe in it anymore.'

'So, do you consider driving better than philosophy? Perhaps as an escape?'

'Of course not. I don't consider driving as an alternative to anything else. It's a job I like and I'm enthusiastic about it. I was first interested in cars before philosophy.'

'That's great. Now tell me about your other hobbies. Perhaps some indulgences… Do you have any?'

'I used to like to have a drink before but not anymore.'

'Why not?'

'It was something my wife and I used to do together. We used to like getting a little tipsy and followed it up with making love.'

'OK. Any other things?'

'Well, I like DIY too. I usually repair the little problems on my car myself, and I change the oil.'

'Really?' How do you do that?'

'It's not that difficult once you know how. You just have to get under the car and unscrew the oil drum to let the old oil out, and then pour a new one in after.'

'You make it sound so easy! Now, let's talk about your fears. Is there anything in particular that scares you?'

'Oh yes.'

'What is that?'

'I fear that something bad will happen to me.'

'Something like what?'

'I don't really know what I'm afraid of to be honest, I just have a feeling of something tragic waiting to happen again. Who knows, maybe it'll be a random force majeure or something sent from hell... I'm just afraid of the unknown.'

'You go on the road every day, do you not fear a road accident?'

'Nope, I don't think that's likely, I'm a professional driver, so it's unlikely that I'll crash into anyone. This may sound weird, not that I'm Houdini or anything like an escapologist... I've this notion in my head that I'd be able to escape from any avoidable crash against my cab.'

'That's another positive assertion, and quite an interesting one too. I admire your confidence. So, what do you really hope to benefit from in our session?'

'I want to be able to get over my depression.'

'Of course. About that, I like to tell you as a matter of fact now that even though I may agree that you are saddened by the recurring tragedies that have hit your loved ones, it may not be appropriate for you to assume that you are suffering from depression. You haven't been clinically diagnosed, so let's keep it tentative for now until that is established. Do you agree?'

'Yes, that makes sense.'

'Fantastic. Now to my next question. What do you think you could do possibly to decrease your feelings of sadness? I mean, is there any positive ideas you can come up with if you were to approach it philosophically?'

Xiamen stared narrow-eyed at Adam with his mouth slightly agape. He considered the question and swiftly rummaged in his mind for something to say but only ended up mooning away.

'Hey, it's time for our ten minutes break,' Adam suddenly announced to distract him. 'I am going to make myself a cup of coffee. Would you like one? Or I have tea, juice or water. I've got some snacks too if you are hungry.'

'Tea will do please.'

'Sure. Sugar and milk?'

'I prefer it dark with one sugar please.'

Whilst Dr Griffin was in the kitchen, Xiamen used the time to think. He hadn't expected his session with the psychologist to flow in the way it was going. He had come with an expectation in mind but Dr Griffin was now treating him psychotherapeutically and trying to get into his head. That wasn't what he was hoping for. Dr Griffin returned. He gave Xiamen his tea and went to take his seat.

'I will let you finish your tea before we continue. We are still within our break so let's drink and talk about other stuff. Do you support any football teams?'

'I'm afraid I'm not a football enthusiast.'

'Me neither. But I like the horse races. I sometimes bet on them for fun.'

'Have you ever won?'

'Yes, a couple of times but nothing major. I have a horse at home too, her name is Betty. She's not a racing horse though. I take her riding some evenings and on weekends.'

'Where do you keep her?'

'In a stable in my yard.'

'Oh wow, do you have a large compound then?'

'Yes, my land covers 1800 square metres.'

'Woah! That's massive! Where do you have such a land?'

'Just outside Norwich in Sheringham.'

'It must be pretty expensive to maintain a horse.'

'In my opinion it's not. I reckon a car cost's more to maintain. But of course, a horse cannot do the work of a car.'

'Do you have a family?'

'Unfortunately not. Adele, my wife, died not so long ago.'

'I'm sorry to hear that. How long since you lost her?'

'Three years. Betty was Adele's so I kept her as a reminder. I have kept up all Adele's routines with her too.'

'That's admirable,' Xiamen remarked, admiring the woman in the frame on Adam's desk.

'It is indeed. Our break time is up. Let's delve back into our session. So, what's your thoughts to my earlier question?'

'I haven't reached anything concrete on that yet.'

'Never mind about that then. Tell me what difficulties you currently experience?'

'I'm just generally unhappy about everything.'

'Would that include your driving work too?'

'No. That's the only thing that keeps me going.'

'So, it might actually be a source of escape after all?'

'Well, thinking about it now, I'll say kind of. It's what gets me out of my house. I hate living there now because of the emptiness.'

'Is it a big house?'

'It's a three bedroom across two floors. Clara and I bought it some decades back. I plan to downsize soon as I'm not able to look after it now. It's just too big to clean by myself.'

'I am sure you can get a domestic cleaner to help with that.'

'I did previously. I had a housekeeper employed that was doing the work, she was there when I was looking after my son at home... I let her go after Simon was rehomed to cull the money for his nursing care.'

'So, when was the last time you cleaned your house?'

'I haven't done that for a while to be honest. There should be little or no mess about anyway as I'm hardly ever there.'

'Perhaps that is true if you follow that logic. But I would like you to take a critical look at the house when you go back there again and appraise its current state of cleanliness. Can you do that for me?'

'Sure. I'll do that today when I get home.'

'Brilliant. So, apart from what you've discussed as the possible causes for your current mental state, do you consider any other matter responsible for your unhappiness at all?'

'No.'

'Very well. Let's assume that's true, that your unhappiness is centred on how you feel about everything that's happened... would I be right if I said your state of unhappiness is how you think about it all?'

'I don't follow.'

'Let me put it this way. Since you understand philosophy, I will take a cue from one philosopher to make my explanation clearer. Did you ever come across the Latin dictum, "Cogito, ergo sum"?'

Xiamen lifted his brows in surprise. 'I know what that means of course. It was coined by the French René Descartes in his discourse on method, as a first step in demonstrating the achievability of certain knowledge, and he particularly used it to expatiate his theory on methodological scepticism.'

'That is correct. What does it mean?'

'The Latin dictum translates in English as, I think therefore I am.'

'You are indeed brilliant. I think it will be easy for you to understand my analogy now. I cited René Descartes' dictum because the statements support the theory that a person is who they are, because they think. Do you agree?'

'Kind of.'

'Good. So, if a person is who they are because they think, would you say every person thinks in the same method?'

'Of course not.'

'Thank you for that honest answer. If you agree that every person doesn't think in the same way, then it will be right to assume that every person is responsible for how they think, right?'

'That's true.'

'Now here's where I am going with this. When people are put in the same circumstance, be it good or bad, would it be sensible to assume they won't think the same way when trying to interpret their situation to themselves?'

'Most definitely.'

'Very good. If that were so, do you think they would all feel the same way about it?'

'I don't think so.'

'Why not?'

'Because every person is different and has a different mental ability to another.'

'Very correct. In your opinion, how do you think people should use their mental abilities to process the issues that affect them?'

'I'd say they should apply it in their best interest.'

'Thank you for that fantastic answer!' Dr Griffin made notes on his jotter before he continued. 'Let's come back to you now. Earlier, I asked if it would be right if I said your state of unhappiness is related to how you think about everything that's happened, and you said you didn't get me. With all we have just discussed, and by your positions on how people should think about their issues, do you get where I am going with this discussion?'

'Yes.'

'So?'

Xiamen momentarily averted his eyes and bit his lip. Dr Griffin gave him some time to process his thoughts whilst he made some more notes on his jotter. He returned his look to Xiamen and observed him. Xiamen remained disconnected, still dwelling on his own thoughts.

'Oh my, it's break time again. Would you like another cuppa?'

'No, Thanks... I'm good.'

'That's fine. I will make myself a cup and come back to you in a jiffy.'

Xiamen acknowledged him with a nod of his head and Dr Griffin disappeared into the adjoining kitchen. Now on his own, Xiamen resumed chewing on his lip and staring into space as his thoughts waltzed around.

'I'm back,' Dr Griffin announced from his chair, breaking into Xiamen's thoughts.

Xiamen looked at him surprised. 'Sorry. I hadn't noticed you'd come back. I was just thinking.'

'That's what we are here for of course. Our task today is purely to think together, with me at the steering wheel. My aim is to guide you to your own mind so that you can have power over it and make it act in your best interest. What were you thinking about just now? Feel free to share it with me, it doesn't matter that we are still on break.'

'Alright. To be honest, I was only thinking that I had not been thinking properly.'

'What makes you think that now?'

'Many things I guess.'

'Such as what?'

'I can't explain it. My thoughts are all over the place at the moment so I can't give you a sensible explanation.'

'Do you think you have to make sense of everything you think and say?'

'Yes of course.'

'Why do you think that?'

'Because it'll be foolish not to.'

'Would you agree with me that foolishness is a perceived perception of one who thinks they, or another, are not acting wise?'

'Yes.'

'Very well. So, if you choose not to do something because you consider it foolish, do you think it might be due to your perceived opinion and conduct of that behaviour, or how you think others will view you'

'Both I suppose.'

'Now if I ask you to tell me what you are thinking and promise I will not consider it foolish, would that make you feel free to express your thoughts to me even though you think it is foolish to do so?'

'I guess so.'

'Now that you have said that, I want you to know it's okay not to talk complete sense when it comes to expressing how you feel about something. What you feel is true to you. You mustn't deny yourself the liberty of expressing your true feelings, especially if it's regarding a matter which concerns you directly. However, how you feel and how you think need to be separated. A person does not allow themselves to steal a loaf because they are penniless and hungry. In your case, you should not allow yourself to feel hopeless about the future because of the ill fate of the past. That's the essence of self-control. Negative emotions often make you feel bad or low of yourself. Anyone who is able to lead their thoughts out of the dungeon of negative emotions will have the power to influence their thoughts positively. By that I mean in their best interest. Do you get all that?'

'I do,' Xiamen said in a solemn tone.

'Perfect. I will leave it at that for now and end our session for today. Do you have any questions you would like to ask?'

Xiamen took a moment to ponder before he replied that he didn't.

'Ok, I have one for you. Do you think you have benefitted from our session today?'

'I have.'

'That's good. I am pleased to know that. How have you benefitted, if I may ask?'

'It's obvious. As I'd said before, I've realised I haven't been thinking properly.'

'Do you mean you haven't been thinking in your best interest?'

'That's it apparently.'

'It's good you have realised it for yourself. Now that you have reached this point, it's up to you to decide if you want to have another session. What would you like to do?'

'I'll think about it.'

'Alright. Do let me know when you are ready so we can pick an agreeable date.'

Xiamen got to his feet and fished out his wallet. He took out some money and passed it over. 'Here's your payment. Thank you very much.'

'Thank you for seeing me,' Dr Griffin replied, receiving the money before seeing Xiamen to the door. 'Here's my card. Give me a call anytime you are ready, we can arrange an appointment then.'

'Okay. I'll have that in mind. Cheers.' Xiamen left.

Chapter Nineteen

After dropping off a passenger at Blofield Market Place, Harrison Powell left the Broadland district and headed back to town on the Northern Distributor Road. The road ahead was clear so he pressed his foot on the throttle, taking advantage of the 70mph speed limit. As the car accelerated, Harrison revved the engine and the RPM needle quickly shot to the red line area on the tachometer. An alert beep suddenly went off. He glanced over the dashboard. There was a warning light on the gauge to indicate that the fuel had plunged into reserve. Harrison eased his foot on the accelerator and stole a glance at the chronometer. Glimpsing the time, he thought to head home.

A short while later, Harrison was parked up in his compound. He didn't see any lights on in the house, a sign that his wife had already gone to bed. Alighting from the cab, he walked to the back of the car. He opened the boot and lifted the carpet off the floor, reaching for the spare tyre. He managed to heave the tyre up enough to dip his hand underneath. He fished out a flat spanners bag, straightened up and zipped it open. The bag had ten spanner pieces that were all laid in individual pouches. Behind the spanners was Harrison's secret hiding place where he securely hid his guilty pleasure. Shifting the spanners out of the way, he fished out a ready-made joint and a gas lighter. He slipped the items into his chest pocket and returned the spanners pouch. Once the car was locked up, he strolled to the garden and sat in a lawn chair.

Harrison retrieved the items from his pocket and lit up the joint. When he was done, he got up and threw the roach in the bin nearby before heading back to his cab. He opened the glove compartment and took out his mint mouth spray and disinfectant wipes. he wiped his palms with a wipe before spraying two squirts from the odour suppresser into his mouth. He returned the items back to the compartment and left the gas lighter there, then headed for the house. Upon entering the sitting room, he locked the door after himself. He turned on the light and almost jumped out of his skin.

'Welcome home, Harry, I've been waiting for you,' his wife Imogene greeted him. She was sitting on the sofa and smiling impishly. An empty bottle of wine sat next to a full glass on the stool beside her.

Harrison momentarily gawked at his wife as he struggled to think clearly. This was rather odd. Imogene was always in bed from 8:30 PM due to the sleeping pills she took. Why was she drinking and waiting up for him at this time?

'What's going on here, Imogene?'

'I already told you I was waiting for you. Didn't you hear me before?'

'I did. But I am surprised to see you like this. What's going on?'

'You will need to sit down to hear what I have to say. Please, take a seat.'

Harrison humbly perched on the other end of the sofa and stared on at her with a troubled expression.

'What's this about, Imogene?' he demanded.

'I know about it, Harry.'

'What do you mean?'

'I know you've been smoking dope.'

Harrison instantly recoiled. 'What are you talking about?'

'Don't you even dare try to deny it. I have been keeping tabs on you and have known for some time. I know you've just been at it in the garden. I can smell it. You always dump the residue in the bin there. I have been taken them out and keeping them as evidence in case you might want to call my bluff. You thought I didn't have a clue, but you've been wrong about that.'

The unexpected indictment threw Harrison into a storm of surprise. His guilt momentarily spread all over his face and he hung his head in contrite.

'Are you just going to sit quietly with your tail between your legs? Go on then, admit it.'

'I am so sorry,' he mumbled.

'That will do. It's over between us. I don't wish to be in this marriage anymore. I want you out of this house by morning. If you don't comply, I will do it properly and invite the police. You will be prosecuted for using an illicit stuff and I will put that on my divorce petition. That would be worse for you so I'd advise you leave without any fuss. It's your call.'

'Why are you doing this Imogene?'

'You want to know? I will tell you. First of all, you can't give me a baby. I am fed up with our hit-and-miss IVF attempts and I don't wish to continue messing up my womb with the frozen specimens of random men. Secondly, you are a two-faced schemer who has been leading a lie with me. Who knows what other secrets you are keeping in that mind of yours, or inside your cab!'

'I am sorry about the performance of my reproductive cells. There's nothing I can do about that. As for my weed addiction, there's no way I could have told you I was indulging in an unlawful act. You would be abetting me and that would make you an accomplice. That's why I'd kept it from you.'

'Well, it doesn't matter now. Just make sure you're out of this house by morning. You can take your secret lover somewhere else to continue indulging in the hobby. I won't say a word of it to anyone.'

'But where will I go? I have nowhere else to go.'

'You will have to figure that out before morning. You should probably sleep on it.'

'I am truly sorry about my addiction and for deceiving you. I' will seek help, all I need now is your support. Do not ditch me now Imogene. Please reconsider.'

'I am sorry too. I have been observing you these past months as you've lied and pretended around here. You disgust me. I wanted to do this earlier. Now that I've finally let the cat out of the bag, there's no going back. I want out.'

'Imogene, don't do this to me please. I have nowhere else to go.'

'That's on you, I'm past caring. I will go to bed shortly. Don't bother coming into the bedroom because I have put all your stuff out to the other room. My door will be locked until I get up in the morning, I don't want to see you still here by then. I hope you will cooperate. Don't you dare try to test me or you'll be sorry.'

Imogene finished the remaining wine in the glass and slammed the cup on the stool. She got unsteadily to her feet and scowled at Harrison with a look of smug satisfaction. 'Hic! So long now Harry. Goodnight to you and… Hic… goodbye.' She hiccupped again and wobbled out of the sitting room.

Some time went by and Harrison remained sitting in limbo, staring into space like a scared cat. Finally, with his thoughts still whirling in a vortex, he lifted himself off the chair and went into the guest room; he was too flustered to remember to switch the light off.

The following morning, Harrison was up by six o'clock. In a temper and without remorse for his noisy movements, he bundled up a few of his possessions and crammed as much he could into his car before speeding out of the compound. He wanted to catch a friend at home before they left for work. After twenty minutes of driving, he reached his destination and drove into the premises. He parked his car in the closest available space and went to the door.

Xiamen had just stepped out of the shower with a towel clad around his waist, when the doorbell went. Unsure he'd heard correctly, he stood still, cocking his head. The bell sounded again. He glanced at the clock in disbelief, wondering who it could be at such a time. Grabbing a dressing gown, he went to open the door.

'Good morning, Xiamen. I am sorry for disturbing you, I couldn't think of anywhere else to go.'

'Morning Harrison, this is a surprise. What's going on with you?' Xiamen asked him.

'I've been thrown out of my house. I'm now homeless.'
'What?'
'My wife kicked me out for good.'
'Why would she do that? Did you do anything wrong?'
'Well… in my opinion, What I did wasn't in any way a direct wrong to her. I will tell you what she said but can I please come in first?'

'Of course. Come in, but I'll need to get on the road soon so make it snappy.' Xiamen moved out of the way to let him in.

Harrison entered the lounge and perched on a chair. Xiamen shut the door and turned to face him.

'Thank you bruv. I didn't know I had a mean nasty woman for a wife. What she did last night was uncalled for.'

'So, what did she say?'

'You know that I smoke weed, right?'

'You did mention it.'

'The truth is, I kept it from my wife and thought she didn't know about it all this time until last night when she confronted me. She accused me of loving weed more than her and leading a double life. She said she is fed up with me and asked for a divorce. She gave me an ultimatum to vacate the house this morning or she would call the police and report about my secret if I wasn't out of there by the time she woke up. The marriage is over.'

'So why have you come here?'

'Leaving on short notice has put me in a homeless situation… I was kind of hoping you could put me up until I sort out another place to live.'

'Why would I want to let you stay here?'

'Why wouldn't you?'

'Why would I? I've got no reason to.'

'Come on bruv, help a mate out. You're all alone in this big house. Aren't you lonely? You did tell me you were unhappy staying in this big house alone, you could do with some fresh company!'

'So I did. But why would I want the company of a cannabis addict? Do you mean to make me your partner in crime?'

'Don't put it like that bruv. You don't have to be judgemental. I told you I use the stuff as a friend desiring to help another friend. Now that I am in a jam, the last thing I expect from you is to leave me stranded because I was open to you. I need your help now bruv, please. I promise I will not use the stuff around here if you let me stay. You will never see or smell it around here I give you my word on that.'

'I'm not sure about this.'

'Don't you worry. Be rest assured that I will never again try to persuade you to try the stuff, so, just disregard all I had told you before.'

'And what if I want to try it?'

'Excuse me? What did you just say?'

'I said what if I want to try it?'

'What?'

'I would like to try the stuff'

'What?'

'You heard me right.'

' Harrison shifted uncomfortably and looked at Xiamen with a troubled expression. 'But why?

'I want to, that's all.'

'I don't think you should bother with it really. Just forget everything I told you about it.'

'It's too late to say that now mate. I've carried out my own research and my findings tally. Many people use the stuff to relieve their pain, so I figure it could be good for me too. I even heard a psychologist tell someone that.'

'I am really sorry but I can no longer be responsible for initiating you into it. At least not when you are providing me a shelter to stay.'

'And why not?'

'Look bruv, you can disregard everything I said before. I am not about that now. I am just here because I need your help. I won't entice you to smoke it anymore, okay?'

'Well, it's too late. I've already made up my mind and I was going to meet you to sort it sooner than later anyway. If you won't help me then you might as well go find yourself somewhere else cos I won't have you here. So which do you prefer?'

Harrison recoiled, feeling a chill up his spine. He started to say something but stopped himself and stared at Xiamen with a perplexed expression. The look in Xiamen's eyes told him he was dead serious.

'Well, if this is what you really want to do, I can't stop you. However, I won't be the one to provide it for you. You can meet me at the taxi rank by Mendes Club later. I will be on my lunch break between one and half one so I can wait for you there… I'll take you to a guy who would be happy to provide the stuff to you for a cost.'

'How much?'

'Not a lot. He sells a wrap for ten quid or you can have a pre-rolled for fifteen.' Seeing the confused look in Xiamen's face, Harrison explained further. 'A wrap is a small quantity of weed sold in a generic packet which you have to prepare for smoking yourself. The pre-rolled joint, or blunt, is already prepared in a rolling paper ready to light. It's pricier and might come spiced with other buzz that adds to the cannabis high. You can get the same deals for half the price at the street depot.'

'Where's that?'

'Not so fast bruv. I can't let you in on everything all at once. This business is strictly based on trust so a trusted client will have to recommend you to a dealer. No pusher will sell you the stuff without a referral. Every dealer in the game has to protect themselves from being set up by a snitch or an undercover agent, as no one can really be sure about who's who. They are very careful who they sell to.'

'So what's the plan?'

'As I said, I will refer you to someone who will sell to you when you meet me this afternoon. You will buy it from him and keep it at your own risk. I recommend that you get a wrap so you can make a light roll for yourself as a first-timer. After work later we can sit down somewhere together and have a puff so I can help you roll and make sure you take in the vapours without any hassle.'

'That sounds like a good plan.'

'It's the best I can do at this stage. If you want to continue with it after that I can let you in on other bits so you will be responsible for everything yourself. You will need to keep the act coded and away from anyone who might make a fuss about it. And of course, you must be clever about how you store the stuff. If the wrong person finds it in your possession that will be raw evidence to use against you, so be wise of that. If you are nabbed and face prosecution, do not divulge any information to the authorities about where and who you got the stuff from, no matter what. You must take the rap alone without implicating anyone else. This is the only condition I want you to agree to in order for me to be your referee. Are you cool with that?'

'Yeah I guess so,' Xiamen answered offhandedly.

'Listen bruv! Say it like you mean it. I need you to understand that there can be no snitching, else the dealers will mark you. So let me ask you again. Do you agree to take the rap alone if you are nabbed?'

'Yes! Do I look like a dobber to you?'

'Of course not. I'm only just making sure that you understand before you get into it.'

'You have my word.'

'That's fine. We're all good now, right?'

'Sure.'

'One thing though.'

'Yes?'

'As cabbies, we don't want to be driving under the influence or reeking of weed. The stuff is illicit so it would be foolish to be carefree about it. Smoking weed at night is the best way to keep it private and ensure that it doesn't interfere with work. Besides that, doing it before bed is nice anyway cos you can take the euphoric effect into your dreams. Do you get me?'

'Loud and clear.'

'Cool then! Have you got any spare rooms ready please? I want to take my things up before we leave for work.'

'Of course, come with me.' Xiamen led him out of the sitting room.

'Can I be cheeky and also request a coffee? I'm dying for one'

'I don't drink coffee so I haven't got any here.'

'That's not good bruv. You might want to get some in the house for us if you want to really enjoy smoking weed. Coffee goes well with dope trust me.'

'We'll see about that.'

Xiamen showed Harrison to Simon's former bedroom and helped him move his stuff in, then the pair left the house for work. Later that night, both of them went to a nearby woods and fulfilled their verbal pact. During the initiation, Xiamen let out a few spontaneous coughs when he inhaled too quickly, so Harrison coached him on how to do it properly. He picked it up well after that and was elated by the feeling he got out of it. He was immediately convinced it was just what he needed. He and Harrison further engaged in the act from that night forwards after they returned from work.

Eventually, Xiamen gained experience and gathered all the info he needed to source his own supply. It took Harrison two months to find a small flat to rent and a further month to equip it before he fully moved out of Xiamen's.

Xiamen continued smoking nightly after Harrison had left, fully embracing the new hobby and making it part of his daily routine. As he became more dependent on the weed, the cooling off period grew shorter; it equally became harder for him to reach his illusive high. He gradually increased the quantity of spliffs he puffed until he pretty much worked himself into an addict. After six months of his induction, he would be yearning for a smoke every evening as if a cannabis-craving parasite lived in his blood. He was smoking the weed with a devil-may-care attitude.

Chapter Twenty

Xiamen hadn't realised how hooked he was on the weed until the product became scarce. He couldn't get any at the street depot for a few days and became restless. Out of desperation, he sought after Harrison once more and met him at the taxi rank where he usually waited for passengers. Harrison listened to his cry for help and told him not to worry; he rang up another taxi driver called Kymani Sanchez. Kymani drove up shortly and Harrison brought him up to speed.

'Yah man, me can provide yuh enough ganja, nuh worries about dat. But ganja price has gone up right about now because of the supply shortage.'

'How much?' Harrison asked.

'Me can flog it for fifteen a piece.'

'Is that for a wrap or a blunt?'

'Nuh man. Me only do de likkle wraps right about now.'

'But I prefer to have them pre-rolled cos it stresses me out rolling the stick. I aren't that patient to do it,' Xiamen put in.

'Yeah man, Kymani, we don't really like the stress of rolling up a joint after a long day so we would prefer them pre-rolled please,' Harrison added.

'Listen man, nuh dealer like to bother with de distro for pre-rolled ganja right about now because of cost of de rolling paper and time to roll it up. But nuh worry man, me can roll it up for a likkle tenner more if yuh buy up to ten. Wah yuh say?'

'Okay, make it ten then,' Xiamen confirmed his order.

'Alright man. Give me a likkle time. Me gwan to roll it up and bring it for yuh in about twenty minutes. Let me have the hundred and sixty man'

'You want all of it now?'

'Yah man.'

'Xiamen glanced over at Harrison who nodded his approval. Then he said, 'I don't have all that money on me right now, but I can give you 100 and let you have the rest when you deliver.'

'Nuh man. Me never do biz like dat. Me want all de cash now, nuh play. Me and Harrison go back lang time, him know how me run things.'

'It's okay. I will make it up. You can give it to me later Xiamen,' Harrison threw in.

'Great, thank you.'

Xiamen took out some money from his pocket, counted the notes and gave them to Harrison. After adding the remaining balance, Harrison passed the money over to Kymani who quickly palmed the cash and slipped them into his pocket without bothering to count. Then he turned to Xiamen.

'Do yuh ever listen to Bob Marley?'

'No.'

'Will yuh do me a likkle favour and listen to de song Kaya? There's an original advice in de lyric from Marley himself, who truly believe say a man got to have what he got to have. Maybe yuh can make Marley's philosophy your mantra too.' Kymani saluted in Xiamen's direction and proceeded to fist-bump Harrison before he left.

Out of curiosity, Xiamen sought after the track Kymani told him about and listened to it. he interpreted the song his own way. It made perfect sense to hold an emergency stash for the rainy days to cater for his smoke needs. He would never run completely short if he emulated the squirrel's act of stowing away so he decided to start buying bulk orders and stashing them.

That evening after finishing work, Xiamen parked up in his compound at his usual time. Typical of him, he went straight to the lock-up garage beside the main building and pressed a remote key to slide the roller door up so he could enter. The garage was jam-packed with heaps of disused belongings that were lined up orderly on top each other, like fillets in a tin of sardines. Two bicycles, that previously belong to Clara and Simon, were propped up against the wall in the corner. Simon's old wheelchair huddled beside them, propping up a CD rack which bore all his music collections; the Queen CD gift from Wilson was first on the rack. Two suitcases containing Clara's and Elisabeth's personal stuff were stacked on top each other on the floor, along with their wellies and other footwear. There were several large items clogging up the remaining space, including a set of white goods, a treadmill, a lawn mower and a dressing table. A large bookshelf was stacked with various portable tools, among other things. Xiamen viewed the items of his loved ones and momentarily recollected past memories. A spate of emotions suddenly clouded his thoughts and he freaked out like a distressed elephant, swaying his head from side-to-side.

Xiamen composed himself after he'd had his moment. He took down a watering kettle from the bookshelf, reached his hand through the opening to the washing machine and pulled out its soap drawer. Straightening up, he took out three cannabis rolls. Noticing that there wasn't much left in the stash place, he made a mental note to purchase some more as soon as possible. After he'd returned the drawer, he walked over to a coat hanging on a hook beside the door. He immediately wrung his nose with a grimace whiffing the stale malodour of burnt hemp that reeked from the coat. Mentally noting to wash it, he fished out a small cigarette case from the coat's pocket and lined the spliffs inside. He switched his coat with the one in the garage, tucked the cigarette box into his pocket and stepped out.

After shutting the garage door, Xiamen walked towards the main house to his kitchen to make himself a coffee. Once brewed, he poured it into a disposable cup and placed the lid on before sauntering out of the kitchen. Going through the rear of the house, he walked towards the pathway that would lead him to the woods, hummin the Kaya song.

Chapter Twenty-One

There had been reports of a major fall out between two rival gangs in Norwich over the last two weeks. Local police had responded by initiating a raiding spree to clamp down on substance pedlars, in the hope that this would calm things down. Several major narcotics pushers had been busted, apprehended and detained in police custody. Plain-clothed officers were now prowling the streets to map out the remaining bad guys. As a result, most of the narcotics traffickers were lying low and not dealing in their usual spots.

Due to the widespread scarcity in the underground distribution, the regular users were having a hard time finding a supply link. Unfortunately for Xiamen, he couldn't procure any new supply since the shortage started. He'd had to cut down his daily puff to two spliffs until he could obtain a new source. Now, the stack of cannabis he used day-to-day had run dry; he was down to his last resort.

That Friday evening, Xiamen finished his work for the day and drove home. With his mind set on the weed he'd stowed away for the rainy days, he arrived at his house and headed for his garage straight away. Inside the garage, he shifted the bookshelf to one side. With the cabinet out of the way, he reached for the tumble dryer, grabbed it by the rear and pulled it out turning it around so that its front faced him. Bending down, he pulled the steam collector out of the tumble dryer and straightened up.

Xiamen placed the steam collector on top of the tumble dryer. He pulled the soap drawer out of the washing machine and placed it beside the steam collector. He then picked up the steam collector and peeled off the adhesive tape that he'd taped on its back to seal a hole he cut there. He crumpled the tape in his palm, slipped it into his trousers' pocket and fished out a black cellophane packet he'd stashed inside the container. He tore it open and took out neatly wrapped foils that contained rolled joints. He carefully transferred all the joints to the drawer, mentally counting them and calculating they would last him for at least 20 days'. He considered the idea of limiting his ration to one until the supply situation improved, then grinned shaking his head.

Xiamen took two spliffs for the evening and went to his other coat for the cigarette case. After lining the spliffs inside, he switched coats and went back to the tumble dryer and resealed the steam container before replacing it and returning everything else he'd ruffled back to their original positions. Exiting the garage, he headed towards the kitchen for a coffee.

Saturday morning, Xiamen woke up with a splitting headache. This was the cephalalgia that followed after his nightly intake of weed; it would often persist like a migraine for a few hours before it dissolved away. Getting up from the bed, he went to the toilet to relieve himself. Sitting on the WC, he pressed his palms tightly to the sides of his head, still feeling the headache terribly. After he'd finished his business, he washed his hands and went to the kitchen to seek a quick remedy for the ache in his head.

Xiamen opened the upper door of the double refrigerator and eyed the contents inside. He made mental notes of what he was short of and took out a carton of milk. He filled a cup up and placed it in the microwave. The enlivening buzz of the microwave suddenly dispelled the tranquillity in the kitchen but not for long; it dinged after a short while. Xiamen got out his cup of warm milk and drank it all in one go.

Drinking a cup of warmed milk was Xiamen's self-derived solution to his morning migraines. His headache shortly vaporised after he drank it one time, so he believed it worked for him and stuck to the tradition like a dogma. Now, he instantly began to imagine the headache was dwindling as he waited for the milk to work its magic. Today was Xiamen's scheduled day off and he had plans to visit Simon; he dedicated every other Saturday to visiting his son at the nursing home, spending most of the day there.

Tender Care Nursing Home was a six-storey block of bricks located on the outskirts of Norwich in Bungay, about 46 miles from Xiamen's address. The residence was mainly funded with government grants and it specifically catered for people who required full-time personal care. It was currently occupied by 80 residents with varying needs of support. The rooms in the building were small and fashioned into self-contained units with their own built-in conveniences. Each room accommodated the basic furnishings of a nursing room alongside specific equipment for the current occupant. Simon's room, which was situated on the top floor, had a standard electric nursing bed, a hand basin and a rubbish bin among other fixtures. The special equipment in his room included a set of ventilators and an assisted wheelchair. There was also a repositioning glide sheet and an electric mobile hoist with an accompanying transfer sling. Simon even had a custom-built wheeled commode with a fitted cabinet that was packed with toiletries for his hygiene needs.

Simon was completely bed-bound Being a tetraplegic. To help him breathe, he had a surgical tracheostomy done to link a ventilator to his trachea. Although he did not technically require invasive ventilating, the procedure was carried out on him since his face was the only part of his body he could use to communicate. He was still able to perform all evident facial expressions such as blinking, pouting, roll his eyes and furrow his brow. Most precious of them all, although he seldom did, was the ability to smile! Other than that, he had no control over his body's actions. He was at the mercy of his healthy autonomic purges 24/7. Simon's urinary incontinence was managed long-term by a surgical procedure; his urethra was connected to a catheter which then emptied into a urine bag. He was always clad in an incontinence pad to trap his rectum discharges. Unfortunately, nothing could be done about his anus winds. His winds huffed miscellaneously without tact or discretion, which Simon himself found both annoying and demeaning to his personal manners.

That morning, Simon was alerted by a brief knock on his door, shortly followed by the emergence of a trolley being pushed by the duty domestic staff. Aradhana entered and gave Simon a cursory glance. Without saying a word to him, she started transferring some of her cleaning stuff from the trolley to a small bucket. Simon trailed his eyes on her as she collected what she needed. She disappeared into the bathroom and he heard the scrubbing noises she was making as she cleaned. He returned his eyes to the trolley to look for the bottle of water Aradhana often brought with her in her trolley every time she came to clean, but he couldn't see it. He wondered if it had been placed somewhere out of his view. As far as Simon could remember, he had always watched her pause and take short drinks at irregular intervals in-between her chores. He was gladdened by the absence of the water bottle and reckoned she would spend less time around him if she didn't have to take drink breaks.

Simon didn't like Aradhana much because she was the only employed domestic worker that totally ignored him. The others made an effort to chitchat with him or warn him about the noise before they used the vacuum cleaner. Aradhana simply treated him like a statue. Simon begrudged her in his heart because of that.

Aradhana came back into Simon's view as she popped out of the bathroom with his dirty laundry. Making for the trolley, she placed the soiled materials into a holdall laundry basket and threw an inspecting glance around the room without meeting Simon's eyes. Simon observed as she rested her look on his bedside cabinet. She approached it and took out one of his cups.

Just as Simon started to wonder what she was up to, Aradhana walked to the washbasin, filled the cup with some water and raised it to her lips. Simon creased his brow into a frown. Aradhana finished drinking and returned the cup. She then got out a vacuum cleaner, plugged it into a socket and began to hoover. Simon wished he could have cupped his palms over his ears to block out the annoying noise of the vacuum cleaner. He counted the minutes and prayed they'd go faster so he'd be rid of her. Thankfully, Aradhana finished her work on the carpet and returned the vacuum cleaner. To Simon's annoyance, she went for his cup again and fetched herself another drink.

Aradhana emptied Simon's bedsitter bins into the rubbish container on the trolley before replacing them with fresh liners. She dashed into the bathroom once more. The steady dribble of liquid dropping into the WC, plus the absence of any other sound in the toilet reported what

Aradhana was doing. The toilet flushed eventually and she returned with her bucket of cleaning stuff. After positioning the items back on the trolley, she surveyed the room again, looking everywhere but at Simon's face. Seemingly satisfied there was nothing else to do, her job there was done. She reversed her trolley to leave.

Simon heaved a sigh of relief but he was momentarily thrown aback when Aradhana made for the cabinet again and got out his cup. His disapproving look couldn't have been fiercer as he watched her help herself to another drink. Shortly after Aradhana left, another knock rapped on Simon's door followed by two carers, Leslie and Judy.

'Hey Simon, how was your night? Did you sleep OK? Looks like you did. We have come to tidy you up, OK?' Judy, the older carer, soothed as she approached his bed.

The younger carer went for the mobile hoist and rolled it closer to the bed. 'Are you ready to bathe, handsome?' she asked, smiling at Simon.

Simon offered a small smile and blinked an eye.

'Very well my prince. I will go get your bathroom throne so we can transfer you there,' she beamed and went into the bathroom.

'I have to check your pad now, mister. Are you OK with that? Are you now, hah?'

Judy asked Simon cheerfully, but he reciprocated with a blank stare.

'No blinking? Of course, you don't like that very much, do you? So, how are you doing down there? Have you been holding it all in? Let me see for myself.' Judy unbuttoned his PJ and looked into his pad. 'Brilliant! Hey Les! Your prince's pad is clean. Come and help me with transferring him please!' she called out and began to strip Simon down.

Leslie wheeled in the shower commode from the bathroom. She retrieved the sling from the hoist and stood by Judy. Judy handed Simon's custom-made pyjamas to Leslie who promptly took them to the basket in the bathroom; she returned in a moment and stood beside her colleague again.

'OK Simon, I am going to roll you on to your side now so I can position you on the sling.' She folded Simon's hands across his chest. 'There we go.' She gently rolled him towards the wall. Leaving him in that position, she took the transfer sling from her colleague and spread it on the bed. 'OK Simon, I am about to turn you to your right side now. Ready?' She rolled his frame towards herself to get him on one part of the sling, then she spread out the other part behind him and rolled him on his back. She gathered the loops of the sling and attached them to the hand of the hoist, then she picked up Simon's urine bag from the floor and looped it on the commode chair before straightening up.

'You can take him now Les.'

'Up you go, handsome,' Leslie said as she switched on the hoist. The hoist immediately went into action and raised Simon out of the bed. Guiding the sling, Leslie steadied his frame into a sitting position and operated the hoist to lower him to the commode chair. She unhooked the loops of the sling from the hoist and slid it off the chair before propping Simon upright and smiling at him. 'Well now my prince charming! Looking graceful on your throne, aren't you?'

Judy moved forwards and quickly switched Simon's ventilator to the portable one. 'There Les, he's all yours,

'If you are ready to roll now prince charming, on your mark. Get set. Off we go!'

Leslie wheeled Simon into the bathroom and left him over the WC. Bending down, she looked into Simon's eyes with a wide smile spread on her lips. 'Alright my man. I'm going to start my little romance on you now. You know the drill already.' She undid the velcro fasteners on Simon's pad and slide it out from under him. She detached his urine bag from the chair and placed the end of the connecting tube into the WC. She wheeled the commode chair to one side, unhooked the urine bag from the commode, emptied the urine into the toilet and repositioned the chair. She proceeded to drop his pad and urine bag into the bin. 'There you are! All set to go. Let it all out now if you can. Gosh! Your beard just grows too quickly. And your hair is even long now. I'll have to give them a trim before I bathe you. And you need a trim down there too. Meanwhile, I will go let the nurse know you are ready for her. Be back soon.' She left the bathroom, making for the door. 'Hey Judy, I am stepping out to let the nurse know Simon is ready for her.'

'That's fine Les,' Judy replied as she stripped the bedding off Simon's bed. She gathered the bedlinen and took it to the bathroom. 'Are you doing OK there, mister?' she asked Simon. She dropped the beddings into his laundry basket and returned to make the bed. The door shortly opened and Leslie entered with the nurse.

'Good morning Nurse Bridget,' Judy greeted her.

'Morning Judy, you alright?'

'Yes, I'm good thank you.'

'How did he do in is pad? Zero, in-between, or messy?'

'Absolutely zero, not even a stain.'

'Oh really?'

'Yes, his pad is spotless this morning. He's done brilliant.'

'Oh wow! That means more work for me now, doesn't it?'

'Sorry Nurse Bridget, I'm afraid so,' Leslie chimed in with a giggle.

Leslie and the nurse headed for the bathroom whilst Judy continued making up Simon's bed.

'How do you do today, Simon?' the nurse asked, entering the bathroom.

Simon returned her greeting with a blank stare.

'Not very chatty today, are you? Anyway, I have come to do your enema so that you will be sorted for the next couple of days. Sounds great, doesn't it?'

Simon' didn't alter his expression.

'Don't look so cold, prince charming. Aren't you happy today?' Leslie enthused.

Simon blinked his eyes then.

'Oh, I see. Well don't you worry now, you can tell me about it later. But right now, we are here for you this morning and we've got all your immediate needs covered, so try to be cheerful for me just a little please,' Leslie soothed.

Simon' suddenly flashed his teeth in a grin.

'Bravo my prince charming! That's more like it. You look more handsome than ever!'

'You do have an effect on him Leslie, don't you?'

'He is my prince of course! I have a soft spot for him. He is just so cute!'

'I don't see what you see Leslie, but I do use glasses so my sight isn't as good as yours. Anyways, let's crack on with it. Bear with me a moment Simon. I have to flush your urinary catheter first.'

Bridget opened Simon's bathroom cabinet and took out a syringe. She picked Simon's urine tube from the WC and disconnected it from his catheter. She inserted the syringe into the holding tube in the catheter, drew out the water from the fixing pouch and slid the catheter out of his penile duct. Retrieving a new catheter from the cabinet, Bridget slid it into the duct and injected water back into it to hold it in place. She fixed the new catheter on the urine tube and returned it to the WC, throwing the old one in the bin.

Opening the cabinet again, Bridget took out a polystyrene bag which had two linking tubes attached to a nozzle and a pressure pump. She drew water from the tap into the bag, stopping when it filled up to 700 ml. Bending down, she pushed the nozzle's injector right into Simon's rectum and started pumping up the water. It took her two minutes to empty the bag; once complete, she pulled out the injector, rinsed it in the sink and placed the enema kit back into the cabinet.

'Leave him on for 45 minutes this time since his pad was clean,' Bridget said, turning to Leslie.

'Okay Nurse Bridget, I will.'

'Thank you. I will leave him in your hands now.'

Bridget left the bathroom and Leslie followed after her. Simon was left alone in the interim to give his rectum enough time to cleanse. In a short while, all the congested waste would flux and spill out in water torrents, ridding his bowels of everything that randomly defaced the integrity of his pad. This procedure was carried out matutinally every three days: it helped to reduce the inconveniences of his faecal accidents and the cleaning task for the carers.

Xiamen arrived at the nursing home shortly after 11 AM. After checking in at the reception desk, he proceeded to the long corridor that led to the staircase. He preferred to avoid the lift because, from previous experience, when he called the lift it was either in use or he had to wait a long time for it. Sometimes it would already be occupied by mobility-deficient residents being transported. After experiencing this a couple of times, he reasoned within himself that the lift service in the building was designed primarily for the disabled residents who live there, so he thought better to leave it to the ones that needed it the most. He pretty much opted for taking the stairs.

Truth be told, Xiamen kidded himself; he didn't really mind waiting for the lift. What really put him off was meeting the severely disabled occupants being transported by the carers; that made him feel really uncomfortable. On the occasions he'd shared the lift with some of the incapacitated residents, he'd felt awkward by the thorough look they gave him. He hadn't known what to do for the best, whether to return their gazes with a greeting or look away. He avoided being put in that dilemma by using the stairs every time he came to the nursing home. He didn't mind trekking the 200-foot corridor to the stairwell, or the laborious climb up that followed.

Eventually, Xiamen reached Simon's room on the sixth floor and let himself in. He glimpsed the familiar view of the cubicle; it still had the same old things in the same old spots in the two years he'd been visiting. He'd never appreciated the monotonous room apart for the fact that it was fully functional for his son.

'Hello, Si!' Xiamen greeted his son, beaming a smile.

Simon's expression suddenly glowed like a smiley emoji at the sight of his father, his silvery grey eyes sparked with feelings. Xiamen's heart leapt with joy when he saw his son's radiant look. He walked to the bedside and touched his face. Simon lifted his eyes to his father's and they exchanged sentimental smiles.

'You're looking great, Si, how're you doing?' Xiamen asked, welling with affection.

Simon blinked an eye.

'You're good, ay? I see you've had a haircut and a shave. They're really looking after you well here! You really look handsome!'

Simon arched his brows to say thank you, then he puckered his lips into an O-shape pointing them towards his father.

'I'm alright myself, my business is doing great and everything is good at home too.' Xiamen paused with an expectant look at Simon.

Arching one of his brows, Simon moved his lips and mouthed his reply. Though Xiamen couldn't lip-read, he watched the lips' gestures understandingly, nodding his head like he got it all.

'Well, I'm pleased to see that you are all smiles today. I've brought you your favourite treat. You were expecting it, right? I'll give it to you in a minute. Let me wash my hands first.'

Xiamen went to wash his hands in the sink and dried them with a paper towel. After tossing the towel in the bin, he opened up his backpack an pulled out two tubs of vanilla rice pudding. Placing the tubs on the bedside cabinet, he took a spoon out of the drawer, peeled off the seal from a tub and began to spoon-feed Simon. Treating Simon to the pudding was Xiamen's exclusive paternal routine; he used it as a way to bond with him, never missing to perform it during his visits.

After feeding his son, Xiamen disposed of the rubbish and pulled out another gift from his bag. He showed Simon a miniature bottle of Ciu Ciu Piceno Libation wine.

'I got this for you as well. Actually, it's for both of us. I know you like it as much as me. I was aware the whole time you were pinching shots from my bottle in the kitchen cabinet back in the day. I guess you thought I didn't know what was going on. But I didn't mind you taking a few you know. My father never complained about my nicking his drink too. I guess his own dad hadn't raised a stink either. So, this is for us to share. Happy?'

Simon flashed him a grin delightfully. Xiamen went on to unscrew the bottle and took the first sip. He brought the bottle to Simon's mouth who helped himself to a swig too. The father and son took turns in drinking from the bottle. After they finished the contents, Xiamen brought out a mini USB player and placed it on the bedside cabinet. He inserted a USB stick into the port, pressed the play button and sat down in the chair beside Simon's bed as the audio narrator began the intro.

Simon's face lit up with surprise when he heard the narrator introduce his favourite fantasy fiction of all time. He beamed at his father in appreciation. The narrator's voice announced the beginning of chapter one and Simon began to listen attentively. Feeling satisfied with himself, Xiamen sank into the chair and joined in listening to the audiobook.

Two-and-half hours later, the book had just rolled into the fifth chapter when a slight knock sounded on the door. A carer came in carrying a tray with a lidded bowl and a spoon on it. Xiamen promptly paused the USB player.

'Good afternoon Sir. I've brought your son his lunch. I'd like to feed him now if that's okay?'

'Please let me do that as am here.' Xiamen stood up.

The carer gave him the food tray. 'Thank you for helping.'

'It's my pleasure.'

'I'll come back for the tray later.' The carer smiled and left.

Placing the tray on the meal table, Xiamen lifted the lid off the bowl. A serving of diced boiled potato, tuna bits and mixed vegetables in a washy soup were portioned inside. Xiamen picked up the spoon to taste the bland-looking meal. He tried hard not to spit it out and he forced himself to swallow the mouthful, knowing Simon was watching.

'Would you like me to feed you now Si? he asked' enthusiastically.

Simon blinked his eyes.

'You're not hungry?'

Simon blinked his eyes again.

'Okay, no worries. Maybe later.' Xiamen rolled the meal table to one side.

'Right, let's delve back into The Lord of the Rings now. Are you enjoying it?' Xiamen asked, shooting Simon an expectant look.

Simon stared back at him sadly.

'What is the matter?'

Simon altered his expression to a look of plea.

'Come on now Si, don't you go there now. I've already told you I won't agree to it. Please leave it alone.'

Simon's face became more ashen with sadness. He promptly shut his eyes so tightly that they crinkled at their corners. He remained like that and sank into his bitter thoughts. He desired to end his own life and wanted help out of his misery. He had even got as far as asking his doctor for some guidance on the matter. His doctor responded that he wasn't professionally bound to advise him and that the deed was actually illegal. The doctor had notified the relevant authorities about Simon's request and recommended him for a mental evaluation and suicide watch. Xiamen was also notified about Simon's desire so he was forced to speak to him about it. Simon confirmed his wishes and asked for his father's support but Xiamen disagreed outright.

Somehow the information had got around and reached a human rights organisation that fought for the cause. Out of the blue, somebody from the NGO paid Simon a visit. The agent asked Simon if he wanted to further his right to decide for himself whether to be kept alive or die with dignity. Simon affirmed he very much wanted that.

After the first visit, the visitor returned with a lip-reader to make their communication more fluid. They explained to Simon he would be provided with funding to cover the costs, should they determine from his financial assessment that he could not afford it himself. Simon agreed and the NGO started the process. With the lip-reader's help, a testament of what he wanted was drawn up. Later, they got back and informed Simon that it wouldn't be possible to implement the procedure in Britain due to the legislative act. However, it could be done in a relatively close European country if he could get the consent of a guardian to accompany him. The agent, at Simon's request, had briefed Xiamen but he was met with a flat-out rejection. Ever since that moment, Simon had been pleading with his father but to no avail.

Watching his son's defiance made Xiamen feel bad. He knew it was Simon's way of showing he was angry. He couldn't possibly see reason with Simon on that matter, how could he allow his son to die? He moved over to Simon and touched his face. 'It'll be okay Si,' he said to him reassuringly.

Simon opened his eyes and tears squirted down his cheeks. He fixed a scornful look on his father, gazing at him with all the pain he could muster with his eyes. Though he had felt his father's affection through the tender touch of his palm, he equally saw the pity in his eyes. He knew he was only alive because of the care provided to him.

Simon didn't understand why he was saved from death, only to be put in a dehumanising condition. He remembered how his mother's life was snuffed out without any delay, so why wasn't his? Especially if it was his own wish. He didn't see any good reason for living in his condition when he served no benefit or purpose to the world. Why wouldn't anyone listen? He didn't want to remain a shut-in for the rest of his life. It just made him so furious inside and he was helpless to do anything for himself. He was at the mercy of everyone; he must be the one to respect everybody's wishes and not the other way round. He was angrier now than he'd ever been with life's unfairness.

Looking at Simon's tearful eyes totally weighed Xiamen down; he could see the urgency in his son's facial plea and felt guilt, as if it was his own fault. He would never be able to bring himself to fly Simon out of Britain for the euthanasia. As far as he was concerned, it wasn't a thing to be done. He averted his eyes and thought bitterly.

Xiamen wasn't the sort of father who could consciously agree to the legal manslaughter of his son. That would mean agreeing to have him put down like a sick animal? Why would Simon even choose to die on him? Doesn't the lad realise that he was his only surviving family? What a selfish choice to make. Besides, Simon was still a young man with his whole life ahead of him. Xiamen couldn't imagine how he would permit the procedure, let alone accompany his son to have it done. He was resolute. Still averting his son's eyes, he sank into the chair again and resumed the USB player.

Chapter Twenty-Two

A few days after Xiamen's visit to the nursing home, he found that his guilty pleasure stash had drastically run low; he needed to top up before he was completely out. Today, during his lunch break, he went to the street depot to try his luck. Walking hurriedly, he passed several short lanes and connecting backstreets heading for Metrodame; a slum vicinity situated away from the city centre. It was only in this neighbourhood that he found the pedlars who sold the goods to him at the cheapest price. After walking for about fifteen minutes, he turned into an alley. The alleyway led him to a T-junction and he turned left, walked three yards up and made a sharp left into a cul-de-sac. He followed the blind alley to the end and took a paved pathway at the bottom to Luna Crescent.

With less than 5.5 metres width, Luna Crescent, codenamed MaryJane Lane, wasn't as broad as a typical residential lane. Although the ground was tarmacked, it wasn't accessible to vehicles because of the bollards that were fixed at each entrance. The crescent-shaped street was sandwiched by stories of low-cost flats that snaked along its curve, making it look narrower than it actually was.

Luna Crescent was a street mall for the cannabis hoi polloi. The strong scent of burning spliffs filled the air from the faceless persons who were puffing in shadowy corners. They were hustling traffickers standing idly about on the kerbside; some of them attempted to lure Xiamen as he walked past but he ignored them and carried on walking. He passed some more of the hustlers and they tried to engage him.

'Oy, nice day, innit?' said one hustler.

'Can I do anything for you, matey?' another asked.

'I'm here for you pally if you need anything!' a third hollered at Xiamen.

'Greetings, posseman, wah yuh want?' one of two Caribbean guys standing together asked Xiamen in patois.

'Nuff respect man. yuh like to try our MJ buzz for free? A likkle try guh convince yuh me tell yuh.' His mate added.

Xiamen strolled on ignoring all the hustlers until he saw the person he recognised chatting with a bushy-haired guy whom he didn't know. He approached them. Billy Osborne looked in Xiamen's direction when he was a few metres away. Xiamen halted and gestured to him touching the bridge of his nose with steepled fingers. Billy excused himself from the company of his confrere and walked to Xiamen.

'Big up posseman! Heaps of ten, innit?' Billy asked quietly, now standing face-to-face with Xiamen.

'No, I'd like twenty or thirty today please.'

'I can't anchor that much at the moment. The best I can arrange for you right away is fifteen.'

'But didn't you give me your word last time that you'd deliver more when I came again?'

'I might've. Unfortunately I can't deliver as promised. There's not enough in the field for all the customers so we are rationing the grass. Sorry posseman, my hands are tied. The best I can do is fifteen rolls per bag,' Billy said giving Xiamen a take-it-or-leave-it look.

'All right, I'll have it,' Xiamen capitulated.

'That's game, hand over the cheese and I'll sort the order for you.'

Xiamen brought out a wad of £20 notes and gave them to Billy. 'Here.'

Palming the cash, Billy swiftly counted them and slipped them into his pocket. 'Do you see my mate over there? The one wearing a high-neck collar.' He pointed to a shaggy-haired guy in a black polo-neck sweater who was standing with his eyes fixed towards them.

'Yes.' Xiamen nodded, Looking at where he was pointing. '

Billy swiftly gave some coded hand gestures to his mate; his mate signed back nodding, then Billy turned back to Xiamen. 'Head down to him for collection.'

'Okey-dokey, thanks,' Xiamen said and promptly walked towards Billy's mate. As Xiamen passed the guy whom Billy had been with earlier, their eyes met; he grinned knowingly and Xiamen muttered a greeting at him.

Xiamen reached Billy's shaggy-haired acquaintance, who told him to wait there before he disappeared through a path gate into a compound behind him. Xiamen used the interim to stroll further up the lane, crossing to the unpaved side and standing in a corner to wait. From his spot, Xiamen got a good view of the lane and trailed his eyes around. Not far from where he was stood, two guys were chatting. One of the men's outfit particularly caught his attention as he observed the colour coordination. The man wore a chevron-collared cashmere cardigan over a dusky brown shirt and a matching necktie, which were complemented with manila chinos and taupe brogues. The stranger was fairly stocky and a vivid redhead in his late - thirties. The dandy manner he was dressed suggested that he doted on his appearance. Xiamen guessed he was probably a user talking with the dealer.

Five minutes later, Billy's mate reappeared and quickly passed a black cellophane packet to Xiamen who snappily received it without a word and promptly started walking back the way he had come. With the goods safely tucked inside his coat pocket, he felt relieved but not entirely happy. He had wanted more to top up his rainy-day stash but Billy failed to deliver his promise. He would need some more sooner than later and was thankful for the ones he got anyway. His smoke for the days ahead was guaranteed.

Humming a melody from Bob Marley, Xiamen briskly walked to the car park where he'd left his cab, oblivious that the dandy man in the cashmere cardigan was on his tail. Unbeknown to the local traffickers in Luna Crescent, the dandy dude was an undercover agent who'd been patronising dealers at the depot pretending to be a user. He strolled casually as if to look like he was going on his way, but in reality he was surveying Xiamen's movements. He tactfully followed Xiamen to the car park and stood out of sight. He watched Xiamen got into his cab and reversed out of the parking space, making a note of the registration number as the car drove off.

Two weeks later, having smoked through the last supply, Xiamen returned again to Mary Jane Lane for some more of his guilty pleasure. Today, however, he was more anxious than ever before. He'd had to ration his last stock of spliffs and hadn't even had enough to satisfy his usual daily allowance in the days running up to this visit. Xiamen made his way to purchase through his regular contact Billy Osborne. The guy in the black polo-neck wasn't around today. Instead, a big dreadlocked guy in a Rastafarian hat was there to dispense the goods. He handed Xiamen the black cellophane packet. He once again tucked it into his coat pocket before swiftly leaving to return to his cab.

A short time later as Xiamen walked along his usual route, his phone suddenly started to ring in his coat pocket. He stopped walking, hurriedly took out the phone and hit the answer icon. A woman's voice on the other end asked to speak with him. Xiamen acknowledged he was the one speaking and she carried on.

'Good day Mr Christopher… I'm Janet Stewart, one of the admins at Tender Care Nursing Home. I have a message for you from your son. He requests that you urgently visit him this week, the sooner the better.'

'Is there a problem? Is there something going on with him?'

'There's no problem with him as far as I am aware. I think it concerns his travel to Belgium. He wants to see you before he leaves."

'He's going to Belgium? Who's taking him there and what for?' Xiamen sounded apprehensive.

'Mr Christopher, the human rights agency advocating your son's request for euthanasia has officially received power of attorney for their agent to act as his accompanier to Belgium, so they plan to take him there soon for the procedure. Your son has the intention to discharge himself from our care… he's scheduled to fly out early next week.'

Xiamen instantly stiffened, standing stock-still like a scared mouse.

'Are you still there Mr Christopher?' The caller's voice nudged Xiamen to his senses.

'Yes… thank you for letting me know. I shall come over to see him ASAP.'

After the caller rang off, Xiamen's body jittered and he struggled to remain upright. Conveniently, a lamppost was positioned next to him; he quickly placed a hand on it to brace himself, clutching his phone tightly in the other hand. Several seconds ticked by as Xiamen stood there. Eventually, he remembered where he was and composed himself. Without tarrying any further, Xiamen walked as fast as he could to his car he got in and drove off. Fear gripped him and he freaked out.

'What the hell? Simon is not being considerate! Doesn't he realise he's all I have left now? I'm never, ever going to let him die. Never!'

Still fraught with morbid agitation, Xiamen continued his grumblings inwardly as he drove along in autopilot. All of a sudden, the uproarious blare of a siren shot out of the blue and rudely yanked him out of his thoughts. He looked in his wing mirror. A police car was speeding up from behind as the other vehicles were pulling over to let it pass. He quickly pulled up in the shoulder of the road to allow the patrol car to drive past him too. Through his rear-view mirror, Xiamen saw the driver wave another car on before he drew up close to his cab flashing the headlights.

The police car parked a few yards away from Xiamen's cab. The siren was turned off, but the globular light continued revolving. Xiamen watched the two policemen in the front seats keenly observing him. Before he had time to digest what was happening, they exited the vehicle and approached his cab.

The police? What do they want with me? Shit! I've got a bag of weed in my pocket! Oh God... how am I going to get out of this one?

With his adrenaline rushing like a rapid running river, Xiamen swiftly thought of how to get rid of the incriminating evidence. Before he could think of something spontaneous, the two uniformed officers were beside his front doors looking at him suspiciously.

'Good day Sir. May I see your driver's licence and registration, please?' the first policeman by the passenger door demanded politely.

'Good day, officers. I hope am not in any trouble as I don't recollect causing any. I can assure you there's no issue with my particulars. Bear with me, I'll get them out from the glove compartment,' Xiamen spoke light-heartedly to suppress his jitters. He fetched the documents and gave them to the officer.

'Where are you coming from?' the other policeman beside his door asked.

Xiamen met the blatant probing stare of the officer who was scrutinising him like he could miss something if he blinked and felt a chill run up his spine. This clearly didn't look like a random routine check. He was scared, but he chose to play it cool.

'Why, officer? I wonder why you'd be interested in where I'm coming from. But if you must know, I've just got back on the road after my break time.' Xiamen noticed the first policeman he gave his papers to was sneering at him without bothering to look at the documents.

'So, cabman, where were you during your break time?' the policeman by his side further probed.

At this point, Xiamen got it. They were on to him, what business was it to a policeman where he was during his break time? He figured they knew something, so he chose to be evasively brusque.

'I went for a shit around the corner. Do you require me to tell you exactly where the toilet is, officer?'

'Okay, feller, let's cut to the chase,' said the policeman with Xiamen's documents. 'We know you were at Luna

Crescent. We believe you are in possession of a contraband item that was acquired from a dealer within the past few minutes. We want you to produce it willingly right now so that we can formally arrest you and speed this whole process up.'

That's right cabman,' the other officer butted in. 'We would appreciate your cooperation and we shall make note that you willingly cooperated. So, in the name of the law, we ask you to produce any illegal item you have on you now.'

Knowing he was cornered, Xiamen bit his lip in hapless surrender. 'Okay. I'll get it out,' he said without further hesitation.

Xiamen dipped into his coat's right pocket for the package but didn't feel anything there. He searched the left pocket too with no luck. He went back to the right pocket again and thoroughly ransacked it fruitlessly. He then began a frantic feel of the other pockets of his coat but they were all empty. Perplexed, he felt his pockets all over again for the umpteenth time with no luck.

Xiamen further took the search to his trousers' pockets. He felt the front ones but they were just as empty. For where else to look, he fumbled on the floor between his legs and where his hand could reach under the seat, but the package wasn't there either. Getting really flustered now, he inclined his body sideways and tilted leftwards and rightwards to feel his trousers back pockets. Xiamen had never searched for anything as he was so doing in that moment. Out of his own puzzlement, opposed to a police request, he started to search his pockets again frantically.

Watching Xiamen perform the roundabout search on himself, the policemen couldn't fathom why he was acting so befuddled. They found his drama entertaining and continued to monitor his antics with amused irritation. To their further surprise, Xiamen started fully turning out the insides of his pockets. He first turned out the ones in his coat, then the ones in the front of his trousers. He unclasped his seatbelt and started to lift himself up so he could reach his back pockets to turn them out too, but the officer father from him put a stop to it.

'What are you doing?'

'I'm looking for it,' Xiamen replied earnestly.

'Looking for what?' the officer threw at him again.

'For it, I guess,' Xiamen said feebly.

'Look fella! Quit messing about, We haven't got time for this!' the officer closest to him snarled impatiently.

'But I was truly looking for it, officer.'

'Step out of the car right now!' The officer ordered. He stood to one side to give Xiamen room to open his door. 'Take off your coat, hand it to me and place your hands on the hood of your vehicle!'

Xiamen got out of the cab. The other officer came over and patted him down whilst his colleague ransacked the pockets on his coat. After a thorough search, the policemen began to get desperate. The first officer opened the cab door and scanned inside the vehicle with a detector.

Lost in wonder, Xiamen watched the officer as he determinedly combed the inside of his cab with precision swipes. He expected the officer would find the evidence he was after soon enough, but after watching him search the car fruitlessly, he could not understand why the package had still not been found. The stuff wasn't in his cab and it was definitely not on him, so where was it? He wondered foolishly.

'There's nothing in the car,' the officer said finally.

'Are you sure? The Intel said he received a black packet from a dealer at the crescent,' his colleague affirmed.

'That's what they said. So far it's not here. Maybe he dumped it.'

'I can't see how, we had him in sight right until we pulled him over. I think you should look in the boot.'

'Yes of course. Go open your boot, cabman.'

'Officer, it can't be in there, I haven't been to my boot at all,' Xiamen said honestly as he went to open the boot.

The officer with the device proceeded to scan the boot. After he'd thoroughly swiped the device inside the boot, he straightened up, looking slightly baffled. He turned to his partner. 'The detector hasn't been able to locate the substance in the car.'

'I wonder why,' his colleague returned, equally looking perplexed

'Do you want me to call in Narco-forensics to take the car in for a clean sweep?'

From the exchange between the policemen, Xiamen figured out the police officer who'd been standing back and holding his coat was the superior of the two officers. It was he that had to make the call whether to take the search to the next level.

The superior officer turned to Xiamen. 'Where is it?' he shot the question at Xiamen with a fierce look.

Xiamen just stood speechless. Though he couldn't fathom how it could have happened, he was certain the packet wasn't in his car or in his pockets. His mind suddenly began to work. He reckoned that, if the officers didn't find any evidence, they would have nothing to pin on him and wouldn't be able to charge him with anything. This line of thinking brought him a newfound comfort as he concluded the packet must have vaporised. He instinctively swelled with bogus boldness. Bracing himself, he looked the officer straight in the eye.

'Pardon me, officer. Where is what?'

Welling with indignation, the superior officer gave Xiamen a nasty look and growled, 'Where is the item that you received from Luna Crescent?' His sharp tone could have easily sliced a loaf of bread in two.

'I don't know what you're talking about officer,' Xiamen lied defiantly.

'Look fella, quit playing! You said you were getting it out, so where is it now?' the younger officer threw at him angrily.

'Well, officer, I really have no clue what you're talking about. It baffles me that you are indicting me. I am sorry if I've wasted your time... actually, to be fair, you should be the ones apologising for wasting my time. Now officers, if you don't mind, I'd like to get on with my work please. I've already lost good money on account of you pulling me over. Let me go now or take me in if you've something to charge me for.'

The policemen glared indignantly at Xiamen for his sudden cheeky attitude. It dawned on them that they had been out-smarted. As much as they would have liked to take him in, the superior officer weighed the odds. He could call in the Narcotic squad and take Xiamen in for further investigation, but this would cost the police both time and labour that could be better spent on taking down the real bad guys. On the contrary, if Xiamen was taken in without a charge, he could slam the force with a lawsuit and demand a redress for the loss of wages during the time he was detained. This was a dicey situation. The superior officer made a decision.

'You got lucky this time. My advice, steer clear of patronising those guys at Luna Crescent. You might not be so lucky next time.' Without another word, he flung Xiamen's coat at him.

Xiamen caught his coat and looked expectantly at the other officer who proceeded to give him his car documents. The officers left him and walked back to their patrol car. Once inside they switched off the revolving light and continued to sit in deep discussion, their eyes still fixed on Xiamen. Xiamen was massively relieved he was off the cliff's edge. Without putting on his coat, he got back into his cab and scowled at the policemen through the rear-view mirror. He turned his ignition back on and set his cab back on the road.

Driving along, Xiamen wasn't in the best state of mind to continue work so he didn't bother to turn his passenger dispatcher panel back on. He was still shaken and wallowing in the mystery of his missing package. How had he escaped the close shave and got away scot-free? Should the police had found that quantity of cannabis on him, the rest of his day could have gone south. Most likely, they would have taken him into custody and slammed him with a double charge of possession of a ban substance and intent to supply. His cab's licence would be repudiated and he would later be convicted in court. A criminal record would mean he'd never be able to work as a cabby again. 'Whew!' He whistled in relief.

Xiamen looked in his rear-view mirror and was relieved when he didn't see the police car trailing him. Regardless, he turned into several backroads spontaneously and scanned the rear-view mirror every now and then, but he didn't see a suspicious tailer. He let out a triumphant sigh and relaxed. Now a bit more settled, Xiamen focused his mind on the missing packet and gave it a serious thought.

Where the hell is the weed really? I could have sworn that I put the package in my pocket... then poof, it just vanished! How did it just disappear into thin air? Could it be the magical work of the Caribbean fellas? Not that I believe in voodoo or snake god powers, but one can never really know with these West Indies guys... that Billy's mate today looked like some freaky Rastafarian. I've no clue what the Rasta cult is all about, but if it was responsible for the mysterious disappearance of the package then I'm glad for the mystic in today's circumstance; the force that made it happen sure saved me today. Perhaps I should look into the Rasta philosophy and figure it out. Anyway, enough of that jazz. I've got a serious problem now... I'll have nothing to smoke later. What am I going to do?

'Damn those coppers!' Xiamen swore as this realisation dawned on him. Overwrought with rage, he slapped the steering wheel with the aggression of a gorilla.

For crying out loud, cannabis isn't a dangerous substance! It's only a plant I use to enhance my senses. If I smoke weed, it's because I need it... because it's good for me... it should be a thing of freedom of choice for us all. I mean, weed should be of the people, by the people and for the people? What nonsense to deprive me of something that I need to clear my mind? Are chocolate and alcohol really any better? In my opinion they're worse, yet there're no restrictions on their consumption. So why put restrictions on cannabis... a nature's gift from mother earth? Excuse me, all you crucifiers out there, kindly stop trying to nail me on a cross for fulfilling my one need an enjoyment on this sorry earth. Quit your infringing, live and let live!

Still incensed by his loss, Xiamen continued to brood bitterly. He wished he lived in a liberal country where he could have the fundamental right to puff his spliff without being treated like a criminal. Now he was going to sleep tonight, and the subsequent nights, without any supply. Suddenly, his phone rang and startled him.

Xiamen stared at the phone lying on top of the dashboard as if he didn't know whose it was. Usually, he would have reconnected the phone to the car's Bluetooth system, but other matters had took over his mind. He sighed irritably as he saw the caller ID. It was the manager at the taxi-booking office. He was sure the manager was calling to ascertain why his cab's dispatcher panel wasn't turned on. His first instinct was to ignore the call, but his disciplined cabby mind wouldn't let him. Moreover, Spencer Davidson was a bloke he liked to chit chat with, though he was never able to pronounce Xiamen's name right. He picked up the phone and connected to hands free.

'Hello boss man!'

'Hey Xiamey, are you okay?' the manager's voice buzzed inside the car like a bee.

'Yeah I'm alright Spencer.'

'You haven't switched your dispatcher log back on, are you still on break?'

'Not really, it's just that I don't feel too good right now.'

'Oh dear, what's wrong?'

'I think I've got a stomach bug, My bowel has been running like a tap… I've been to the toilet more than three times,' Xiamen lied extemporarily.

'Ah! That's not good. Sorry to hear that. Are you dehydrated?'

'No… er, I mean yes I guess so.'

'I don't envy you. You must be going through a lot of sufferation right now,' Spencer sympathised.

'Suffer what?' Xiamen retorted, laughing out loud. 'Is that a real word, or did you make it up?'

'Of course not! Sufferation is a real word!'

'Is it in the dictionary?'

'Yes of course, but maybe not in the smaller volumes.'

'Oh yeah?'

'Sure! You will find it in the larger dictionaries. It means the same as suffering and it's commonly used in the West Indies.'

'I think it's more like a Rastafarian's jargon, like when they say… bumbbaclat rudeboy … guh small up yourself inna dat likkle chair.'

Spencer's belly laugh boomed out from the speakers before he composed himself. 'Well, I dare say that was really funny. So, Xiamey, why didn't you ring me up to alert me that you were sick at least?'

'Sorry boss, to tell the truth, I totally didn't remember. The diarrhoea completely threw my mind off course.'

'Ok, fair enough. So what is the way forward now? Are you done for the day?'

'Good question. I actually don't know, but I kinda feel better now.'

'Just like that?'

'Yes. Talking to you has made me feel better.'

'I'm glad I am able to affect you positively. So what does that translate to?'

'I'm going to turn my dispatcher panel back on.'

'Just like that? Didn't you just say you are purging like a tap?'

'I do feel eased up now, although I'm not quite sure how the dice will turn. I want to give it a roll, nonetheless.'

'Great! I'll keep an eye out for your dispatcher to come back on then.'

'Give me a few minutes, I'll pull myself together and get my mojo working again.'

'Sure thing, just like the Terminator, eh?'

'Yes, no problemo.'

'Hasta la vista then, see you on the other side.'

'You'll see me.'

'Okay Xiamey.' Spencer rang off.

The call ended and the quiet in the car brought Xiamen back to himself. Having had his mind temporarily taken off the loss of his treasure, he felt much better and thought he might as well go back to work. With a resigned sigh, he turned the dispatcher panel on. It was then that a thought suddenly flew into his mind that sent his adrenalin rushing at breakneck speed. His heart was racing like a driver in hot pursuit of Lewis Hamilton at the Grand Prix. He promptly turned off his dispatcher panel and pulled over.

Xiamen cut off the engine. He curtailed the explosive thought in his mind as a gust of hope burst loose within him. He realised what might have happened to the bag of weed. Trusting he was right, he mumbled a prayer of faith. In this frame of mind, he turned on the dispatcher panel. The panel had no sooner come on than a ping from Spencer hit the display and the location of a waiting passenger danced on the screen. Xiamen rolled his cab back on the road and headed towards that direction.

Chapter Twenty-Three

Later that evening, Xiamen drove straight home after work. He reached his compound at about 7:30, parked his cab and stormed into his house. A few minutes later, he came out wearing an anorak and made his way to his garage. Opening the door, he went in and rolled out a recumbent racing bike that belonged to his son. He set the bike outside the garage. After ascertaining the tyres were ridable, he locked the garage door and rolled the bike towards his driveway.

Mounting the bike, Xiamen raised the hood of his coat over his head and pedalled towards the main road. The bike rode pretty well even though it hadn't been used for some time. Simon used to do a lot of riding on it when he was agile. After his accident, Xiamen relegated the bike to the garage and had only used it a couple of times when he didn't wish to use his cab. Now the bike had come in handy once more, he was thankful he had not gotten rid of it.

Propelled by Xiamen's swift pedalling, the sports bike gathered speed and glided easily along the tarred road as Xiamen rode against the wind. He knew his destination was a long way off so he needed to make it snappy. He navigated to the city centre, detouring as much as possible through the backstreets to avoid the main roads. He could feel the chill from the windy dark night slapping his face as he sped along. His mind bobbed with unpredictability as he focused on his mission. Although he wasn't a hundred per cent positive, it was certainly worth a shot and he remained optimistic.

Eventually, Xiamen's zealous pedalling brought him to his destination. He stopped right by the lamppost where he'd answered his phone earlier that day. The lamppost was now switched on, illuminating the area. Barely two steps away was his missing packet, lying like a dead blackbird on the tarmac!

Xiamen's heart was leaping with joy. He looked around and scanned the length and breadth of the street to check the coast was clear. Without getting off the bike, he leaned down, snatched up the found treasure and rode away beaming from ear to ear. Xiamen couldn't believe his luck. How the bag had dropped out of his pocket without him knowing didn't matter now; he was only too glad to have recovered it. He sped through the lanes pedalling with less zeal, feeling as joyful as a lottery winner.

After Xiamen reached home, he quickly went into his garage and sorted out his new supply of weed. He switched his anorak with the other coat and went back into the house to make his coffee. In a few minutes, Xiamen came out with his cup of coffee in hand and swaggered to the woods in high spirits.

Barely enough light shone from the waning moon and stars in the sky. Darkness shrouded the atmosphere like a coin dunked inside a cup of black coffee. Even darker was the underwood, where the branches of tall trees canopied overhead like hanging parasols. Despite the pitchy ambience, Xiamen made his way along the footpath through the brush, heading for the exact spot where he usually carried out his act.

A short while after, Xiamen reached a fallen tree trunk. He climbed on to the large woody stem, navigated to his favourite sitting spot and hopped off the trunk to hit the ground. Sitting down, he hurriedly drank his coffee. He emptied the last mouthful into his mouth and gargled before letting it flow down his throat. He tossed the cup away and fished out his cigarette case from his coat pocket. He took out one of the joints and stuck it between his lips, fumbling in his pocket for a lighter.

Lighting up the joint, Xiamen sucked on the roach to help it ignite. The spliff came aglow and he inhaled deeply before exhaling the carbon vapours. After a few more deep drags, the psycho active fumes from the coarsely ground hemp inspired his sensory cortex, kindling his mind and stirring his thoughts psychedelically. Suddenly, he was entwined in his own thoughts and began to soliloquise.

'So, who does the universe truly belong to? I wonder if it's to a God, or a group of them? If so, which ones? It's confusing with all the many faces of religion that proliferate. I doubt which one to look to. Then again, don't the atheists take every opportunity to say there's no God? What then? Everyone should chew their own food in the controversy, or what? That'll pretty much encourage discrimination against beliefs, wouldn't it? So, how could we ever digest a universal God? How can anyone truly know?' Xiamen paused to nurse his joint. He sucked in a long draw, filtered it with his lungs and exhaled the refined fumes before resuming his monologue.

'Can anyone really tell who controls the behaviour of the universe, or produce a passkey to unlock the mystery? I reckon not. If the almighty universe was an asset to be acquired, it would likely be owned by the richest country on earth... or perhaps the Group of Eight would've amalgamated liquid capital in a conspiracy to buy it? But then, who can sell the universe if no one owns it in the first place? If a concrete owner can't be proved... I suppose that's why people just make up abstract ones for the mind.

After all, anyone can give whatever name they so choose to their dog, so I can as well call my personal view on the matter.'

Xiamen paused again, taking a moment to recalibrate his thoughts. He sucked hard at the roach, dragging in a long puff until the joint was finished. He threw the residue away and discharged a cloud of mainstream smoke through his nostrils as he fished out his cigarette case for another spliff. After lighting up, he continued to talk to himself.

'I think it's possible that the universe owns itself, therefore, it is its own boss. Perhaps that's why it can take whatever action it chooses. Why would Anybody want to figure out why the universe randomly distributes luck or ill luck to people in the world if they aren't insane? Where would they look? Perhaps they could get some answers from the sun if there was a spacecraft brave enough to venture there… or perhaps from the stars if there was a rocket resilient enough to do the mission. No one should bother themselves about such an impossible quest… whether one meets luck or ill luck in their path… is just how the universe randomly distributes fate… which I dare say is the que sera sera of life.' Xiamen paused again to puff and recalibrate. He remained silent and gazed at the evaporating side smoke at the glowing end of his joint for a brief time, then continued to talk.

'The universe has recorded several historical phenomena and it still continues to bring forth phenomenal events that baffle my comprehension. Some of these I've seen occur in my lifetime and others I recollected from history. While some wreck irremediable tragedies in places… some cause traumatic life-changing problems for the affected. Who can prevent natural disasters, or reverse irreparable disabilities, or even heal incurable diseases? No one can decipher why human calamities keep occurring, and even more puzzling is the fact that no one can filter what the universe has in store for them. If fortune tellers could tell their own destinies, I doubt that they would settle for reading other people's palms... if predicting the time to one's destiny was as simple as forecasting the time to one's destination, then couldn't we all predict how long we will live?' Xiamen fell silent once more, puffing as he mused.

'Nevertheless, I cannot judge the universe as all bad... it has some fateful fortunes too. The sun is a great example... it's the greatest extra-terrestrial providence we've been blessed with... the world would be impoverished without it. The sun gives warmth to the tundra plains... it heats the seas and vaporizes its waters... those waters condense and come down as godsent rain... yes, that's right, the rain is a saviour! We're grateful for its buckets... without it, the deserts, savannas and forests would be dehydrated... even the seas would be depleted too...' Xiamen momentarily puffed his joint before carrying on.

'I've no clue how the universe makes it possible for living species to procreate and repopulate the world, thus life and living is a continuous creation. Even more, the universe provides the world with Hominidae; humans that have language abilities and the brain capabilities to encode and decode complex tools. As a result, scientific and technological breakthroughs by human intelligence are conquering some of the vicissitudes of the universe. Some of these innovations are even altering the universe's nature and causing mass avoidable climate change. Though the almighty universe is working round the clock to fix these rising challenges in its stratosphere, it's not able to adjust the equilibrium. No one, and nowhere, is safe anymore from getting hit by a piece of random fate. The universe is therefore going to author and finish everyone's fate... whether it'll be good, bad, or ugly, your guess is as good as mine.' Xiamen finished another spliff and threw the roach away. Taking out the third roll, he lit it and spent some time puffing it as he mulled. After a while, he talked on.

'The universe and all its eternal matters will remain perpetually extant with it... whereas all living species, myself inclusive, shall only live here once upon a time. Some have theorised that the universe shall end one day, but how can they say something will end when they never understood how it began? Why do they even bother to proffer suppositions to mess with people's heads? Why do they want to mould how we think about the universe when they don't know for sure how it came into existence? If there is no concrete philosophy of a beginning, can there be one about an end?'

Xiamen rounded off his monologue as he puffed the last toke of his final joint of the night. Throwing the roach away, he was now ready to head back home. He stood up slowly to avoid a head-rush. High as a kite and feeling light-headed, he kept his keeling legs steady, stomping them on the forest floor like a jackhammer; the carpet of leaves rustled protestingly beneath his feet as he squashed them. Feeling at peace with no melancholy in his mind, he whistled along a Bob Marley song and bobbed his head to the rhythm. He was ready to go to bed and immerse in his euphoric dreams.

The following morning, Xiamen didn't wake up as early as usual. He got up around 9:30 and pursued a glass of warm milk to cure his morning migraine. He didn't plan to go to work that morning because he wanted to visit his son at the nursing home. He had resolved to go there and talk him out of embarking on his death mission. Whilst having a shower, he reflected on the incidents of the day before and grinned to himself. After all that panic and tension, it had ended with him having the last laugh. He thanked the universe for intervening in the scheme of things and doling him a good fortune. Only the universe could create unexplainable enigmas; that was why the call from the nursing home miraculously came in the nick of time to dispose the proposed plans of the police. This was Simon's doing, the lad created the catalyst that saved him from handcuffs.

The jubilation in Xiamen's mind suddenly quietened and he became engrossed in the matter of his son's mission to Belgium. Simon had been adamant about his wish to go by assisted suicide and now he had succeeded in finding a way to achieve it. He only wanted to say his final goodbye. What if he wasn't able to talk him out of it?

But I just can't let Simon die. I can't bear to lose the only family I have left… I just can't bare it. What sort of father would support his child to die? I'd be the killer then for sure. I simply can't permit it… that would be over my own dead body.

After Xiamen got ready, he was soon out of the house and driving to Tender Care Nursing Home. Thinking about what to say to his son, he fully understood why the lad was requesting to be relieved of his life. Deep down, he believed that Simon's wish to die was a gallant thing to do, albeit he couldn't accept it.

Xiamen couldn't possibly agree to his son's request. Simon was only in his thirties, certainly not a ripe age to die. Why would he want to go when he was in good hands at the nursing home? He should be grateful for that at least. He didn't die in the fall so was destined to live. Why would he not be thankful that his life was spared and enjoy the privilege? What pleasure would he derive from death when he could stay and have carers pander to his needs?

Xiamen didn't want his son to die; he didn't want to be without any family. He imagined he would bring Simon home eventually after he retired from work. They would be together again and he would dedicate his time to care for him. Xiamen mused Simon would be delighted to hear of his future plans and hoped the lad would change his mind after he told him about it.

Xiamen momentarily checked his rationale and criticised himself for making it about his own wishes. He began to reshape his perspective.

Hadn't Simon chosen this for himself? The lad is deeply unhappy... I'm not the one that's feeling the pain. Perhaps I should respect his decision and give it my blessing... I should not deprive him of his right to die with dignity. He figured it out all by himself after all... I doubt I'll be able to talk him out of it anyway. He knows I'm fully against it, but he still made arrangements to go ahead. It isn't up to me anymore. The universe knows best... maybe this is one of its courses. I'll go say farewell to my boy and give him a hero's hug.

With the thought of conceding to his son's will, Xiamen drove in silence feeling somewhat better. He didn't feel an iota of sorrow; not even a tiny tear wet his eyes. Considering how he'd been emotional about it previously, his machismo side was apparently now in force.

Xiamen had a sudden urge to hum "We Are the Champions," Simon's favourite Queen song. The tone of his humming made it sound like a requiem. He soon got into the groove of the song and upped the tempo to a lively whistle, bobbing his head in sync. In a lighter mood, he drove into a petrol station for some diesel and topped up his tank still whistling. After filling up his tank and paying for the fuel, he got back on the road to Bungay, whistling and bobbing to his son's glory.

Chapter Twenty-Four

The clampdown on narcotic traffickers and users had heightened in Norwich City since Xiamen's close-shave with the police. Some users who weren't as lucky had been nabbed with narcotics in their possession and were facing prosecution.

The police dragnet was closing in on a number of drug dealers who'd been implicated by apprehended users, and the undercover agents tactfully waylaid them around the city. Luna Crescent was currently devoid of all peddling activities as most of the dealers were lying low to minimise risk. As a result, getting a supply of weed was like digging for shrimps in the Sahara Desert.

Despite the risk involved in distributing cannabis to users, some moneygrubbing dealers cashed in on the scarcity situation, supplying the product at exorbitant prices. These die-hard pedlars ripped more profits to commensurate the risk taken.

Due to the short supply and greater demand for the product, the market forces were no longer able to regulate the price so the monopolising supply chain took complete control. The asking price was sometimes doubled or tripled without notice and the patrons were at their complete mercy.

For the fast money, artful quack dealers suddenly appeared on the horizon too; they bastardised the distribution with doctored cannabis, dealing the stuff to the most desperate users. Some of these charlatan dealers even went as far as contaminating the grass with false greens or doping it with other addictive narcotics; they would conceal the additions in ready-made joints and blunts.

Some crafty weed brokers took their chances on busy pedestrian street corners, scouting for patrons like flea market vendors.

Finding pure weed in these times was a real jackpot. Dealers with the genuine product were hard to distinguish as each one claimed they had the pure grade without allowing any tasters. Since these dealers traded on take-it-or-leave-it terms, the vulnerable addicts were taking the adulterated cannabis away to quench their cravings.

Now, the use of narcotised cannabis was widespread in the city; a grade of weed doped with crack cocaine was even being circulated. It had increased the addiction dependency and caused euphoric mental problems in some users. For this reason, special undercover narcotic agents were prowling the streets daily, desperate to get the situation under control.

Tonight, it had been over a week since Xiamen had narrowly escaped an arrest. He was on the road driving home after a long day at work. Being very wary of another showdown with the police, he never went back to Mary Jane Lane. They had already warned him he wouldn't be so lucky next time and he didn't want to bet on it. The last spliff from his last supply would expire in a fortnight. He would have to figure out where else to get it before long.

Eventually, Xiamen's weed stock ran out and he went to Harrison to ask if he could get in touch with Kymani for some assistance. He and Harrison drove to the taxi rank where Kymani usually waited. Whilst there, they gathered some news from another taxi driver, a friend of Kymani called Henry. He told them Kymani had been taken into police custody and was awaiting trial. After they left the taxi rank, Harrison suggested to Xiamen to try the pedlars in the high street and he told him which corners to find them.

Xiamen took the advice and headed for the high street. He was shocked to learn of the dealers' asking price and he tried haggling with them, to no avail. In the end, he bought the goods off two sellers to make up the quantity he required. He travelled home brooding about the rip off. He went back a couple of times after to buy more from them too; each time their asking price was unpredictable. The weed pedlars just hiked the price at random and refused to sell for a fraction less. This annoyed Xiamen so much so that he wanted to tell them to go to hell, but he was a slave to his own needs. He ended up paying the dealers the asking price and got his beloved guilty pleasure. *A man got to have what he got to have anyway.* He mused to himself as he walked away.

The scarcity of weed in the city prolonged further and the demand grew even greater. The supply chain became ruthless with their prices and operated as oligopolists. Even though Xiamen was able to afford the goods at the current rate, he was having a hard time keeping up; the prices kept getting dearer each time. He purchased a few more times out of necessity but the dealers' cut-throat extortion made him unhappy. Now, he was low on cash, low on weed and he had not been able to procure enough quantity to restock his rainy day stash.

Xiamen wasn't coping well with the situation. Not only was weed scarce to find, but it was gradually becoming unaffordable to him. The hiked prices didn't make it easy for him to purchase his guilty pleasure conveniently. Some days, he didn't find anything to buy at all. On the days when he did find it, he wasn't willing to pay the asking price of the dealer and he had to go without a smoke. On such days, he would feel miserable and have a restless night's sleep.

Xiamen persisted despite everything and eventually found a supplier he was happy with. From the first puff he'd experienced a different heady feeling. He appreciated the buzz he got from the weed more than any he'd previously puffed; These latest spliffs gave him a new kind of euphoric high he hadn't experienced before. The sensation even lingered into the following day. It was so powerful that Xiamen was back to his more cheerful self, humming as he commuted passengers and looking forward to the evening for his next puff. At night, Xiamen's dreams became more hallucinated as he re-lived family moments of the past. Sometimes, his dreams were filled with futuristic moments with his family too.

Xiamen's current state of mind helped him cope with his son's demise. Although he was sad about losing him forever, his heady bliss helped to tone down his grief in the days that followed Simon's passing. On the day that Xiamen had gone to say goodbye to Simon, he was fortunate enough to meet the NGO's advocate and the lip-reader; their presence allowed him to communicate with his son in those final moments. Whilst there, he told Simon he was proud of him and commended him for his courage; he also apologised for not agreeing to his wishes earlier. Simon said he understood his reason and that he wasn't offended by it. Simon told him to try to find himself some companionship, maybe even a wife, so he wouldn't be alone for the rest of his life. Xiamen had chuckled at the advice and responded that he would get a dog instead.

Later, Xiamen was particularly impressed when he read Simon's after-death declaration; he learnt that Simon had donated his useful vital organs to the organ bank and the rest of his body was donated to anatomical research. He was so touched by the compassionate act that his eyes had watered. He gave Simon a hug and called him a gallant hero.

The following week, Xiamen went to the high street to buy his next fix. He'd missed the news about the recent clash between undercover police and a band of dealers. It had happened only the day before and had involved a gun exchange, resulting in the death of one police officer and a sniffer dog. The police force was infuriated and revengefully released a squad of undercover narcotic agents into the city. They secretly kept the streets under surveillance, waiting for the right minute to pounce. Some of the smarter dealers had received a tipoff and steered clear that day, but the novices among them came out for business as usual without a clue.

Xiamen did not see his regular source on sight that afternoon, so he resorted to buying from one of the other pushers hustling in the area. He confirmed his order and passed money to the dealer. The brokering dealer alerted his mate by text and told Xiamen the supply would be brought shortly. His mate came after a few minutes to deliver the goods, completely unaware of the undercover policewoman on his tail. She pointed her gun and bawled at them to surrender. The delivery guy instinctively tried to run and the officer instantly downed him by shooting him in the leg. In a flash, two other gun-wielding detectives appeared and surrounded them.

Arresting the culprits, the detectives read Xiamen and the others their rights before taking them away in handcuffs. Xiamen and the brokering dealer were taken into police custody whilst the wounded dealer was taken into hospital arrest. Later, they went through the formal protocols of having their mugshots taken and they were interrogated separately. Xiamen had never been collared to the police station before, let alone sat in the suspect chair inside an interrogation room. He knew from watching crime movies that a suspect was better off keeping mute if the police didn't have any obvious evidence. He said no comment to all the questions without hesitation. The police released him the following day after eighteen hours of detention.

On Xiamen's way out, he met with the brokering dealer who told him that neither he, nor his mate, had cooperated with the interrogators. Because they hadn't found any evidence on him, they'd let him go but he said his mate may have been kept in because of the quantity found on him. When Xiamen went to collect his taxi, he didn't find it in one piece. The forensic crew had ransacked it and left it in a mess. He got into the cab and drove home, feeling plundered and unhappy about the time wasted.

Forwards from that day, the drug enforcement squad made things pretty tough for the narcotics pushers and users. Things got pretty scary in the streets as the undercover agents tracked and netted the retailers and bingers, one after another. Several arrests were made and the guilty suspects were prosecuted. Consequently, the dealers themselves disappeared from the face of the street and went underground. It was now too risky for both the pedlars and the buyers to be out in the street doing their shady deals.

The users were once again having a hard time coping without their fixes. Xiamen himself had grown shy of going to buy weed since his last encounter with the police. He tried to get in touch with Harrison but was taken aback to learn the police had nabbed him and found a significant amount of cannabis in the boot of his car. As a result, they slammed Harrison with a substance trafficking charge and he was sentenced to two years in prison.

Xiamen was devastated by the news of Harrison's incarceration. He developed cold feet and was scared of another arrest. Having already had two close-shaves, he was wary of a third, which might just be the one that would break the camel's back. He toyed with the idea of how he could get his fix and speculated whether to go out to scout for it, but he wouldn't dare risk another face-off with the law.

Xiamen knew his indictment and biometrical data were now stored in the police database and they probably wouldn't spare him if he got into trouble with them again. Above that, he didn't think the dealers would risk selling to him for fear he might be under surveillance. He was certain that, if he wasn't careful, it would be his turn next to languish in jail. Any conviction on his DBS profile could make him lose his cabby licence, the only part of his life that still gave him some satisfaction. Getting weed in the future was going to be dicey and it bothered him.

Xiamen went without a smoke in the days that followed and his whole persona changed. All his sorrows returned to his mind and he took solace in grieving Simon's death. Within two weeks, Xiamen had dunked himself into his anhedonia, like a mouse trapped in a WC. He resumed grieving for the other members of his lost family too. Without any more weed to fuel Xiamen's illusive high to sustain his heady bliss, he was left in a sorry state. His mind crumbled into a rubble of melancholy, brimming with dark thoughts. He felt as hopeless as a mouse flushed down the sewer.

Chapter Twenty-Five

One evening, Xiamen went shopping for groceries in Aldi. Whilst pulling an item from the shelf, he heard a familiar voice behind him and turned to see Kymani Sanchez standing beside a store trolley.

'Whoa... Kymani! Where did you spring from?'

'Me was right behind and stocking up right after yuh all along. Not once yuh look back man.'

'Sorry, I didn't realise. How're you? It's really been a long time.

'Yah man, it's been a lang time, true.'

'So, what are you up to? Are you working here now?'

'Yah man. Me just run things here for de time being.'

'I heard some story about you getting into trouble with the police, then I didn't see you tooling on the road after that. Did you quit driving?'

'Nuh man, not dat me quit, just dat me driving licence has been suspended. Me can't drive now until after one year.'

'I'm so sorry to hear that,' Xiamen said, then, he lowered his voice and asked, 'Did they find any grass on you?'

'Nothing of such man. De police nuh find even a likkle ganja on me when dem pull me over.'

'Why were you arrested then?'

'Dem police give me a breathalyser test and me nuh pass it. Me had a likkle rum earlier dat day. De judge who sat upon me case suspended me licence and give me three weeks of community work for drink-driving. Me finish dat, so me just running things as a packer here for de time being.'

'I didn't know that's what happened. I'd thought otherwise.'

'Dat is what most people who nuh know de true story think. Me case was just a traffic offence… nothing to do with the bust on de ganja massive. Well, it was nice to see yuh again, posseman. Me have to go back to me work now. See yuh man.'

'Okay, Kymani, it was good to see you too. Take care.'

Kymani walked off and Xiamen continued his shopping. An idea suddenly flashed into his mind. He turned back and went after Kymani. Kymani was bending down by a shelve and restocking it when Xiamen found him. He waited for him to finish.

'Hey, Kymani, do you have a minute?'

Kymani looked at him in surprise as he straightened up. 'Watt a gwan?'

'I've a request to make. Can we meet to talk later?'

'Wah yuh want talk about?'

'I need some supply, but I don't think here's a good place to talk. When do you finish work?'

'Nuff respect man. Me understand wah yuh say. Give me a likkle ten minutes, me take a cigarette break and meet yuh outside in the corner. We can chat all about it there.'

'Thanks, I'll do that, see you shortly.'

When Kymani joined Xiamen outside, he briefed him of his encounters with the police. He explained he was in dire need of a supply and didn't know anywhere else to go or anyone else to turn to. He asked Kymani if he could get him some stock.

'Nuh problem man. Me can easily do dat for yuh. How many wraps yuh want?'

'As much as you can get me this time, but I need a good price please.'

'Nuh worries man, Me can bring yuh the sinsemilla you need, but yuh have to buy well over nuff to get it at a cheaper price.'

'I don't understand.'

'I mean that yuh have to buy plenty of it to get the wholesale deal. Yuh understand now?'

'Yes. So, what quantity are we talking about?'

'Nuh likkle than three kilo.'

'How many rolls will five kilo be?'

'Maybe eighty or ninety, or more than dat. Me can't tell how many exactly. De scale will give de accurate keys when de dealer weighs it, but it also depends on how much quantity yuh wrap up in a roll.'

'Okay. Work out what it will cost and I'll bring you the cash so you can get it for me.'

'Dat is easy man. Me can tell yuh dat off the top me head right about now.'

'Brilliant, tell me then.'

'Five keys of pure original ganja will cost yuh one thousand, one hundred pounds. The hundred on top is me likkle commission.'

'For real? Kymani, that is too high!'

'Which one? Yuh mean de cost, or me commission?'

'Umm… er… can't you do it for any less?'

'Pay attention now. Dis is a wholesale deal. A whole lot a things are involved. Me can only get yuh that much tonight before all of dem are sold. If yuh want it, yuh have to bring me the cash today before 6 PM. Maybe the distro merchant can throw in some extras if me can persuade him, but me can't guarantee dat right now.'

'Okay, I'll bring you the cash today. Where do I meet you?'

'Just here. Me finish work at 5PM and wait for yuh. Me nuh guh be here after quarter past so be wise of dat.'

'No problem, I'll be here in time.'

'Make sure of dat man.'

'I'll be here.'

'Me see yuh then. Me have to go back to work right now.'

'Okay, see you later Kymani.'

'Yah man, laters, bless.'

Kymani left. Xiamen finished his shopping and went home. He later went back to give the money to Kymani. They exchanged numbers; Kymani promised to deliver the goods in two days and said he would call to arrange a meeting place. After two days, Xiamen hadn't received a call from Kymani as per the agreement. He tried Kymani's line and wasn't able to reach him. Xiamen became anxious and was compelled to come to his place of work. He walked around the shop with the hope of running into his acquaintance but was unsuccessful, so he decided to approach a store clerk to ask of his whereabouts.

'Good evening. Sorry to bother you, I just want to ask after my friend Kymani. I helped him order an item and wanted to deliver it to him, but I can't reach his mobile. Do you know if he is on duty today?'

The store clerk eyed Xiamen suspiciously before she said, 'Kymani stopped working here yesterday. I don't know what happened but I think he may have resigned.'

'That's a surprise. So, do you know how I can reach him?'

'I don't, sorry. Please, I'd like to go back to my work now.' The store clerk turned her attention back to the shelves.

Xiamen turned around and walked away. Outside the shop, He got out his phone and tried Kymani's number again. He heard the buzzer repeatedly ring, and then the voicemail assistant telling him to leave a message. He hung up in exasperation. He was now getting worked up and didn't know what to make of Kymani going AWOL. He had no idea where he lived or where else to look for him. The only person he knew who could tell him something was in prison. Suddenly, a brainstorm from the blue unexpectedly flipped through Xiamen's mind as he thought of Harrison. He remembered Henry, whom Harrison had taken him to once when they were looking for Kymani. This was a headway at least.

The following morning, Xiamen drove to the taxi rank where Henry often queued and found him inside his taxi waiting in line and he tapped on the front passenger's door to get his attention. Henry slid down the window.

'Howdy, mate,' Xiamen greeted him.

'What's up with you bruv, you need a taxi or what?'

'Nope, I'm only looking for information. Do you mind if I pick your brain for a moment?'

'Of course. I'll be too glad to fill you in if it's within my repertoire.'

'I am looking for Kymani. Do you know how I can find him?'

'Oh yeah? What do you want with Kymani?'

'That isn't proper. I thought I was the one here seeking information.'

'Sure thing. I am just curious because I dropped him off at the airport last night. He said he was jetting to Montego Bay. Is there a problem?'

'He's gone to the Caribbean, for real? When did he say he's coming back?'

'We didn't have that discussion, so I don't know. But I think he might've said in passing that he will chill there till he can drive again. Did you know his licence was suspended for a year?'

'Yeah, he told me. Well I think he might've just have tricked me and made away with my money.'

'Holy Mary! How much?'

'Uhm, well, never mind about that. I'll have a bone to pick with him when he returns.'

'Gee! So sorry about that bruv, I didn't know. Otherwise I would have alerted you.'

'Don't be sorry. It isn't your fault. Well, I'll be on my way now, thanks for the tipoff. Cheers.'

'Cheerio to you bruv.'

Xiamen flounced back to his cab like an angry lion. How could he have been so trusting of Kymani? Now the Jamaican had bailed with his money, and what's worse, he couldn't tell anyone about it. No one would sympathise with him if they knew how much he'd advanced to Kymani and what it was for. They would laugh at his stupidity and say it had served him right. He was even worse off now, his hard-earned cash was gone and he had no weed to compensate for it.

Two further weeks passed; by that point it had reached a month since Xiamen enjoyed a puff of weed and he desperately craved for it like a junkie. The absence of his beloved guilty pleasure began to tell on him. Since he could no longer attain the illusive high that helped manage his sad mood, his melancholy gained control of his mind and made him lugubrious about everything. All his woes eventually crept back into his mind and would torment him like a plague.

Day after day Xiamen's sad thoughts would oscillate nonstop like a grandfather clock. There was nothing he could do to get a fix for his craving. The balance between his nucleus accumbens and prefrontal cortex could not stabilise. He reverted to mourning his losses, though he was more sorrowful about losing his beloved guilty pleasure. His mind was in chaos and his perception of reality altered drastically. He was losing his mind without the slightest clue about it.

One day whilst Xiamen was pining, he remembered the psychologist and thought he might as well pay him another visit. He searched for the business card Adam Griffin had given him previously, but he couldn't lay hold on it. He hadn't thought to save his number at the time and mused about what else to do. He recalled seeing Dr Griffin's phone number on the nameplate that was fixed on his door. Xiamen opted to go try his luck at the premises; even if Dr Griffin wasn't in he could get his number at the very least.

He arrived at the counsellor's office and was immediately alerted of his absence. There were unclaimed newspaper deliveries lying by the foot of the door and a letter was sticking out from under it. Xiamen just assumed the psychologist was away on holiday. Taking out his phone, he copied the phone number on the door and saved it. He turned around to head off but his eye caught a glimpse of the headline on one of the newspapers. He peered closer at it and his curiosity was roused. Picking up the tabloid, he glared at the news in disbelief.

ADAM GRIFFIN NAMED AS THE VICTIM IN THE RIVER WENSUM CRASH. The police have released the identity of the driver whose vehicle plummeted into the River Wensum just before 09:00 GMT last Tuesday night, on the Halfords roundabout approach. 43-year-old Adam

Oscar Griffin was a practising psychologist from Sheringham village. The emergency services carried out a rescue operation on his grey Toyota Corolla, holding up traffic for over two hours and causing heavy delays during the rescue. Unfortunately, they were unable to save Dr Griffin and he was pronounced dead at the scene. Though the cause of the accident is still unknown, the police included in their report that traces of a psychoactive substance had been found in his system. The police are appealing to anyone who may have witnessed the accident or has a useful information about the victim to come forward...

Chapter Twenty-Six

Xiamen completely lost it in the days following his discovery of Dr Griffin's accident. He felt more depressed, losing sleep; melancholy ravaged his happiness like a swarm of locusts defoliating a bush. He was so mentally disturbed that he had not gone to work for three days, or anywhere else for that matter. In three days of solitude, he had not bathed, cleaned his teeth or changed his clothes. Consequently, he was adrift, slobby and smelly, looking like a homeless person in his own house without being aware of it or even caring.

One thing Xiamen did still manage to do was eat. Although he hadn't cooked anything in three days, his microwave had been busy churning out whatever he could scavenge out of his cupboards and fridge. As a result, his stock of canned and cold food had gone down whilst his rubbish bin was overfilled with the remains.

It had just past three o'clock in the afternoon and Xiamen was just waking from a deep slumber, which was induced by the sleeping pills he took. He didn't sleep a wink at night due to insomnia; he'd eventually drifted off at 7AM and had remained asleep until now.

Today would be the fourth day of solitude if he remained indoors until the end of the day. Rising from his bed, he glimpsed the notification light blinking on his phone and reached for it. Taking the phone with him, he trudged out of the bedroom to relieve himself.

In the toilet, Xiamen looked in the mirror but he didn't pay any attention to his reflection. The man in the mirror had put on weight, his hair was fluffed up and his unkempt beard were spread over his face like seaweed. Xiamen pulled down his joggers and sat on the WC.

The water closet made rapid plonking sounds as Xiamen's excretory products dropped into it. He sniffed and wrung his nose, irritated by the smell. He flipped through his phone to check the notification and saw a voice message from Spencer. He called his voicemail and listened.

'Hey Xiamey, what's up with you? Are you still unwell? For goodness sake, I'm worried about you! It's been four days now since you called in sick. I haven't seen your dispatcher panel on since then. Let me hear from you if you're alive.'

The message ended. Xiamen cut off the voicemail and put the phone down on the toilet floor. He peeled out some toilet paper and wiped himself. After pulling up his pants, he picked up his phone and left the toilet without washing his hands or flushing his excrement away. As he walked back to his bedroom, his phone began to vibrate. He heaved a sigh of irritation when he saw the caller ID. He answered the call.

'Hello, Spencer.'

'Hey Xiamey, thank God I have finally got you! Where the heck are you? You have been AWOL, just like that. Are you OK?'

'I guess so.'

'Why do you sound like that? Are you still sick?'

'I'm fine.'

'But you sound barely human. There's no life in your voice. Where are you right now?'

'I'm at, er, I'm away.'

'I beg your pardon? Away where?'

'I'm away on holiday.'

'You mean that you are out of town?'

'Yes.'

'What the heck Xiamey, you never mentioned you were going away… or did you?'

'I can't remember. If you didn't know, perhaps I didn't remember to let you know. Sorry.'

'I'll be damned if you tell me you're having a great time there. You sound like a broken toy. Why can't I hear any life in your voice? Is everything okay?'

'As I said, I'm fine.'

'Okay Xiamey if you say so. Well then… when are you coming back to work? It's been pressure down here. I'm short of reliable cabbies and it's not looking good without you on board. I really need you back on the road, can you tell me when this can happen?'

'Well, to be honest, I'm sorry to tell you that I actually don't know.'

'Come on Xiamey, what's going on? Be real with me man.'

'Nothing's going on… I just can't give you an answer right now.'

'Come on now Xiamey, I need you on board! You are one of the reliable cabbies we have. I need you back on the road asap. Can you please do something about that for me?'

'I'm really sorry Spencer, I can't do anything at the moment. As I said, I'm away so can't do otherwise.'

'When are you coming back from holiday then?'

'I don't know.'

'What do you mean?'

'I mean that I don't know when I'll be coming back to work. I'll let you know as soon as I'm ready.'

'Are you not okay, Xiamey? Why don't I hear any vibe in your voice? This is very unlike you.'

'I'm not sure I know what missing vibe you're talking about. I'd like to go now if you don't mind. I've some things to attend to.'

'That's fine. Give me a call as soon as you are back.'

'Okay Spencer, I sure will. Bye.'

'All right Xiamey, bye for now. By the way Xiamey, do you—'

Xiamen hung up to let himself off the hook before Spencer could finish the sentence. He walked into his bedroom. The air there reeked of a stench that was no better than a skunk's glandular emission. The floor was strewn with filth, like a beach had been attacked by marine debris. The area beside his bed was cluttered with empty packets and tubs of the snacks from his binge-eating sessions. A half-empty bottle of juice and some unopened packets of crisps nestled in the rubbish. Plastic wraps and dirty clothes were littered across the carpet too. Xiamen ignored the popping hisses from the splitting cellophanes as he stepped on them to get to his bed. Sitting down, he pushed a bowl of half-eaten cornflakes on the bedside cabinet out of the way and reached for a bottle of water that'd been lying there doggo. He finished the bottle and tossed it in the pile of litter beside his feet.

Getting up from the bed, Xiamen wandered to the window. He looked out at the woods and espied the canopies of tall trees standing like pylons. He gazed on forlornly, wondering when he would go there again to smoke. A pang of hunger suddenly distracted him. He left the bedroom and went downstairs to the kitchen.

The dining table had been equally transformed by detritus out of Xiamen's negligence. His preferred sitting side of the table was polluted by croissant flakes. The coat from his garage had been left there and was nestling uncomfortably on one end of the table with one of its sleeves drooping to the floor. a train of worker ants seizing the opportunity, was using the droopy sleeve as a track to cart away crumbs from the table.

The table was also cluttered with crumpled tissue sheets, a chalice bowl, two glass cups and two plastic bottles. The bigger one litre bottle had some water in it but no cork, whilst the other 75 cl bottle had contained orange squash but was now empty and lying flat. One of the glass cups still contained some water whilst the other one was empty and soiled with stale squash. A dirty tea mug, that was used two days prior, sat next to a saucer which held a teaspoon and some soggy teabags. The chalice bowl was sitting askew with a mix of berries and grapes inside, some of which were starting to go off.

Xiamen absentmindedly kicked a box of cornflakes that was left on the floor beside his chair as he walked to the dining table. The box rolled across the floor spilling out some of its contents. He stood by the table, not caring about the disarray. He flicked the fruits in the chalice around, picked out some edible ones and tossed them into his mouth.

Xiamen opened the fridge and surveyed its contents. He took out a pack of ham, cheese slices and a tub of margarine. He opened the freezer section and pulled out a pack of frozen rolls. Without tearing off the wrapping, he tossed them into the microwave and set it to defrost mode for a few minutes.

Walking over to the coffee maker, Xiamen opened it to make a drink but remembered he was out of coffee pods. He shuffled to the electric jug and turned that on instead.

When the water heated, he made a cup of tea using the mug from the dining table, without rinsing it. The microwave shortly dinged and he took out the rolls. After preparing the sandwiches, he placed them and the tea in a tray and took the brunch to his bedroom.

Later that evening, Xiamen was sitting in the kitchen drinking tea from the same mug. He was dressed in the other coat from the garage with the hood up like he was about to head out. This was the time he usually went into the woods to smoke, but weed was far from his reach as the sky. If only wishes were horses.

Downcast, Xiamen fixed a thoughtful gaze to the dark beverage in the mug, looking as sober as a man that'd lost all his life savings. A dark thought he'd been nursing was now cooking in his head, boiling like magma that was about to burst from a fissure in the earth's crust. He' figured out a way to end his problems. He mulled over the plan to perfect it.

'Don't be so sad, Dad. Brighten up!'

Xiamen looked up as he heard the voice and saw an apparition of Elizabeth sitting there with him. He ignored it and continued to stare at his black tea.

'She is right, Dad. You shouldn't just lock yourself and close off the world. Be cheerful and live your life.'

Xiamen looked up again and there Simon was, sitting on the chair next to Elizabeth. He looked from one to the other and went back to gazing at his tea.

'Liven up, honey. You can't just sit there and mope. It's about time you seek help for your addiction. You should do something before you go down the drain. Like Si said, you have got to live your life. The world can still offer you so much without us.'

Again, Xiamen looked up and saw it was the ghost of his wife talking to him. He didn't return to his cup of tea this time. Instead, he fixed his look on her lustfully. He reached out his hand to touch her but she suddenly vanished, along with the other apparitions. Without any provocation, he swung a backhand swipe across the table and the contents flew to the floor with a clattering noise. He charged to his feet and stormed out of the house to his cab.

Speeding out of his compound, Xiamen drove on the road with a set mind. He sped out of Attleborough and headed out of Norwich, driving east towards Great Yarmouth. He had gathered some intel from the internet so he knew exactly when to be at his destination. He had concluded what he was going to do and reckoned his mission would be dead easy to implement.

Driving into the north part of Great Yarmouth, Xiamen headed towards the south of the town. A few minutes after, he was soon approaching the high functioning bascule bridge that he used to love watching. Lately, there had been a problem with the platform on the south wing of the bridge; it wasn't lifting due to some mechanical fault. As a result, only vessels small enough to fit through the space on one side were able to pass through the crossing.

Though inconvenient to the operators of bigger vessels, there was no hindrance to the smooth flow of traffic across the bridge.

Reaching the bascule bridge, Xiamen drove across it. Shortly after, he found a clearing to turn. He reversed and drove right back towards the bridge. When he was within a few yards away from the traffic lights, he pulled over to the side and stepped on the brake. Where he stopped was restricted to licensed taxicabs only. The rule only allowed cabbies temporary parking for dropping off or picking up passengers. Sitting behind the wheel, Xiamen left his hazard lights blinking. He checked the dash clock. There was time.

Five minutes later, Xiamen quickly pulled into the road, signalling late and cutting in front of an oncoming vehicle. He'd forced the driver to suddenly slow down. He had done it with utter disregard to any consequences, but thankfully the oncoming car managed to avoid a collision. He was lucky; the first step of his plan was complete.

The lights turned red. Xiamen was positioned at the front of the queue and was in close proximity to the barrier that had swung down to block vehicles driving any further. In the interim, the traffic had formed long lines on both sides of the bridge. They were now waiting patiently for the bridge to be lifted to let the oncoming vessel pass.

With one foot completely depressing the brake, Xiamen pressed the clutch and accelerator, revving the car for action. The infra-red traffic lights were as bright as ever, but Xiamen had his eyes fixed on the north wing platform without blinking. He was very focused and didn't want to miss his chance.

The force of the bascule mechanism started hoisting the platform and it gradually headed up to the point where it would stay suspended. Without waiting for the platform to finish lifting, Xiamen selected the first gear, took his foot off the brake then swiftly ascended the gear to the max. The car jerked away like a projectile from a cannon and cracked through the traffic barrier, snapping it without the slightest resistance.

Fast and furious, Xiamen's cab supersonically leapt on and zipped across the faulty lowered platform. He was heading for a collision into the bottom of the raising platform. Suddenly, Xiamen stepped hard on the brake, simultaneously drawing the handbrake. The car stopped short in mid-air and hung suspended over the water, halting the deadly headlong crash.

Upon sighting the car attempting to sky dive across its route, and with no automatic brake feature, the oncoming vessel did the only thing possible. It blasted its horn wildly, which went off like the trumpeting of an elephant running from a bushfire. Xiamen's cab plummeted with a splash that sent water into the sky and the car was submerged instantly, spreading ripples that almost toppled the oncoming vessel. Still blasting its thunderous horn, the vessel reluctantly went over the spot where the car had dived in.

In that moment, pandemonium was unleashed. Everybody in the proximity was thrown into a fit of hysteria. The horns of vehicles were honking and tooting rampantly. People came out from their cars and formed crowds, crying and screaming at the top of their voices. The unfortunate vessel had turned off its propeller and was now quietly floating on the waves nearby. Dismayed-looking crew members were gathered on the deck as the sirens of police cars and rescue services drew closer.

In the midst of the chaos, the hanging bascule platform remained steady on its tenterhooks, calmly watching the unfolding events from its bird's eye vantage. This was going to be a long night for the waiting traffic!

The End

Wake up and
Wake up and turn I loose

Wake up and turn I loose
Wake up and turn I loose
For the rain is falling
Got to have kaya now
Got to have kaya now
Got to have kaya now
For the rain is falling
I'm so high, I even touch the sky
Above the falling rain
I feel so good in my neighbourhood, so
Here I come again
Got to have kaya now
Got to have kaya now
Got to have kaya now
For the rain is falling
Feelin' irie I
Feelin' irie I
Feelin' irie I
'Cause I have some kaya now
I feel so high, I even touch the sky
Above the falling rain
I feel so good in my neighbourhood, so
Here I come again
Got to have kaya now
Got to have kaya now
Got to have kaya now, Lord
For the rain is falling.

("Kaya", released in 1978 by Bob Marley)